MW01129540

# REBELLION

### THE RESISTANCE TRILOGY, BOOK THREE

## K. A. RILEY

**Disclaimer**

**Cover Design**

www.thebookbrander.com

# A NOTE FROM THE AUTHOR

Dearest Fellow Conspirator,

What you have in your hands is one-ninth of what's called an *ennealogy*, a rare and hard-to-pronounce word meaning "a nine-part series." It's basically three sequential, interlocking trilogies. (Think *Star Wars* or *Planet of the Apes*)

Here is the Reading Order for the *Conspiracy Ennealogy*...

#1: **Resistance Trilogy**
   *Recruitment*
   *Render*
   *Rebellion*

#2: **Emergents Trilogy**
   *Survival*
   *Sacrifice (Coming in November 2019)*
   *Synthesis (Coming in early 2020)*

#3: **Transcendent Trilogy**

*Travelers*
*Transfigured*
*Terminus*

I'm glad you chose to join in the Conspiracy! Enjoy the revolution!

— KAR

*To my brothers and sisters, ravens all.*

"War does not determine who is right—only who is left."

— Bertrand Russell

"Ravens are the birds I'll miss most when I die. If only the darkness into which we must look were composed of the black light of their limber intelligence. If only we did not have to die at all. Instead, become ravens."

— Louise Erdrich, *The Painted Drum*

# PROLOGUE

THIS MORNING COULDN'T BE ANY MORE NORMAL.

The five of us wake up, roll reluctantly out of our warm beds, and pad off—the three girls first, then the two boys—to the shower room just off of our sleeping quarters. Once we're clean and dressed, we straighten our white sheets and green army blankets and sit at the foot of our low cots that we've arranged in a circle like the spokes of a wheel. Stretching our arms and arching our backs to work out the knots in our muscles, we compare notes about the dreams each of us had last night. With his dark hair still wet and with a soft yellow towel draped around his neck, Brohn says he had a dream about running through the woods. "Only I couldn't tell if I was being chased or if I was chasing someone else," he tells us. Behind her cowl of wavy brown hair, Manthy's dark, brooding eyes perk up at this, and I ask her if she had a similar dream. She shakes her head and mumbles something about how she never has dreams anymore. I can't tell if she's bragging or if she's sad about that fact.

Leaning back on one elbow, Cardyn rubs his stomach and licks his lips. "I had the most delicious dream ever. I was stuffing myself with chocolate-covered yucca buds and rolling around in

1

a juicy buffet of mountain sage and wild strawberries." Pretending to bask in the satisfaction of satiety, Cardyn licks his fingers one at a time. "You can keep your terrifying dreams of being on the run in the woods," he says to Brohn with a dismissive wave of his hand. "We've already done that for real. Mine is a dream I'd love to see come true!"

Sitting cross-legged and drawing her straight black hair back into a slick ponytail, Rain gives Cardyn a poorly-concealed eye-roll, which makes Cardyn scowl. "What about you, Rain?" he grumbles. "Let me guess. You dreamed about beating all of us in chess."

"Better than beating all of us with her bare fists," Brohn says, and we all laugh. In addition to being the smartest of our group, Rain has recently taken it upon herself to fight pretty much anyone who tries to cross us. In Reno, a stranger tried to grope her, and she responded by breaking his nose. Yesterday, she took down a soldier who was on guard duty for the Patriot Army. I didn't get a chance to see her in action that time, but I saw the results: a cluster of perfectly round knuckle imprints where the guy's face used to be. For such a small girl, she really packs a wallop.

"Actually," Rain says, looking at Card like he's a bug who just scurried out from under the floorboards, "I dreamed we were all back on the run when we decided to stop to assemble a giant jigsaw puzzle in the middle of the desert floor. It was a picture of the original eight of us from our Cohort of 2042, including Terk, Karmine, and Kella."

We all go quiet for a minute and bow our heads at the names of our friends who aren't with us anymore.

Rain still has her head down when she adds, "But the puzzle still had one piece missing."

"Oh yeah?" Cardyn asks. "Which piece?"

Raising her head, Rain points over to the top of the big

antique armoire where our clothes for the day are stored and where Render is quietly preening himself. "It was him."

We all look over at the large raven who must sense that he's suddenly become the center of attention. He lifts his smooth feathered head and cracks out a series of coarse *kraas!* which sound way too loud for this early in the morning, and I'm wondering if the Insubordinates, our fellow rebels who are sleeping in the dozens of other rooms on this floor, think we're in here running an aluminum garbage can through a corn-thresher.

Manthy clamps her hands over her ears, and Cardyn puts his finger to his lips in a pointless effort to tell Render to be quiet.

Render barks out another string of raspy *kraas!* and then spreads his wings and suddenly seems gigantic, like a prehistoric flying dinosaur or something. I don't need to activate my psychic connection with him to know what's on his mind: he's hungry, and he doesn't like being cooped up. It was comforting for me to know he was in here with us all night but having lived his life in the boundless mountain air, he's not a big fan of walls or ceilings. I hop up from the end of my cot and go over to the window. I've barely got it open when the familiar woosh of feathery purplish-black whizzes by my face, and Render is soaring out over the quiet city with the first pinkish rays of the morning sun lighting him up like a glistening missile.

This is our first time in such a big city, and I panic for a second as I watch him disappear into a forest of tall office build-ings of reflecting black glass and synth-steel. I let out a long, soft breath when I spot him banking and circling as he happily scouts around the city for something he can scavenge for breakfast.

I turn back to Brohn and the others just as the door to our room creaks open on old-style metal hinges to reveal Wisp and Granden, and I'm suddenly shaken out of the illusion that we're all just a bunch of normal teenagers in a normal situation getting ready for a normal day at school. There's nothing normal about any of this or about any of us. We're five homeless and parentless seventeen-year-olds who have been dodging death for nearly our entire lives. As we discovered over a month ago on our last day of captivity, we're what's called Emergents. Manthy and I are, anyway. And possibly Brohn. I don't know about Cardyn and Rain. We have certain abilities we didn't ask for and don't completely understand. We're hunted, hiding out, and one week away from war.

If 'normal' has an opposite, we're it.

Shaking the last lingering bits of slumber from our heads, we all rise and greet Wisp and Granden, who inform us they're going to take us downstairs to the Intel Room to begin our strategizing sessions in preparation for the battle ahead. In the happy commotion of the "Good mornings!" and gleeful, overlapping questions about how everyone slept, I realize I never got to tell the others about *my* dream.

In it, I was soaring over the city—confident and free. Then the clouds parted to reveal the world below in chaos and flames. I could have flown off and left it all behind, but something I couldn't see or hear but only feel pulled me down toward the burning fields of battle and bodies. Unable to fly, but also unable to land, I hovered in the air, helpless, weightless, and I was forced to watch the world I hoped to save descend, instead, even further into a pit of apocalyptic violence. Buildings were twisting on their foundations and disappearing into dust, and people were running for their lives as the deafening crack of gunfire filled the air. There was a mysterious figure in a red cloak and a tall soldier with cruel eyes, and they were laughing as they killed the only people I love left in the world.

Back in the Valta, I once read a book where a psychiatrist claimed that humans have some sort of self-preservation mechanism in our brains that doesn't let us die in our dreams.

Last night, the searing pain in my head and the sound of my

own screams ringing in my ears just before everything went black proved that guy dead wrong.

Unlike Cardyn's dream, mine is a dream I really hope doesn't come true. The scariest part is that it didn't even feel like a dream.

It felt like a vision.

1

---

With Wisp and Granden looking on, we finish getting ourselves dressed in the form-fitting, five-button olive-sweaters and the multi-pocketed black combat pants from the armoire. I'm lacing up my boots when Wisp and Granden, waiting patiently and proudly in the doorway, remark about how nice and clean we all look. Wisp stands on her tiptoes and throws her arms around her brother's neck, and I can tell it's taking all of Brohn's strength not to let her go. He finally releases her, though, and Wisp says how happy she is to see us rested and healthy. She scans us up and down. "Better than ever," she exclaims.

"Well, cleaner, anyway," Granden adds with a twinkle-eyed smile playing at the corners of his mouth.

I'm still astounded at the odd couple Wisp and Granden make: Wisp, short, rail-thin, and practically drowning in her baggy khaki cargo pants and lime-green hoodie; Granden, decked out in pleated black pants and a crisp white dress shirt under a tactical military jacket, towering behind Wisp's shoulder like a vigilant bodyguard. He's handsome like Brohn, but he has silvery eyes and a certain soldierly coldness about him that tends to mask what he's feeling, which makes me a little nervous around him. Wisp, on the other hand, exudes a happy, positive, and almost mystical energy, which makes me imagine what a prancing baby unicorn might be like. Together, the two are quite the pair. There's something sweet about the image, but there's something scary about it, too. Like they're a unified entity with twice the power to kill you if you dared to threaten either one of them.

It used to be Wisp and Brohn who were never apart with Brohn standing guard over her like this. When we were growing up in the Valta, he was her protector, the one always within reach to lend a helping hand, an arm to lean against, or a shoulder to cry on. If he's feeling any jealousy or weirdness about being replaced by the same man who taught us how to kill, he isn't showing it. Instead, he strides confidently out of the room with me, Cardyn, Rain, and Manthy right on his heels.

Wisp with her sprightly steps and Granden with his determined strides escort us down the long, wide hall past a series of closed doors on either side. Outside, this building, affectionately called the "Style," looks old. A former office building housing the legal headquarters for a team of immigration lawyers, it's five floors of cracked bricks and crumbling mortar under about a hundred years' worth of age and grime. We only got glimpses on our way here last night, but there are some amazing buildings in this city. Tall towers and streamlined apartment complexes with green lawns on the terraces and everything. There are long, wide roads—clean and pristine. Silver mag-tracks, a hundred feet high, snake through parts of the city and connect the taller towers to each other. A lot of the businesses were closed when we got here, but some of the ones that were still open—a bakery and a bunch of bodegas—had glowing pink holo-ads shimmering out front that fizzled when we ran through them.

This neighborhood we're in now, on the other hand, isn't so nice. Since we got here yesterday, we've seen some dark rooms and some pretty creepy corridors. Fortunately, this fourth-floor hallway Wisp calls the Dorm is wide and long with at least twenty closed doors on each side. The floors and walls are illuminated by a gentle light glowing from thin halo-strips lining the ceiling. The light has a slight purplish tint to it, and it takes me a second to realize that it brightens almost imperceptibly as we walk down the hallway and then dims again behind us. I'm sure it was like this last night, too. I was just too tired to notice and way too happy to care.

I have faint memories of hallways like this in the school I went to before the drones destroyed our town and orphaned us. When I was six, school was a bustling throng of happy, jostling kids with our teachers, who seemed like benevolent giants at the time, constantly herding us between rooms and from one activity to the next. After the drone strikes, the only rooms left were in Shoshone High School, one of the few buildings left standing and the only one safe enough to live in. For the next ten years, we called that building home. We set up bedrooms, stocked supply closets, nailed scrap materials onto the windows, and even designated parts of the crumbling space as classrooms where we taught each other anything and everything we could from academics and sports to music and mechanics. Cardyn used to joke about how our studiousness and civility was all just a front and that we'd likely descend into a hostile and anarchic Lord of the Flies society before too long. But that never happened. Instead, our small community of survivors, bonded by a common fear but also by a common sense of compassion and by a stubborn refusal to surrender, managed to eke out a living and save ourselves from the brink of extinction.

When the five of us—me, Brohn, Cardyn, Rain, and Manthy—went back a few months later, the school had been destroyed along with everything and everyone else in the town. Except for Wisp, as we discovered only yesterday.

As we follow her and Granden past each door, I think about all the normal things I missed out on in those ten years. Things like going to classes, goofing around with friends, and enjoying each day without worrying it might be my last. I give my head a good shake to clear it of the distracting things that might have been but never were.

Wisp flicks her thumb toward the series of closed doors as we pass. "The others aren't up yet," she explains loud enough for us to hear her over the gentle echo of our footsteps on the tiled floor. "We figured we'd let them get one more night of solid sleep before we start them on their training this morning. It's going to be tough on them. I don't expect all of them to stick around. You, on the other hand, are kind of the key to everything we're about to do, so it's best you know everything there is to know. And that means lots of work and little sleep for the rest of this week."

"We can handle anything you throw our way," Brohn brags.

"I don't doubt that," Wisp says as she pushes up the sleeves on her oversized hoodie. "It's what the Patriot Army is going to throw our way that worries me."

Cardyn yawns, stretches his arms out wide, and says he wishes he could join the sleeping Insubordinates behind these doors. "I'm not sure which I'd like more right now, food or some more sleep."

"Unfortunately, Cardyn, we don't have a ton of time for either," Granden says evenly, his voice resonating with the air of authority I remember so well from our time in the Processor. He may be on our side now, but he's still military through and through. Everything about him—rigid posture, steely gaze, raised chin, unwavering focus, total lack of self-doubt—has been forged by his time as a soldier. I don't think he could conceal it if he tried. As one of our trainers, he pushed us hard and turned us into the unyielding survivors and warriors we've become. On top of that, he has the dubious honor of being the turncoat son of President Krug, who is probably the worst person in the world. I'm still not one-hundred-percent sold on Granden as an ally, but it's hard to doubt him right now. After all, he risked his life, twice now, to give us clues about where we needed to go and what we needed to do after our escape from Hiller and the Processor. It's largely because of him we're who and where we are. Whether that turns out to be a blessing or a curse remains to be seen.

Granden gestures toward a doorway at the end of the hall. "We'll have a quick meal in the Mess Hall, but then we have to head straight downstairs to the Intel Room and get to work. We have a lot of planning to do. We only have one shot at getting this right, and failure could mean..."

His words linger in the air. He doesn't need to finish. We all hear the barely-concealed urgency in his voice, and we know full well what the consequences of failure are. Not just for us, either. If there's even a sliver of truth to what Wisp and Granden told us last night, we could be facing the total takeover of San Francisco, the permanent installation of a sadistic military dictatorship, a base of operations in the West for Krug's government, and basically the end of everything we thought our country was and what we hoped it might still become.

Beckoning us forward and with her brown hair tied back in a jaunty ponytail, Wisp leads us into what turns out to be a large room set up with six rows of long metallic-blue tables arranged in orderly lines. The lights flicker on as we step into the room. Wisp strides over to an input panel on the wall and skims her fingers over its shiny red surface.

"I hope coffee and a tofu and spinach breakfast wrap are okay," Wisp calls out to us over her shoulder.

Cardyn licks his lips and slides onto the bench seat of the nearest long table. "I can't speak for the rest of you, but *my* dream is coming true!"

Granden invites the rest of us to sit as well, which we do, our mouths dribbling with anticipation. It's only just now occurred to me that the last thing we ate was tofu-stew back at Caramella's shack in Oakland nearly two days ago. That was right before we snuck into San Francisco and discovered that Brohn's dead sister Wisp was not only alive but that she had become the small but somehow very powerful and supremely confident leader of an underground resistance movement.

While I'm marveling at this, in front of us, a panel on the top of the table whooshes open, and an oval platter, neatly arranged with seven cups of steaming coffee and seven fat breakfast wraps, rises to the surface. Personally, I'm even more stunned by the tech than I am by the prospect of having a proper meal for a change.

"Pretty impressive," Cardyn beams.

"Mag-tray delivery system," Wisp boasts as she joins us at the table. "Thanks to Olivia, we've got mag and grav networks threaded through every floor. You wouldn't know it from the outside, but the whole building is rigged with them. We've got better tech here than they have in some of the government buildings downtown. Meals are prepared in our kitchen in the basement. We have three rotating crews down there responsible for shopping, food prep, and delivery. Most days, the Rations Team serves everything up in person like they did back in the old days. They've got a delivery coming in right now, so we're going to rely on automation this time. Chef Angelique oversees it all, and, I have to say, she's the one keeping us going."

"If she's the one responsible for feeding us," Cardyn gurgles through a voracious mouthful of breakfast wrap which he's dunked with a barbaric splash into his coffee, "then she's okay in my book."

Rain shakes her head and mutters, "Disgusting" under her breath but still loud enough for everyone to hear.

As embarrassing as it is to watch Cardyn eat, he's right, and I ask Wisp to thank Chef Angelique and her crew on our behalf.

"She'll be happy to hear that, Kress," Wisp says kind of sadly. "She used to be head chef and one of the deans at the San Francisco Culinary School before the Patriot Army came in and started taking away everyone's civil liberties and putting all kinds of restrictions on people's movements. This city has some real beauty to it. It also has some pretty nasty policies going on at the moment. There's deportations. Travel bans. Identity sweeps. Resource rationing. Rescinded health care. Slashed local budgets. A lot of defunded schools. All handed down by Krug's direct order. He's controlled the flow of information around here for years. At some point, we'll need to get you out on the streets so you can see it all for yourself. It's not as dangerous here as you'll find in some of the other New Towns. People still shop and socialize and live their lives. But that could be changing very quickly."

"How so?" Rain asks.

Wisp takes a sip of coffee and shrugs. "The city is resisting a push by Krug to return to gas-powered cars instead of the electric and mag-cars and the bicycling initiatives they've had in place here for nearly twenty years. He wants to reduce pollution controls like he's done all across the rest of the country. There are curfews here now. And no gatherings of three or more people allowed in public at any time. All in the name of safety for the citizens. No one likes it, of course. But they're victims of a slow, imminent death, and when Krug and his army get here in a week, they'll put the final nails in the people's coffin."

"Sounds like he's trying to gain total control out here like he has everywhere else," Brohn observes.

But Wisp shakes her head. "His goal isn't control. It's chaos. The more mess he makes, the harder it is for anyone to figure out what's happening, what to do, or how to do it. While we're reeling, he's ruling. A few weeks ago, the Patriot Army even tried to close the church Angelique and her family went to. No real reason. Just to see what they could get away with. The town council didn't allow it, but the whole thing threw a monkey-wrench into her life and drove her to us. Now she's promised to do whatever she can to help in the cause."

"She sounds like a great asset to have," Brohn says, rubbing his hands together in the steam swirling above his coffee cup. "Fighting for equality and human rights is hard enough without having to do it on an empty stomach."

On the opposite side of the table, Cardyn and Rain raise their coffee mugs in a toast to that.

Although I know we'd love to take our time and enjoy the rich coffee and the savory spinach and tofu-filled wraps, we eat quickly, the urgency and momentum of our mission driving us relentlessly forward.

## 2

AFTER FIVE MINUTES THAT SADLY FEEL LIKE FIVE SECONDS, WISP pushes herself to her feet and heads toward the door. With happy stomachs but heavy hearts, we follow her as she leads us down one flight of stairs to the third floor and takes us back into the Intel Room where we parted company just last night.

The large, windowless room is the same odd blend of dark gloom and halo-glow I remember from the night before. Some-how, the reflective surfaces of the dozen viz-screens on the walls and the linked lines of input boards illuminate the place without making it seem any brighter. A bank of spherical glass monitors floats in a semi-circle around a central console where Olivia, the half-human, half-machine Modified we met yesterday, sits in her hovering mag-chair. Thin, multi-colored tendrils ripple and roll from her wrists where her hands used to be. Undulating in wavy bundles like mountain hay in the wind, the vibrant filaments ebb and flow into the hovering spheres and through the various panels of black glass in front of her.

The shock I had from meeting Olivia yesterday has given way to a kind of morbid curiosity this morning. With her legless body apparently connected by a web of fibrous cables to her hovering mag-chair, I wonder how she moves around the building. Or even *if* she moves around. I've only seen her twice now, but both times, she was planted firmly in her chair at the head of this conference table as if this were the only possible place for her to be. She seems so plugged in right now that I can almost imagine her as part of the tech she's in charge of. The patchwork of fused skin and circuitry making up her face and her hairless head looks like it must hurt. And those odd eyes. Mine are brownish-green flecked with specks of goldish-orange if you look closely enough. But Olivia's eyes are a whole different level of unusual: They appear gray at first glance, but then, on closer inspection, her irises are revealed to be made up of tiny, alternating black and white squares like you'd find on a chessboard. Although she explained to us how she came to be a Modified, there are still so many questions I'd love to ask: What does it feel like to be so much machine? Is there any point where you stop feeling human? Would you trade the techno-human hybrid you are today to return to the pure flesh-and-blood human you once were?

I don't ask any of that out loud, of course. And the truth is, I have a lot of the same questions about myself. If what Granden said about me yesterday is true and as I've been slowly discovering over time, my psychic link with Render might not even depend on the maze of black circuitry running through my forearms. Which means that my father had another reason for implanting me with what Granden claims is the key to bringing down Krug and the Deenays and all of their plans for control over the future of humanity itself. It's too much for me to deal with this early in the morning, so I give my head another fog-clearing shake and turn my attention to Olivia, who rotates around in her chair to greet us with a bright smile and that haunting, slightly tinny voice of hers. "Nice to see you up and about. I'm looking forward to working with all of you."

"Us, too," Cardyn says, his eyes wide as he sweeps his head

around to take in Olivia and all the busyness of this strange room. Olivia's cluster of tech casts streaks of hazy light on the long oval table of black glass in front of her. The table's mirrored surface distorts the reflection of everything in the room—including us. Surrounded by her monitors, screens, and spheres, Olivia sits in a cut-out at the head of the table like a CEO presiding over a board meeting. The chairs around the table are a mix of old-style office chairs with wheels and silver mag-chairs that hover idly above the floor.

Wisp steps over to Olivia and traces her finger along one of the consoles. "We need to get our friends here up to speed. Can you call up the Armory?"

"Initiated." Olivia swings back around, and the black table in front of her glows a flickering carroty orange as a detailed 3-D schematic of the city of San Francisco materializes in the air. Although her body doesn't move, Olivia's tendrils continue to weave and snake through the air seeking out micro-ports in the viz-screen and along the surface of the shimmering, floating orbs around her head. Granden invites us to gather around as the hovering schematic over the table zooms in to a single spot until a twinkling image of a large building comes into meticulous focus. We all take seats at the table and stare at the imposing structure, which consists of a clunky, four-story rectangular building with octagonal turrets forming its four corners. Its windows are narrow and tall, its entire surface pimpled with dark red brick. Attached is a slightly taller structure with a similar brick façade and a smooth white domed roof arching high into the air like the back of a whale. I've never seen a sports stadium in real life, but this is kind of how I imagine they must look. Parts of Olivia's models are missing with pixilated patches and blacked-out sections giving the whole thing a kind of partial, blasted-out feel that reminds me of the destruction we witnessed in the Valta.

Olivia apologizes for the incomplete images, but Wisp tells

her not to worry about it. "You've done amazing work getting us this much."

On the streets around the Armory, a few human figures, fizzling in and out of focus, walk between buildings and along walkways or zip along the city grid on mag-bikes. It's busy and bustling, even this early in the morning, but there's something so safe and normal about it that it makes me want to be part of it all.

"This is real time?" I ask.

Without looking at me, Olivia nods her head. "You're looking at a typical morning in the city of San Francisco."

"It looks like a pretty normal city, doesn't it?" Wisp says through clenched teeth. "But what you don't see from here is the infection of tyranny already in its system."

Olivia gives a quarter-turn in her mag-chair. "I can tap into some of the existing surveillance systems in the municipal grid. Some, but not all."

"We have to be careful," Granden warns. "Wisp's right. The Patriot Army is in the process of corrupting established security protocols and taking over the city grid. And they're getting better about securing their own communication and surveillance networks. If they catch Olivia snooping around like this, it won't take much for them to backtrack along her neural-network path and find their way here."

"I can cover my tracks," Olivia says with what sounds like a hint of defensiveness in her hollow, metallic voice. "But not completely," she admits after a brief pause. "And not for long. For now, I'll keep giving you what I can."

Wisp slips past Olivia to join us around the table. She leans forward, her arm extended, and begins to poke at the image with her index finger. The spots on the schematic of the imposing building pulse green where she touches them. "These are the three targets we've identified as vital for pulling off this rebellion: the Munitions Depot, the Communications Center, and the Command Headquarters, all located in the San Francisco

Armory. The first two targets are important, but it's the Command Headquarters here on the mezzanine level of the Armory that will be the real key. If we can take all of this, plus their Command Headquarters, we can prevent them from taking total control of the city."

"Wait," Rain says, "you're saying they have their three strategic branches all in one confined location?"

"Yep. For now, anyway. But they're in the process of fixing things, digging themselves deeper and more permanently into the city and its systems."

Looking deeply contemplative, Rain presses a finger to her chin. "That's a point in our favor. A centralized objective with the primary tactical targets in a cluster."

"This is the Patriot Army we're talking about," Wisp says. "They're armed, not intelligent. Mostly just boys, hardly older than us. They've only been here for the past month or so, and even now they're not really here in an official capacity."

Rain squints. "What do you mean? They're here. They're technically part of the government. How can that not be 'official'?"

Wisp looks from Rain to Granden who clears his throat and explains. "The San Francisco City Council continues to oppose the presence of the Patriots. Quietly. Local law enforcement has been caught in the middle and won't move without specific directions from the mayor."

"And the mayor...?" Rain asks.

"Is just as caught in the middle. His hands are tied. He can't oppose the presence of the Patriot Army without defying President Krug, and he can't embrace them without defying the San Francisco City Council or the Chief of Police and his captains."

"Or many of the residents, for that matter," Wisp adds. "With everyone in the country afraid of the Eastern Order, Krug has been able to roll through a lot of towns without a lot of resistance. This isn't one of those towns."

Granden nods and drums his fingers on the table's glossy

surface. "This city has a long history of following its own path and going against the government's grain. There are still a lot of people here, young and old, who aren't planning on sitting still while Krug tries to destroy that history. The Patriot Army is Krug's personal arsenal of bullies and bodyguards. Make no mistake, they're violent, well-armed, and extremely dangerous. But they're also relatively new in town, disorganized, tunnel-visioned, and arrogant."

Sitting between Brohn and Granden, Wisp stretches her arms out wide. "And that gives them a blind spot about this big."

Rain leans in to survey the flickering, pixilated image more closely. "Then it's a blind spot we need to exploit—hard, fast, and with everything we've got."

Standing and walking around the table so she's right behind me, Wisp puts a hand on my shoulder and looks around the table from Brohn, Granden, and Rain on one side to Cardyn and Manthy on the other. "And that's exactly where you come in. This is Saturday morning. The attack we're planning relies on you, and it happens this coming Friday night."

"Wonderful," Cardyn says. "I've always wanted to know the exact location and day of my death."

Matching Cardyn's sarcasm, Brohn does a pretend half-bow in his seat, hailing Cardyn as "The great and inspiring prophet of doom."

While Cardyn sulks, Manthy stares, and Rain and I laugh, Wisp and Olivia arrange for the schematic of the Armory, flickering in some places and still blacked out in others, to rotate. As we look on, Olivia gives us a bit of the building's history, its structural specs, and its strengths and weaknesses. "They used to have boxing matches there over a hundred years ago. It hasn't been used as an armory since 1976. After that, it sat empty for thirty years. The city's very own white elephant."

"White elephant?" I ask.

Olivia gives me a resonant, lilting laugh. "A 'white elephant' means something that's outlived its usefulness and is now something no one wants."

"Sound familiar?" Manthy says to Cardyn who scowls at her in return.

"In this case," Olivia continues, "the Armory could have been used for housing or offices or retail space, but no one could agree one way or another, so it sat there like an orphan waiting for the right family to come along. Anyway, after that it took a turn as a movie studio for the adult film industry."

Card's ears perk up at this. "Really?"

"Yes. Eventually, the town kicked them out. Turns out that for this particular orphan, having no family was better than having the wrong family. But then it sat empty again for nearly a decade until a tech developer swooped in and turned it into a giant science lab, which the town council soon discovered was a front for some rather disturbing bio-tech experiments."

"Let me guess," I say, "the Modifieds?"

Olivia waggles her polychromatic tendrils in affirmation. "It was set up by Krug to be the western branch of the Deenays' Modified program they had going on in Washington D.C. and in some of the other cities back east. Most of the Modifieds you met downstairs came out of the program here. We saved as many as we could. Brought them to the Style. The rest…"

Wisp hangs her head, and Granden reaches over to put a hand on her shoulder, but she waves him off. "I'm okay."

"After that," Olivia continues, "the Armory got cleared out, so it sat empty yet again until forty-one days ago when Krug's battalion of Patriots arrived and commandeered it as their personal headquarters. We had eyes inside for less than an hour when they overrode the old security protocols, and we lost that tactical advantage. So we switched to a city-cam patch-in. They found that, and shut it down, too. Then we sent out some Insubordinates on a scouting mission. Some of them never made it back. The few who did reported that the place was too secure to get any useful structural or logistics intel. That's why so many of the images are incomplete. Our information about the Armory and the other facilities taken over by the Patriots is partial and outdated at best. At worst, it's just plain wrong. Either way, it's currently useless and possibly even dangerous."

"So how are we supposed to get into *that?*" Card asks, leaning over the table toward the image with his nose practically touching it. The glow from the slowly-rotating hologram highlights his freckles and paints his face a grim yellowish-orange. He waves his hand back and forth through the graphic. "It looks like a flippin' castle."

"No castle is impenetrable," Wisp points out. "And none is indestructible. That's why you don't see many of them around anymore. We have a chance to make this one just as obsolete. With the right intel, the right strategy, and with just the right group of rebels, that is."

"I'm assuming that's us," Brohn says.

Wisp claps him hard on the shoulder. "None other, big brother!" she sings out.

With her brow furrowed and her chin resting in her cupped hand, Rain studies the revolving schematic like a chess player contemplating her next move.

When she doesn't say anything, Wisp leans forward, pressing her palms down onto the tabletop, and lays out her big-picture battle plan. "We'll have multiple Infiltration Teams. We'll need to be coordinated to the second, and we're going to need to know everything about everyone in a lot of places, but especially in the Armory and the attached barracks. Every guard. Every change of shift. Every weapon, security protocol. Every room, nook, cranny, corridor, input panel, fire escape, window-washer's rig, access corridor, janitor's closet, service elevator...the works. If it's in this building, living, dead, or totally inanimate, we need to know about it."

Rain shakes her head. "I don't see too many vulnerabilities in this thing. Plus, there's not a ton of detail. I don't suppose we can just walk up to it and have a look around?"

"Only if you'd like to get shot," Granden warns. "These boys guarding the place are on a hair-trigger and are on high alert for spies, recon drones, or anyone else who might be snooping around."

Rain turns to Olivia who is sitting quietly in a deep shadow among her consoles at the head of the table. "I know you're gathering what you can. But for this plan to work, we'd need to have a better way of getting all the detail Wisp is asking for. Even if we manage to get it, do you really think we can identify the right targets, get in, and take them over without getting caught, shot, and definitely killed?"

Wisp leans back in her chair and swivels it around to face Rain. "We're lucky in a lot of ways. We're outmanned and outgunned, the Armory is a large facility, and it's a variable with a lot of unknowns, and, as you point out, it's pretty much impenetrable. Plus, of course, Krug has reinforcements arriving in six days to coordinate and solidify his Patriot Army's grip on the city—"

"Forgive me for saying so," Cardyn interrupts, "but you seem to have a slightly terrible definition of the word, 'lucky.'"

Wisp pushes up the sleeves of her lime-green hoodie and laughs. "Okay. They have a lot. But they don't have the five of you. We do. And I'll take the five of you over an entire battalion of Krug's army any day."

Wisp stands and begins walking around the glistening black table, gazing at the image of the Armory like she's seeing it for the first time. She runs her finger along the back of Olivia's chair and some of the viz-screens before returning to our side of the table to stand next to Brohn. She kneels down and presses her cheek to his and, in a flash, she goes from powerful Major to doting little sister. "Sure, there are some obstacles we'll need to overcome. But I still say we're the lucky ones. We're together.

Against all odds and against an enemy who has already tried to kill us and failed, we're still together. Never forget that."

Just when I'm getting an optimistic, feel-good vibe about this whole situation, Rain brings us all back down to earth. "Listen, Wisp. I hate to be the voice of reason here," she says, "but as great as luck is, it's still not a plan. The five of us, you and Granden, a room full of immobilized Modifieds downstairs, and I don't know how many untrained Insubordinates you have upstairs against what Granden himself admits is a violent, well-armed, and dangerous army...I just don't see how we have any chance of carrying this off."

Wisp nods her agreement, and I suddenly get the terrible feeling she's going to heed Rain's warnings, pull the plug on the whole operation, and lead us all out of the building with our hands up to surrender to the Patriot Army. Instead, she laughs. Standing between Brohn and Granden, who are nearly as tall sitting down as she is standing up, Wisp tells Rain she's absolutely right. "We're outnumbered. The odds are stacked against us. The cost of failure is death. Not just ours but the final nail in the coffin of our democracy. But there is more to all of this than meets the eye. More importantly, there's more to all of you."

## 3

WE ALL STAND UP AS I LOOK FROM BROHN TO RAIN AND OVER TO Cardyn and Manthy. "More to all of us?"

Wisp reaches out to put one hand on Brohn's shoulder and the other on Granden's. "You've only gotten a small taste so far of what you're able to do. While you're helping us train the Insubordinates, we'll be training you."

"Training us?" I ask. "Training us in what?" I give what I hope isn't too obvious of a dirty look at Granden who was one of our trainers back in the Processor. In the space of three months of intense mental and physical challenges, he and his partner Trench, under what turns out to have been the deceitful guidance of the now-dead Captain Grace Hiller, taught us how to work as a team, how to survive nearly any situation, and how to overcome nearly any obstacle. The two of them also ran us through all kinds of combat drills and taught us countless techniques to kill with a variety of weapons in a variety of ways. It turns out it was all just a failed attempt to turn us into super soldiers in a war against our own people. The whole experience cost Kella her sanity, and it cost Karmine and Terk their lives. I'm not going to feel guilty right now about being suspicious of Granden.

Granden catches me looking at him and turns his attention back to the polished black table where the image of the Armory continues its slow spin.

"I think we've had our fill of training for one lifetime," Rain says, pretty much reading my mind.

"It's not like that this time," Wisp says. "We'll train you how to access your abilities in order for you to become better versions of your true selves."

Manthy is sitting next to Cardyn on the opposite side of the conference table near Olivia and her array of consoles, floating spheres, and holo-screens. Manthy scrunches up her shoulders and cringes at the word "abilities." After she started developing this strange power to link her mind with certain types of digital technologies, my weird psychic connection to Render didn't seem so impossible to believe anymore. I know the last thing Manthy ever wanted was to be in the spotlight for any reason. Now, here she is, one of the people Wisp claims is going to somehow magically win a war.

"And how exactly do you plan on training us?" Manthy glowers, her voice laced with distrust and dripping with doubt.

"I'll show you shortly, I promise." Wisp puts up a hand to stave off any more questions. "We need to get moving. The clock is ticking. As for the actual plan, here's how it will work." She presses her hands down on the table. "As you know, this room we're in is the Intel Room. It's where Olivia is stationed, and it will be strategy-central for the rest of us. Every plan and possibility will go through this room. Over the next few days, Kress and Manthy will work with Olivia on gathering as much information as they can about the Armory and our other key targets in and around the area and throughout San Francisco. That includes the guard posts, checkpoints, and security stations the Patriot Army has scattered around the city. As you can see, we've got a basic overview, but we're a bit short on details. Between today and Wednesday, Thursday at the latest, Rain and I will sit across from you right here at the image-relay station and coordinate a battle plan using the information you provide. At the same time, Brohn, Cardyn, and Granden will head up armed and unarmed combat training for the Insubordinates upstairs on the fifth floor. Then, at the end of every day, it's off to bed for an unfortunately very brief sleep, and the cycle repeats the next day. If we do this right, if we don't cut corners, we can have our troops up and running and ready to fight in time for Krug's arrival."

"That's not a lot of time to gather all the information you say you need and to train a bunch of kids," I point out.

"I wish we had more," Wisp says. "More time and more people. But we don't. And once Krug gets his claws into this city, that's it. The country is his and all of us along with it. If we had more time, I'd take it. But, as it stands, all we have is the time we have."

Wisp hops up to sit on the edge of the table and twists around to face us. The way she kicks her legs as she talks makes her look like a little girl sitting on a pier somewhere without a care or a responsibility in the world. "For the next few days, we'll just be gathering intel. After that, we'll start setting up smaller raids to pick away at the Patriots' perimeter defenses. Friday night at twenty-three hundred is zero-hour. The point of no return. After that, Krug will be embedded, a backup contingent will arrive in the city shortly after midnight, and we won't be able to do anything about anything. At exactly twenty-three hundred hours, we'll have nearly a dozen smaller teams tackling some of the lower-priority targets in a coordinated, simultaneous attack. The only thing the five of you have to do is get yourselves, along with a few of the Infiltration Teams, into the Armory. After that, you just need to let the other teams get started on their takedown of the Munitions Depot and the Communications Center while you break in and assume control over Command Headquarters."

Cardyn whacks his forehead with the palm of his hand. "Oh, is that all?"

Ignoring him, Wisp goes on. "While you're having fun doing all that, the remaining teams of trained Insubordinates, coordinated by me and led by Granden, will take over the Patriot Army's external garrison and commandeer their military vehicles. We'll detain the personnel who offer the least resistance and literally drive the rest of the Patriot Army past their own checkpoints and right out of San Francisco. You've met Patriot Army Staff Sergeant Dennis Kammet. He's one of our inside guys with full knowledge of and access to the army's fleet."

"What about local law enforcement?" Rain asks. "Will they stay neutral? Or will they help us? Or worse, will they help the Patriots?"

"Good questions, Rain. Granden?"

Granden slings his jacket over the back of his chair, undoes the top button of his shirt, and begins to roll up the cuffs of his sleeves with tidy, military precision. "Honestly, Rain, they're a wild card. The mayor, the chief of police, and the chief's captains and deputies don't like the Insubordinates because we're underground and off the grid. But they don't exactly have a lot of love for the Patriot Army either. In addition to helping coordinate the training, I'll also be doing what I can to draw local law enforcement over to our side. I do have to be careful, though. Being the president's son has had certain advantages. Now that I'm gone and presumed dead, sticking my neck out now is a good way to get my head chopped off."

Rain nods her understanding of the precarity of the situation, his and ours. "So we have a short timeline, a limited window, a strategic deficiency, limited and inexperienced personnel, *and* we don't know what side the police are on...?" Rain mutters. I can see the gears churning in her head. She's a riddle-lover, a dedicated mystery-solver, and she's the best I've ever known when it comes to assembling variables, diagnosing a problem, and strategizing a solution. It's why she always beat everyone at chess back in the Valta, and, honestly, it's why we're not all dead out in the desert wasteland so much of our world has become. She squints but doesn't say anything else, which is a good sign. It means her brain is in overdrive, which means whatever problem or problems are standing in her way don't have a chance.

Speaking more quickly now, Wisp asks Olivia to highlight the primary border posts, and two orange glowing points pop up alongside the schematic of the Armory. "After we secure the Armory, we'll position defensive checkpoints here and here at the foot of the Golden Gate and Oakland-Bay Bridges to keep the city safe but supply lines open. With control over the comm-grid and with some cooperation from the harbor-master's union, we can monitor and even control ships coming and going from the Pacific. As for the rest of the peninsula…Olivia, call up the wall."

Olivia says, "Initiated," and the city schematic scrolls sideways until an imposing, curved and white overland wall of synth-steel supported by a line of cable-stays and support posts comes into view. Looking like the bleached skin of a giant, flattened snake, the wall meanders all the way across the middle of the San Francisco Peninsula from what Wisp informs us is the Gulf of Fallarones in the west to San Francisco Bay in the east.

"Nearly a decade ago now—back in 2033—Krug had this ten-mile wall installed along East Market and the old Guadalupe Canal Parkway. As you've seen everywhere from the Valta to the Processor to Salt Lake City, Reno, and Oakland, Krug is all about walls. I know you've heard them mentioned many times on the viz-screens in his weekly national security reports. He calls them 'Safety Partitions.' Just his cute little euphemism for the walls of his city prisons. Until the rest of the troops arrive, this particular partition is under drone patrol. Getting control of the Communications Center in the Armory will allow us to access and commandeer the drones and reclaim the southern San Francisco border. There's urgency to all of this," Wisp says, and for the first time, she looks a little nervous. "All that's at stake is everything. Every freedom we were promised, all the social equality our country is supposed to stand for, and all the justice on behalf of all those who've died or had their lives crushed in the name of greed. We're not just fighting for freedom or even for our lives. If Krug gets his way, he'll have control over life, itself."

I don't know if it's the barely-discernible quiver in her voice or the extra breath she takes, but Brohn picks up on his little sister's apprehension. "Wisp, why do I get the feeling there's actually more to this than you're saying? Control over life, itself? I mean, you and Granden filled us in yesterday about what it means for us to be Emergents or whatever. But I still don't get it. Why us? Why now?"

Wisp and Granden exchange a knowing look before Granden clears his throat. "Brohn, we're at a pivotal point in this rebellion. Pivotal and potentially problematic. Like you, the people of San Francisco have been fed propaganda. A lot. As you know, Krug needs to keep attention focused on the Eastern Order, so the citizens don't see his Patriot Army taking control of their lives right under their very own noses like they've been doing so effectively and ruthlessly everywhere else. Well, that attention has started to stray. Thanks to you, although you didn't know it at the time, the Eastern Order has been called into question. Not just its motivations or ruthlessness anymore but its entire existence. Rumors are going around about a group of escaped super-powered teenagers who have discovered the truth and who hold the key to the future."

"Superpowered? And you think that's us?"

"No. I *know* that's you. Krug controls most of the country's communication networks. Most, but not all. There are resourceful people still out there, people who are finding ways to get to the truth and pass it on as best as possible. A lot of them are getting arrested or even killed for their efforts. But they've poked holes in Krug's stories. People are starting to see the strings above his little puppet show. He knows this, and he's preparing to go all the way to ensure those strings aren't cut."

I raise my hand. "By 'all the way,' you mean…?"

"He's going to stop being slow and subtle about it, Kress. He's been in power for a long time, but he's starting to realize it can't last forever. That *he* can't last forever. His goal now is immortality. He's not just coming here in one week for a stroll around town. He's not even coming here to finalize his control over the West Coast of the country. He's coming here for you. And he's bringing reinforcements."

"Wait," Cardyn says, making a "time-out" motion with his hands. "Coming for *us?*"

"Honestly," Granden says "I don't know if you should be flattered or terrified. But yes, you're on Krug's radar and in his cross-hairs. Dead center, actually. All five of you. Kella, too."

"But we had to leave Kella behind," I remind him. "She's back in the mountains with Adric and Celia."

"And that may be exactly what saves her life."

"Celia said something about them possibly heading east," Brohn says slowly.

Granden sighs and looks at the ceiling. "I didn't know that. That's…unfortunate."

Brohn leans toward Granden and gives him a harsh look. "Why is that unfortunate?"

"I don't think Krug's soldiers would have ever found her in the mountains. But if she heads east…if she and the others make it as far as the Capitol…well, they'll be walking right into the lion's den. It's right where Krug wants her. Where he wants all of you."

Wisp holds up both hands and orders Granden to stop. "Speculation and scaring everyone aren't going to get us anywhere," she nearly snarls. "Let's stay focused."

Granden apologizes and hangs his head.

"It's simple," Wisp says, hopping back down from where she's been sitting on the edge of the table. She turns toward the rest of us and starts to walk in a slow circle around the perimeter of the room, pausing for a second to glance through the partially-shuttered window down to the street below. She stops behind Manthy and puts her hands on the back of her chair. Manthy looks up at her and then back at me though the 3-D model of the city still hovering over the table. I give her a shrug and a reassuring smile as Wisp continues. "Let me see if I can distill this mind-numbing prospect down to slightly more manageable size."

"That would be great," Cardyn chimes in. "You know, for all us dummies in the room."

Wisp gives Cardyn a wink and a thumbs up. "For the dummies, then. Look. Krug is way past wanting political and military power. He has that. He's not looking for total and absolute wealth. He has that, too. He even has nearly complete control over the nation's communications grid. What he *doesn't* have is the key to what his geneticists have convinced him is the next and most important step in the history of human evolution. And I'm talking about since we learned to walk upright and use language and tools. There've been other Emergents identified, but you're the first who've escaped from one of Krug's Processors. You're also the first and only Emergents who've been not just identified but also confirmed to have the altered DNA sequence Krug thinks will make him immortal or omnipotent."

"Confirmed?" I ask.

Granden pivots in his chair to face me. "The first thing Hiller did back in the Processor…"

With a look of realization spreading over his face, Brohn reaches over his shoulder to the top of his back. "Those Biscuits."

Granden nods as Cardyn, Rain, Manthy, and I all reach over to feel our shoulder blades, too. "Those implants, or 'Biscuits' as Hiller called them, you got on the first day in the Processor," Granden tells us, "were more than just simple tracking devices."

I get an odd combined feeling of relief and confusion. "Then why weren't you…I mean, why weren't they able to track us?"

Granden presses his palms together like he's praying. "I wondered that too, Kress. After your escape and after Hiller's body was discovered, I was able to do some investigation of my own. From what I can tell, it turns out Manthy fried the link-up when she was with you and Brohn in the Halo with Hiller."

I remember the exact moment he's talking about. When Manthy tapped into the console with the odd symbols and scrolling text—right after Hiller shot herself in the head—I worried about the consequences of Manthy creating a feedback loop. I still worry about that kind of feedback whenever I initiate my connection with Render. Fortunately, Manthy seemed to be okay, despite her headaches. But now I realize that her connection with the tech back then apparently had other unknown side effects. It worked out fine for us. We got answers, and, as it turns out, the Patriots couldn't track us. But what if my connection with Render is having the same kind of destructive impact on him? I spend so much time worrying about how our connection is affecting me, it never really occurs to me how much he might be suffering as well.

I don't have time to dwell on it, though, as Rain, barely holding back her irritation, whips around to face Granden. "Then if they weren't being used just to track us, what were they for?"

"They were…*are*…SGAs. Spectral Genomic Analyzers. They identified you as potential Emergents. Long before Manthy accidentally scorched them, they'd already fed most of your genetic information back to Krug and the Deenays. You were one day away from being transported to their labs in D.C. when you got away."

"And now," Wisp adds, "Krug will be here soon with his personal armed escort to finish what he started."

Cardyn is still reaching his hand far back over his shoulder and whipping his head from side to side like a dog trying to itch a spot on its back it can't reach. "Can't we just get these things out of us then?"

"Not without killing you," Olivia hums. "They're not sending any signals out anymore, but they are still integrated through active supercoiled microfilaments with your individual genomic and nano-synaptic configurations."

"Great," Cardyn groans, his shoulders slumped low in resignation. "How am I supposed to sleep, knowing I've got a micro-nano-whatever burrowed in my spine?"

"I'm sure you'll be fine," Rain assures him.

"Big baby," Manthy adds under her breath.

Wisp plops back down in her seat. "Listen. Krug has your DNA, but he needs *you*, including your blood, your brains, and your cooperation to make it all come together. The good news is that he needs you alive. The bad news is that he can keep you alive and in a lot of pain for a very long time until he gets what he wants. You're the last pieces in his puzzle. The rest of his army will be just a few hours behind him. If we don't strike before Friday night, we'll be facing impossible odds by Saturday morning."

Brohn holds up five fingers on one hand and his thumb on the other. "That gives us six days to turn this handful of Insubordinates of yours into an army."

"No," I correct him. "It gives us six days to turn them into a Conspiracy."

4

WITH THE PLAN OUTLINED, WISP DOESN'T HESITATE FOR A SINGLE second longer before doling out our duties.

"Olivia, call up the Style."

Olivia says, "Initiated" and complies with her customary speed and cheerfulness. With a flick of her fluorescent tendrils, she patches back into her holo-spheres and monitors, and, before our eyes, the San Francisco city-scape, the long white wall, and the Armory are replaced by a shimmering image of the Style, the building we're currently in. Several dozen heat signatures glow red throughout the basement and the five main floors of the building with small, scrolling info-tags blinking white above each figure.

"What are those?" Cardyn asks, pointing to the ghostly, blue and purple forms congregated on the second floor.

"You met them yesterday," Wisp reminds him. "Those are the Modifieds."

"But why—?"

Olivia looks up from her monitors. "Glitchy neuro-synaptic firing. Distorted thermal and electromagnetic radiation patterns.

Inconsistent atom vibration frequencies. And altered heat-signatures. All side-effects of being one of us," she adds.

Addressing Brohn and Cardyn, Granden stands and points to various spots on the image that light up green as he touches them.

"We have our weapons cache here in the basement. That includes guns, ammunition, body armor, combat knives, and a small collection of explosive devices. There are other supplies, too. Comm-links, zip-cuffs, stun-sticks, argon torches, night-vision goggles...things like that. Not as much or as sophisticated as we'd like, but we have to make do. We have a relay system already in place," Granden informs us, pointing to the fifth floor of the image. "As you can see, there is a team of Insubordinates already moving the supplies from the basement up to the top floor."

Cardyn turns his attention from Granden to Wisp. "And what, exactly, are we supposed to do with these Insubordinates and all these weapons and supplies?"

"If I knew that," Wisp laughs, "I'd do it myself."

"You remember your training?" Granden asks.

Brohn and Cardyn nod in unison.

"Well, it'll be just like that. Only faster. And more difficult. And with a lot less time, less disciplined trainees, less rest, and a lot more on the line."

Brohn leans back in his chair and looks across the table at Cardyn who has begun chewing nervously at the skin around his fingernail. "Don't worry, Card," Brohn assures him. "We can do this. We don't need to turn them into super soldiers," he adds, turning toward his sister. "Just give them the basics, right?"

Wisp gives him a smile and a thumbs up. "Nothing to it. Make sure they know the difference between a knife-handle and the blade, and which end of a gun the bullets come out. That'll already be more than most of them know."

"I've been training them for a while now," Granden says. "A couple of weeks anyway. But I can't do it myself, and, honestly, I can't do it as well as you'll be able to."

Brohn and Cardyn exchange a "what do you think?" look across the table. Card returns Brohn's small, affirmative nod with half-smile and a completely skeptical look of tepid agreement. "When do we start?"

Granden reaches into the image and focuses in on and enlarges the fifth floor, where we see the heat signatures of the Insubordinates unloading a freight elevator. "About five minutes ago," he says. His tone is unmistakable, and he's already ushering Brohn and Cardyn toward the door before his words fade into silence.

Brohn waves back at me and calls out, "I'll see you tonight," and then the door whooshes shut behind him, leaving me, Rain, and Manthy alone with Olivia and Wisp in the Intel Room.

With the boys off to start conducting the training, the rest of us work tirelessly for the remainder of the day and deep into the night to lay out battle plans and organize training protocols for the Insubordinates. At first, Manthy and I mostly sit and watch as Wisp and Olivia talk strategy with Rain. They ask for our input from time to time, but Manthy and I don't have much to add. Manthy can talk to tech. I can talk to Render. Neither of us has ever been very good at strategizing. Personally, I don't know how Rain does it. In the Valta, I once saw her working out a complex logic problem, solving a math equation, and teaching a Juven about the inner workings of the internal combustion engine…*all at the same time*. Even though my memory seems to be getting better and closer to perfect by the day, I still can't apply it to multiple tasks at a time the way Rain can.

Over the next few hours, Rain spins the city image around, asks Olivia for as much detail as she can provide, and makes suggestions to Wisp about approach points and gaps in defensive positions. Wisp taps her comm-link, and, a few seconds later, one of the Insubordinates or another pokes a head into the room to receive instructions.

Wisp is an unhesitating machine of efficiency. She seems to have complete and detailed knowledge of the inner-workings of the entire underground movement. Rattling off names of buildings and lists of streets and neighborhoods, she sends a few Insubordinates on supply runs. She sends a squad of three Insubordinates out to communicate with some other smaller faction hidden somewhere in the city. A few minutes after that, she withdraws a metal box from a small locker over by the door and instructs two boys to deliver a voice-mod synthesizer and neuro-inducer to Caldwell downstairs on the second floor where the Modifieds are being tended to.

At the same she's directing this flurry of activity, she's filling me and Rain and Manthy in on what comes next for us. Following Wisp's orders, Olivia continues to show us as much of the Armory and the other strategic locations in the areas she's able to patch into. Speckling her report with the history of nearly every neighborhood in San Francisco, she calls up image after image of the city and its thousands of buildings. One at a time, she peels back layers of her multiple floating diagrams to reveal everything from subway systems to water lines to electric power girds. She shows us 3-D images of City Hall, the Transamerica Pyramid nestled in with the other towering downtown skyscrapers, the United Nations Plaza, which looks like a five-story capital "D," and Grace Cathedral—one of the Insubordinates' backup hideouts not too far from here. All the structures, bridges, piers, and grid-maps of the city spin and shed their outer layers to reveal the skeletal foundations beneath. It's an information overload made more challenging by all the gaps and missing sections where the intel is compromised, inconclusive, or incomplete.

After a few more hours and with my eyes glazed over from

fatigue, I ask Wisp if it's all right if I head upstairs to check on Brohn and Cardyn's progress with the Insubordinates. Telling me not to be too long because she may need me soon, Wisp gives me the go-ahead. I'm already up the first flight of stairs when it occurs to me how odd it is to be working under the supervision of a girl who used to seem so tiny and frail. Once, when Brohn and I were Juvens and she was still a lowly Neo, she burst into tears because she couldn't keep up with him when he went walking down to the water reservoir. Another time, I watched Wisp, her hair in pigtails, follow a butterfly around the Valta for an entire afternoon. Now, she's called "the Major," people do her bidding, and she doesn't seem to mind having the weight of the world on her narrow shoulders. In fact, she seems to delight in it. It's like size really doesn't matter, and this is who she was meant to be all along.

Grinning, I take the next flight of stairs two at a time and push open the steel door at the top landing.

Stepping through the door and out onto the fifth floor of the Style, I'm stunned. Unlike the dark, tech-filled Intel Room downstairs where I've been cooped up all day, this floor is abuzz with energy, activity, and a throng of bodies in motion. Together, Brohn and Cardyn are a whirlwind of organization. They're working at super-speed with Granden to turn the rooms on this top floor of the building into a fully-stocked training facility. A dozen Insubordinates unload two big freight-lifts at the end of the hall, and a dozen more are busily pushing equipment around on hovering mag-carts as they work to fill the rooms and cordoned-off sections of the wide hallway with training supplies and combat gear. With their high-fives and hearty backslaps, the Insubordinates seem inappropriately happy considering what we're preparing them for.

Striding up to me through the noisy crowd, Brohn greets me with a big smile and a sweaty hug.

"Welcome to training!"

"Well, this is certainly impressive."

"We've already started teaching them some of the basics," Brohn boasts with a broad wave of his hand in the direction of the tittering Insubordinates. "Wisp apparently tracked down some more supplies for us, so we're offloading those before we get back to it."

Cardyn waves to me from down the hall as Brohn starts to explain how they have specific rooms dedicated to certain elements of their training schedule. Pointing one at a time to the series of doorways lining the long hall, he rattles off the purpose of each room like a proud parent bragging about his child's report card. "This room is for hand-to-hand combat training. We have blocking pads and sparring equipment on the way. This room is for stealth operations training. We're going to introduce them to night fighting. This room is to teach them how to communicate with each other and work as a team. And that one down there is a long, double-room that has the target gallery to teach them how to shoot straight so they don't wind up killing one of us by mistake when Friday rolls around."

I nod, impressed. "You really are already whipping them into shape, aren't you?"

Brohn blushes and shrugs. "I don't think I'd go that far. We're just getting started. But I've got a good feeling, Kress. I really do. We're in the process of figuring out what everyone is capable of. Their strengths and abilities and such. We're hoping to get a cascading effect going on a rotational basis where the Insubordinates are able to cycle through certain parts of the training protocols to help each other as we go."

"Kind of like how we taught each other for all those years in the Valta," I say.

"Exactly. Here, I'll show you what we've done so far."

Weaving between throngs of kids, a few adults, and an assortment of wooden and synth-steel crates, we walk farther down the hall, and I get my second sweaty hug as Cardyn trots over, red-faced and beaming. Together, Brohn and Cardyn talk over each other like excited schoolboys about all their plans. Cardyn picks up on Brohn's tour and shows me a room dedicated to edged-weapon combat. Another room has equipment and monitors set up to teach the Insubordinates about communication and code-breaking.

"And this is going to be one of our simulation rooms!" Cardyn exclaims. "Wisp is having some supplies sent over. Granden is downstairs right now to receive them."

"And once you help her get better intel," Brohn continues, "Olivia is going to relay details of the key rooms we're going to infiltrate, and we'll replicate them in here, so the Insubordinates get a chance to preview the targets and the attack plan."

I tell them how impressed I am, and both boys blush like I just told them "Good boy!" and tossed them a treat.

Proceeding with the tour, I continue to be impressed. In addition to the swarms of bubbling Insubordinates, the rooms are loaded with boxes of ammo, tables of knives and handguns, racks of rifles, and a whole array of comm-links for in-the-field communication. Somehow, Brohn and Cardyn have worked together with Granden to turn the place into a proper training facility.

And all in less than a day.

I'm filled with a mind-swirling combination of pride and regret. I'm happy that Brohn has taken on such a leadership role, but I wish I could stay up here with him instead of going back down into that cave of an Intel Room. Although I know how important it is for me to work with Manthy and the others downstairs, there's a small part of me that misses the muscle-straining thrill of sparring and the adrenaline rush of combat, and there's a large part of me that misses Brohn.

When Card goes over to talk to some of the Insubordinates,

Brohn puts his hand on my cheek, and I don't know if it's the heat of his palm or the public nature of the gesture, but I can feel myself blush crimson red.

"I wish I could be downstairs with you," he says, dropping his arms down to take my hands in his. "I miss being able to talk with you about, well, everything."

"Funny," I reply, "I was just thinking how nice it would be to stay up here with you."

"I'll come visit you," Brohn says as he looks around at the busy productivity of the hallway and the rooms around us. "Next chance I get. I promise."

I follow his gaze around the hall at all the laughing and bubbling camaraderie. This could have been us. Under different circumstances. In a different world or in a different life. We could have been the ones bouncing cheerfully down long hallways filled with our happy, energetic peers. We could have been learning new things and sharing funny stories about all of our adventures on each new day. We don't have that, though, and we probably never will. I just hope that in six days, when all this is over, we'll still have each other.

Brohn leans toward me, and three boys standing nearby, probably in their early teens, ooh and ahh as he kisses me good-bye. He shoos them away with a wave of his hand and gives me an apologetic shrug.

"See you later in the dorm?"

"Can't wait," I say. I wave a long-distance "goodbye" to Cardyn who is putting on an impromptu martial arts demonstration to a group of wide-eyed Insubordinates down the hall.

Turning to go, I walk down the two flights of stairs to the third floor, proud of what I'm a part of but saddened that each step is taking me farther away from Brohn.

LATER THAT NIGHT, WE REUNITE IN THE DORM, BONE-WEARY BUT feeling a common sense of satisfaction at having spent an entire day being productive for once instead of moving from place to place and trying not to get killed in the apocalyptic world outside this city. In our spoked-wheel configuration of beds, we laugh together, compare notes about the day, reminisce about the past, and speculate about the future. Well, all of us do that except for Manthy. She tucks her head under her covers with the lower part of her legs exposed at the center of the circle, so we're treated to the full bouquet of her smelly feet.

Cardyn playfully sings out to her, calling her "Manthy the misanthrope." Manthy replies from under her covers by calling him "Cardyn the mucous-y maggot-sandwich."

"Leave her be," Rain chuckles.

"She started it," Cardyn complains. Then he pauses, his finger on his chin. "Oh, wait. No, she didn't. That was me, wasn't it?"

"As usual," Brohn grumbles, leaning across the space between their beds to give Cardyn a half-hearted punch to the shoulder.

At one point, I excuse myself to slip out into the hallway. With my head down so I don't attract any unnecessary attention from the three Insubordinates milling around and whispering down at the end of the hall, I swipe my fingers across my forearm tattoos to engage my connection with Render. Leaning back against the wall, I feel my eyes go black as I enter Render's world. He pushes back against me. He's trying to sleep.

*I just wanted to see how your day was. To make sure you're okay.*

Render responds with a rush of feelings instead of words: *Fed. Flew. Satisfied. Happy. Free.*

I'm smiling and starting to disconnect when I get one more feeling from him: *Fear.*

Before I have a chance to figure out what it means or even if I only imagined it, Render gives himself over to sleep, and the connection is broken.

Shaking off the nagging sense of dread and convincing myself out loud that it's nothing, I head back into our dorm room to chat some more with Brohn, Cardyn, and Rain. They're talking about the Patriot Army and how Krug managed to dupe and assemble so many people into his cause so quickly, but I'm not really paying much attention. I keep thinking about Render.

When it's just me and Brohn left awake, I switch my focus away from Render, and Brohn and I talk in whispers, back and forth across the space between our beds, about what life is going to be like this time next week.

"Who knows?" he says, "Maybe we can go on a real date."

"You mean like with holding hands and giggling over private jokes and window-shopping and everything?" I pretend-gush.

"Well, I'm not sure if either of us is ready to take the next big steps of giggling or hand-holding."

"And the window-shopping?"

"I've never window-shopped with anyone before," Brohn confesses with mock regret. "I just hope we don't become so overcome with emotion that we wind up rebelling against convention and indulging in some madcap browsing."

"I don't know…rebelling is kind of our thing, isn't it? After all, we're here to lead a revolt."

"Well," Brohn whispers with a flick of his head in Cardyn's direction. "*He* can be pretty revolting sometimes."

I press my covers to my mouth to stifle a laugh.

We joke around like that for a little while more, although the parts about us being together, I mean really together—just the two of us—don't sound like jokes. The whole time, we don't say a word about the upcoming battle, the training, or the odds against us.

"When we're out there," Brohn says, "not holding hands, not kissing, not falling in love, and definitely not window-shopping, let's at least make each other a promise."

"Okay. What is it?"

"Let's promise, no matter what happens, that we won't try too hard to be normal, okay?"

"Brohn, I don't think we could be normal no matter how hard we tried."

He smiles, and we reach across the space between our beds to touch hands before I drift off into a quiet, restful sleep.

5

*Sunday*

Sunday, our second day in the Style, starts off much like our first: We wake up, wash up, pull on our clothes for the day, and then, sadly, split up with Rain, Manthy, and me going downstairs and Brohn and Cardyn going upstairs with Granden.

When we arrive at the Intel Room, Wisp welcomes us in with a broad sweep of her hand and informs us that we're ready to engage in the next level of surveillance. Like yesterday, Wisp goes over the city and the plan in increasingly minute detail. Pacing back and forth, calling up image after image on the holo-display, and bantering back and forth with Rain about defining an optimal set of strategies, she's clearly leaving nothing to chance. All morning, she talks, teaches, and quizzes us on everything we've learned so far until my brain feels like a ready-to-burst water balloon.

As I walk over to the table, Wisp ticks off facts on her fingers. "Thanks to Olivia, you now know the basics of the neighborhoods and buildings that are about to be our battlefields. You know the overall plan. You know some of the specifics. You know what's at stake, and you know about Krug's arrival and about the Patriot Army. Now it's time for us to know what *they* know."

Olivia threads her tendrils into one of the glossy spheres floating above her monitors. "From what Granden tells us, you and Render are better than any combat drone," she hums.

"I'd say that's probably true," I agree through a yawn. "Minus the ability to destroy a town."

"Yet," Olivia says without looking up from her monitors.

I can't tell if she's joking or if she really thinks I have the potential or even the desire to weaponize my relationship with Render. Before I have a chance to figure it out one way or the other, Olivia calls our attention to the holo-screen on the panel she refers to as the Central Terminal. She summons me over, and I have to duck under one of her floating spheres to stand next to her. Manthy follows close behind me, and we drop down into mag-chairs next to Olivia while Rain and Wisp sit on the opposite side of the black glass table.

"Up until now, we've had field agents go on sorties to gather intel," Wisp explains.

"Sounds like a good strategy," Rain says.

"It would be. Except, as I mentioned yesterday, everyone we've sent out has either come back with nothing or else…"

"Or else what?"

"Or else they haven't come back at all."

All I can say is, "Oh," as the realization of the gravity of this situation continues to sink in.

"We're at a turning point here," Wisp says. "Honestly, the Patriot Army is close to shutting us down. They've barricaded us in the city along with everyone else, and they have posts set up all over to keep us in check. It won't be long before they make their final move and either root us out or else give up and nuke the whole city just to be on the safe side."

"They wouldn't do that, would they?" Manthy asks, her voice barely audible even though she's right next to me.

Wisp gives her a somber look. "You've been out there. You've seen the cratered towns and cities they've left behind. There is nothing they won't do. We know what they're capable of. But we still need to know what resources they have, when and how they might be deployed...everything."

"In short, we need to get better intel," Olivia says. "We've tried drones, but they keep getting spotted and shot down."

"When they work at all," Wisp adds.

"Let me guess," I say. "That's where I come in."

"Well, you and Render. How much control do you have?"

"Over Render?" I ask, and Wisp nods. "None."

"But I thought—"

"She doesn't control him," Manthy interrupts from her seat between me and Olivia.

"It's a partnership," Rain adds, and I smile at how well these two girls have come to understand me, defend me, and even explain me.

Wisp offers her apologies. "I get it. I guess I'm just used to giving commands these days."

"Speaking of which," I say with a sweep of my hand, "You never really did tell us how you managed to do all this. I mean, no offense, but you're a..."

"One-hundred-pound teenage girl?"

"Well, not to put too fine a point on it. But yes."

Wisp shrugs. "I guess growing up like we did gave us all certain survival instincts."

I expect her to elaborate, but she doesn't. Instead, she folds her hands in front of her like she's praying. "So?" she asks into the silence. "Can I see?"

"See what?"

"What you and Render can do."

"There's nothing to see," I point out. "I just tap into him, and I see what he sees."

"Do you see like a person sees?"

"No. It's hard to explain. It's different. I see more. I see…different."

"And can you hear?"

"Through Render?"

"Yes."

"Sometimes. At first, early on, it just sounded like gibberish. But we've gotten better at it."

"And can you talk? With us I mean. When you're…connected."

"I didn't used to be able to. It was all or nothing. I could be in his head, or else I could be in my own. Over time, I've been able to be with Render but still be me at the same time. It's not always easy, and it doesn't always work how I want. But I think we're…evolving."

"I like that," Wisp says. "Evolving."

Rain urges me to engage my connection, and Wisp watches wide-eyed as I swipe my fingers along the pattern of black lines and dots on my forearm.

"Brace yourself," Rain warns her. "Kress's eyes get kind of weird when she does this."

This time, I slip easily into Render's mind. There's no pressure in my head or dizziness like I sometimes get, especially if one of us is tired or stressed. I blink, and Olivia and Manthy next to me and Wisp and Rain across the table are replaced by a hazy, late-morning sky speckled with crimson-fringed clouds over the expansive grid of the city. I know we've been talking strategy and intel for a while, but it's even later than I thought with the blood-red sun continuing its leisurely ascent over city and lighting up the endless body of choppy white and blue water to the west.

With our connection in full synchronization, I'm able to see and feel what Render sees and feels. He's in mid-flight, and it's exactly the sensation I need, this exhilarating sense of freedom after being cooped up in this room all day yesterday and today.

"Are you connected?" Wisp's voice sounds hollow and far away.

I nod, not wanting to talk for fear of losing my concentration and accidentally severing the connection.

"Do you remember the schematics Olivia showed us?"

I nod again. "I remember everything."

"Perfect. I'm going to ask you and Render to help us scout out certain specific locations. Are you able to do that?"

"We'll try," I murmur.

For the next several hours and as the city continues its descent into nighttime, Wisp calls out the names of streets, office buildings, subway stations, police stations, communication towers. She rattles off lists of restaurants, churches, private residences, grocery ports, cafés, piers and docks, roads, alleys, mag-ways, and mag-tram depots. I ask Render to fly to each place in turn. He soars through the city, looping over buildings and skimming through the streets. He perches unnoticed on window ledges. He even alights on the roofs and hoods of military vehicles parked at various checkpoints around the city. One location at a time, Render sends images to me. From her seat next to me, Manthy intercepts the images by tapping into my implants. Her hand feels comforting and soft on my arm, and I can feel her presence in my head as she gathers up every image Render collects. She then passes that information along to Olivia via her psychic tech-connection.

As the third stage in what Wisp refers to as our "telempathic tech exchange," Olivia inputs the information into a series of holo-pads, and, from what Wisp and Rain tell me, the sketchy images in and around the city are slowly taking shape. I can't see any of this, of course. I'm out there in the sky, weaving between towering structures and landing on tree branches as I conduct what must be the strangest remote recon mission ever.

When I get dizzy at one point and nearly fall out of my chair, I feel Wisp's hands on my shoulders and her voice in my ear. She tells me to focus not on Render's world outside or on our world here in this room. "Instead," she says, "see if you can focus on the space between. It will be a small space. Nearly invisible. A breath. A blur. Think of it as connective tissue instead of as a barrier between one thing and another. If you can find it...if you can land on it, you'll be able to exist more completely in both worlds at once. Without the disorientation or the pain."

I nod, not knowing where Wisp's advice, insight, and understanding are coming from but thankful for then all the same. It's a hard concept to get my head around. Not just the idea. This is the first time I've tried to stay in contact with Render for so long and still engage with someone else at the same time. It's a mental juggling act that consumes every bit of my focus and concentration.

Manthy is doing her best to work as a conduit between me and Olivia but, like me, she's starting to complain about the onset of some pretty terrible headaches. Olivia can't gather the intel without her, though. I do my best to help Manthy while also communicating with Render. It's taking a toll on the three of us and on Render. I can feel him straining to stay connected. He's exhausted and hurting, but he senses my need along with all my hopes and fears, so he continues to soldier on.

Finally, with my head feeling like a jug of mud, Wisp directs me to the Armory, our primary target.

"It's too dark now," I inform her. "Birds don't like to fly at night."

When Wisp asks if I'll at least try, I tell her, "Okay."

It takes Render a few minutes to get from where he's perched on top of the ruins of an old windmill in the west end of Golden Gate Park all the way over to the Armory. After that, in my mind, external images of the Armory come into focus: the huge white dome, the turrets on the blocky part of the building, the exhaust and venting pipes on the roof, black and green wires running in long stretches and coiled up on metal posts, the rough brick of the building's façade, and even a cylindrical yellow waste disposal chute suspended from the rooftop down to a cluster of construction vehicles below.

After a series of loops above the imposing building with the four turrets and the attached dome-like structure, Render dips down, flutters to a near-hover, and slips inside an open ventilation duct on the roof. He pins his wings against his sides and half-walks, half-hops about fifty yards through a pitch-dark corridor of dusty ductwork until he arrives at a small vent. He's able to squeeze through the vertical slats in the vent and hop out onto a lattice of support struts and cables in the ceiling high above the open floor of the Armory below. There are trucks parked down there and clumps of soldiers moving around between various command stations set up with floating viz-screens and holo-displays like glass-walled cubicles in a virtual office building.

The images Render relays to me are hard to sort out. This is one of those times when his sense of sight is too good for my human mind to handle. I'm getting mixed up between what he's seeing, what I think I'm seeing through his eyes, and the swirl of shimmering blurriness all around the edges of my shifting fields of vision. On top of that, I keep getting flashes of the Intel Room where I'm sitting intruding on Render's overhead view of the interior of the Armory. I know Manthy and Olivia are sitting next to me with Rain and Wisp sitting across from us on the other side of the table. I know Wisp is in her lime-green hoodie and that Rain has the sleeves of her compression shirt pulled down over her hands. I see Wisp brushing her light brown hair from her face. I see Rain taking her glistening black hair down from its ponytail and pushing it back behind her shoulders as she looks at me, concern etched on her face. It's what my mind expects to see, so it's trying to see what it expects. Together, it creates a kaleidoscopic effect behind my eyes that is both pretty and painful. I tell Wisp all of this, and I hear her walk back around the table.

"Don't fight him," she says from behind me. "The instinct will be to override his sense of the world with your own. Ask him to take the lead. See if you can envision yourself *as* him instead of only linked *with* him."

With my throat tight, I tell Wisp I'll try, and I get back to concentrating on the task at hand. My lower back is a pool of sweat. I'm a black-eyed, exhausted, and disheveled mess, and I imagine I must look pretty freakish to Manthy, Rain, Wisp, and Olivia.

*Focus, Kress. Imagine yourself as Render. As Render. Ask Render. Surrender.*

I give myself over to Render. No. I give myself over to the *idea* of Render. To the idea that, together and only together, we are more than the sum of our parts.

Zeroing in on the name patch on the jacket of one of the soldiers far below, the man who is clearly in charge here, Render's perceptions become clearer in my mind.

Render identifies the name on the jacket as "Ekker." I relay this information to Wisp who tells us Ekker is the current leader of the Patriot Army. Her voice comes to me in fluctuating waves. "He's a general of some kind. We've heard about him, but we haven't been able to get much. Only that he was hand-picked by Krug for this San Francisco assignment and that he has a reputation for considering civilian populations as expendable assets in the war against the Eastern Order."

"Which we know is just a fake war anyway," I hear Rain say.

Then, I get back to focusing on this man Ekker through Render's eyes.

Ekker is a large man, not heavy like Tread in Oakland or beefy like Crusher in the Processor. No. Ekker is broad-shoul-dered like Brohn, only bigger. Taller. He has the looks of a male model and the body of a prize-fighter. His blondish hair is thick and slicked back with each comb mark visible, giving him a slightly fascist appearance. His face is surprisingly handsome, clean, and scar-free. He's relatively unblemished for someone who's risen to his rank and who has the reputation Wisp claims. Surely, he must have been in combat. But his looks don't reflect that. His attitude, however, does. He strides around in the big open space below, barking out orders and directing groups of uniformed soldiers.

"Who's that with him?" I ask Wisp, forgetting for a second that she can't see what I see through Render's eyes until Manthy and Olivia complete their download. "There's someone with him all the time. Next to him."

"I don't know. Man or woman?"

"I can't tell. It's someone in a red coat with a hood."

Wisp says she doesn't know who it might be. "We've exhausted so many resources and lost so many contacts trying to infiltrate the Patriot Army. Honestly, you've already given us more in the last few hours than we got in the last two months combined. Why don't you go ahead and disconnect."

"Wait," I say. "Some guards just dragged two Patriots in. Ekker is shouting at two men. I recognize them. It's the two guards we took down the other day on our way into the city. I can't hear everything. Just bits and pieces."

"Can you get closer?"

I shake my head. "I don't want Render to get spotted. Wait. Ekker just hit one of the men. I think he broke the man's nose. Now he just hit the other one. The two men are down. They're bleeding. I think they're begging...for their lives. The person with him, the one in the hood, just handed Ekker a gun."

In the Armory, two thunderous explosions rip rapid-fire from the gun and blast a deafening echo throughout the huge open space below. The two kneeling men pitch lifelessly forward as a flash of bright red blood sprays from their heads, and they collapse to the floor. The sound startles Render, and he flutters frantically around the ceiling rafters. The commotion attracts the attention of Ekker who whips his head up and trains his gun on Render. I recognize the weapon. Granden and Trench trained us on one just like it in the Processor. A specialized version of the Beretta DT33 series. With its burnished forcing cone and sleek black lines like a venomous snake in mid-strike, it's every bit as deadly as it looks.

The laser targeting spot glows red from the sight on Ekker's gun. There's another blast of gunfire from the weapon, and my connection with Render goes black.

## 6

WITHOUT MY CONNECTION, THE TWO WORLDS OF THE ARMORY AND the Intel Room smash into one mixed-up mess. I'm in a bone-shaking panic, completely unable to catch my breath, and on the verge of sobbing uncontrollably, when things snap back into focus, and I'm able to say the two best words I've ever said:

"He missed."

"What happened?" Rain asks. She's rushed around to my side of the table and has one hand on my arm with Manthy holding onto my other arm.

I blink the room into clarity and take a very deep, very relieved breath as I look from one of the girls to the other. "Ekker. That general," I explain through a sudden bout of the shakes. "He shot those two soldiers. He spotted us. Took a shot at us. But he missed. Render's still in the Armory. He's okay. Just startled. I need to reconnect."

"No," Manthy protests.

"We're inside," I argue more feebly than I'd care to admit. "We have so much we can find out now."

"No," Wisp says from across the table where the detailed schematics of the Armory are hovering. "We've got a lot, already.

It's late, and it sounds like you just had a too-close-for-comfort call. We'll pick up again tomorrow."

I think I say, "Okay," but it's hard to tell. Render's world and mine are still all mixed up. I can't tell if I'm thinking things in my head or saying them out loud. A wave of dizziness washes over me, and I feel like I'm in the ceiling of the Armory instead of sitting here in the Intel Room, slumped over in my chair.

Manthy stands and helps me up. With her arm around my shoulders, we walk over to the window, which Manthy opens for me with a verbal command that unlocks and opens the black privacy barrier that keeps the room dark and concealed from any of the Patriots' spy drones that might be skulking around at any given time. I know it's a risk, especially considering we need to be as secretive as possible given the magnitude of our objective, but the rush of crisp, cool air is as satisfying as any meal.

I insist to Manthy that I need to keep helping with the planning, and I start to turn around.

She turns me back toward the window and the breeze. "The only thing you need to do right now is breathe."

I never thought I'd need to be reminded to breathe, but here I am.

Manthy has had her hand on my forearm the whole time, and my skin is white and oddly cool where she's been touching it.

"I need to check on him at least."

Manthy looks over at Wisp who nods her tentative approval, and I swipe my tattoos and slip back into Render's mind. He's still up in the ceiling rafters, just about to make his way back to the vent where he slipped in. Ekker and the other soldiers down below seem to have laughed off his presence as nothing more than an amusing and innocent intrusion and have gone back about the business of shipping the two dead soldiers away on mag-stretchers.

After a few minutes, Render bursts from the rooftop vent of the Armory and soars out into the darkening San Francisco evening. I can feel the fear slipping out of him as he pierces the night sky and makes his way back toward the Style.

I disconnect and tell Manthy everything's okay. "He's on his way here. He'll likely find a spot on the roof to get some rest." I offer Manthy a weak smile. "He does seem to be enjoying his new job as a surveillance drone, though."

Manthy gives me a flat, expressionless look before leading me back to the table where I collapse exhausted into my chair.

While I drop back down, feeling barfy and boneless, Rain and Wisp perform all kinds of algorithmic computations based on the information Render and I have been able to provide so far. Clustered around an ever-changing, morphing, and slowly-revolving and evolving series of holograms, they run virtual battle simulations, calculate odds of success given a stream of variables, tap as best they can into the outlying Patriot Army networks, and undertake a preliminary digital infiltration of the army's communication patches.

"It's mostly just test-runs," Olivia explains. "Over the next few days, we'll keep sneaking in, getting whatever information we can, and start installing some sub-routines that will enable us to complete the takeover once you're in the Command Headquarters."

Just the fact of Olivia saying "once you're in the Command Headquarters" out loud gives me a bad case of the spinal shivers.

Standing at the table in the dark but glowing room, Rain and Wisp are illuminated by the detailed schematics and by the real-time images of our various targets in and around the Armory. With their heads practically touching, the two girls assemble all the intel and start to organize a unified plan of attack. It's turned into a very long day. I miss Brohn and Cardyn. I look forward to when I can head upstairs and reunite with them in the Dorm. For now, I sit and stare, trapped in a slog of mental numbness as Manthy and Olivia work their techno-magic while Wisp and Rain refine our plans.

Like Rain, Wisp turns out to have a gift for strategy and logistics, and I'm starting to see how someone like her managed to achieve such a high rank in this underground world of rebels. Rain and Wisp keep flicking their fingers at the schematic. Back in the Valta, I'm not sure the two of them ever even had a conversation. Now, like me with Render, they operate in total and fluid synchronization. Although they consult with me from time to time, I don't really have that much to offer at this point. Everything I saw, I passed along to Manthy who relayed it to Olivia who is fleshing out her new-and-improved schematics at lightning speed. The dozens of gray-green and yellow images grow more detailed before our eyes. It won't be long, I suspect, before we have a perfect simulation of the entire city complete with visual representations of every branch of the Patriot Army's digital surveillance network.

Wisp continues to rattle off battle plans as fast as Olivia can get the images up. "Flank assault here. Enkulette at this point. We'll take down these two guard-posts with a basic Pincer. We'll run a Clear-and-Hold at Mission and 14th. There's a choke-point here and one here. Your team and I will approach from the east and take a position in this park across the street where the Patriots conduct their field training exercises. There's an alleyway here between Mission and Julian Street. City Hall is here between Polk and Grove. This is the pier at the Embarcadero and the foot of Bryant. That's where Granden and I will meet up with Dennis Kammet for the takeover of the vehicle yard once you and your Conspiracy are inside the Armory."

I still don't know exactly what Rain and Wisp are doing, but they seem to be having a fun time doing it. "I think I understood about half of those words," I say.

Wisp and Rain laugh, and Rain waves me over. With more effort than it should take, I push myself up from my chair and leave Manthy and Olivia in the middle of a muted conversation about "intersynaptic techno-neurology," "downloadable parallel arc synthesis," "post-human ethics," and a bunch of other things I don't understand.

Rain pats the seat next to her, and I sit down. "Enkulette is an attack-from-behind guerilla tactic. Clear-and-Hold is normally a counter-insurgency approach, but we're going to modify it a bit to suit our own purposes. You know the Pincer and Flank Assault from our time in the Processor."

"Don't remind me," I say with a blush. "I'm not sure if they filled you in," I say to Wisp, "but Rain and your brother made a habit of wiping out my team in our war games exercises back in the Processor."

"Actually, Rain filled me in yesterday when you went upstairs to check on Brohn and Cardyn," Wisp says. "Don't worry. She didn't reveal too much."

"Whew."

"Only about how her team used to outsmart your team, trick you, turn you around, pick you off one by one, and make bets on how long it'd take to corner you. Oh, and that they won every single time."

"Thanks for not revealing too much," I say to Rain, my voice oozing sarcasm.

Rain throws up her hands. "Don't blame me. We never agreed to keep your horrible battle skills a secret."

Wisp and Rain laugh, and I can't help but laugh with them. With the chaos of rebellion swirling around us, it's nice to remember there's such a thing as light-heartedness, friendly banter, and even good-natured back-and-forth teasing.

Fortunately, I'm spared further embarrassment by Brohn, who taps on the frame of the open doorway. Wisp shouts out his name and waves him in. He strides into the room and walks around the table to put his arm across my shoulders. "What are you all so happy about?" he asks.

"Just taking a little stroll down amnesia lane," I say. "How are things going upstairs? Got those pups ready yet?"

Brohn laughs. "You saw it. It's chaotic. We've barely got the rooms ready. The Insubordinates are enthusiastic. I'll give them that. But we've got a very long few days ahead of us. It's not enough time to do much more than teach them how not to get themselves—or us—killed."

"Where's Card?"

"Still upstairs with Granden. And I have to say, there's definitely something about Cardyn."

"What do you mean?"

"Well, the Insubordinates listen to me. But he has a way of taking their focus to another level."

"You mean they follow his orders?"

"Yes. Well, yes and no. They almost seem mesmerized by him. Like he gives an order or makes a suggestion, and I swear it's like their eyes glaze over, and then they're falling all over themselves to do his bidding. Especially the girls."

When he says this last part, I think I see Manthy's ears perk up, but when I look over, she's still engaged in her conversation with Olivia, so I figure I must've imagined it.

"Plus," Brohn continues, "he makes everyone laugh, which is something I don't think many of them have done in a long time."

"Don't discount the hero-worship factor," Wisp interjects from across the table. "As I think you're learning, you five have become something of a local legend these past couple of months. Ever since you left the Valta with the Recruiters, really." Wisp goes back to rotating the holo-images, exploding them, contracting them, and scanning red lines of attack with her fingers into the glistening, multi-colored images. "Speaking of which…Rain's been telling me about your battle-sims in the Processor."

"Yeah," Brohn says with a wry smile and a wink in Rain's direction. "I think we won every time, right?"

I give Brohn a playful elbow to the side. He flinches and pretends like I just broke half his ribs. "If only you were this tough back in the battle-sims," he jokes. "Of course, we wouldn't be alive if it weren't for you, so I think we can forgive you." Brohn walks around to stand next to his sister and leans in to take a closer look at the holographic images and the dozens of scrolling information tags accompanying them. "So what's going on down here?"

Wisp and Rain fill Brohn in on our little reconnaissance project. He puts his hand to his chin and looks impressed at what we've accomplished so far. At one point, he walks back around the table to stand behind me, his hands on my shoulders as he continues to analyze the scrolling notations about strategy and the technical specs of the different buildings projected in front of us. I tell him about my surveillance missions around the city and about Ekker, the soldiers he shot, and the shot he took at Render.

Brohn sits down next to me, his eyes going wide at this last bit of news, and he asks if I'm okay. I assure him I am, but he's not convinced and begins to ask Wisp if it's really necessary to push me this hard and put me into that kind of danger.

"Technically," I remind him, "it was Render in danger. I was sitting safely here."

"I was about to tell you not to worry," Wisp says to Brohn. "But the truth is that some worry is perfectly justifiable. After all, this is war."

Brohn shakes his head and sighs. "Kress has been seeing some strange things through Render lately. I think she's connected to that bird in more ways than any of us—her included—might realize."

Wisp agrees and says she'll keep an eye on me. "I'll be careful," she promises, and I smile because I can tell she means it. "Now," she says, "about our attack plan…"

As Brohn looks on, Wisp and Rain go over the holo-schematics with me. They throw terms and tactics at me rapid-fire as they detail the elaborate system of simultaneous attacks we're about to undertake in less than five days. They run through every strategy, street, alleyway, and corridor in every building we're preparing to attack.

"We'll need you and Render to gather some more data tomorrow," Wisp tells me.

"Like what?"

"Well, we'll need to know more about their security protocols and the names of every guard and soldier we're likely to encounter."

"I think that's possible," I assure her with a confidence I only partly feel.

Rain fills Brohn in on the major sites we're going to target. "This is the Munitions Depot. This is Communications Central. And this is Command Headquarters."

"And we're going to hit all three, right?" Brohn asks.

"At the same time," Wisp says. "Yes. Among other targets. We'll have nine teams performing different functions, most of them in an around the Armory, although there are some other tactical targets in the city we'll need to address. We can't improvise or take any chances. Coordination will be key. The day before we head out, we'll assign Cardyn and Manthy to brief the Insubordinates and keep them on the same page. Manthy knows the tech part of the plan. And, if Cardyn is as convincing as you say, he just might be the perfect person to help her fill in the gaps."

I look down the length of the table to where Manthy is still immersed in quiet conversation with Olivia, both of them barely visible and apparently oblivious in the deep shadows of Olivia's work station. "I'm not one hundred percent sure it's a good idea to team Cardyn up with Manthy on this project," I say behind my hand to Wisp. "They tend to bicker."

"They also tend to get things done," Rain reminds me. "It was the work they did together on the truck back in Reno that got us this far in the first place."

"True," I sigh. "I just don't want to have this very nice plan of ours go slanted because those two insist on turning into squabbling Neos whenever they're together."

Wisp shakes her head. "I'm sorry we don't have more time. But our window is small. If we don't make our move before the big platoon of reinforcements gets here first thing Saturday morning, we won't have the numbers later on to carry it off. I know it's a lot to absorb. Do you think you can remember all this?"

"Trust me," Rain says, flicking her thumb in my direction. "She'll remember. This one remembers everything."

Brohn agrees and brags to Wisp about how my brain has turned into an infinite data-storage unit.

"I wouldn't go that far," I object as I give him a playful slap on the shoulder. I tap my temple. "Things have just been a little clearer and are sticking around a little longer is all."

"Speaking of sticking around," Brohn says, pushing himself up from his seat, "As much as I'd love to stay here with you, I need to get back upstairs. Cardyn gets so lonely, you know?"

I laugh as Brohn leans over to give me a hug goodbye and a kiss on the cheek and then he's out the door with a backward wave of his hand.

"So this is happening?" Wisp asks, her eyes darting between me and the open doorway where her brother is just disappearing from view. "You and Brohn?"

"It's complicated," I say as I stare down at the table.

"As long as it doesn't complicate things," Wisp says. Her voice is playful, but I pick up on a hint of seriousness in there as well. "Let's get back to work."

Wisp runs through more of the details and issues a dozen orders over her comm-link to the Insubordinates. At least two more hours pass like that until I feel my eyes glazing over. I have no idea what time it is, but between flying around with Render all day and absorbing all of Wisp's and Rain's planning details, my reserves are depleted, and I feel ready to collapse on the spot. Finally, Wisp seems to notice and says we're calling it a night.

Exhausted, Rain and I are just getting ready to file out when Manthy asks Wisp if she can stay with Olivia. For a second, I don't know where the voice is coming from. Manthy has an uncanny ability to blend into the background, and I'm still not totally used to her disappearing-reappearing act.

Wisp shrugs and says, "Fine with me" and then looks over at Olivia who is beaming that pretty smile of hers from her wired-up and pieced-together face. "I'd love some company," Olivia says.

Rain and I say our goodbyes and trudge upstairs on shaky legs. Inside our room, we meet up with Brohn and Cardyn who look as wiped out as we are, and the four of us collapse into our beds.

Cardyn stares for a second at Manthy's empty bed. "Do you think Manthy will be okay downstairs?" he asks through a gaping yawn.

Brohn gives him a crooked squint. "What do you mean? Why wouldn't she be?"

Cardyn shrugs, and it occurs to me that he's not worried about Manthy. After all we've been through, he knows better than that. I think he might be worried about himself. Not in a selfish way. More like in an I-miss-Manthy way that he doesn't want to admit. It's actually pretty cute. I used to wonder if Cardyn and I would stay like brother and sister forever or if something romantic would develop between us like everyone else seemed to expect. It never occurred to me to consider a third option: Cardyn and Manthy. I laugh to myself at how crazy that sounds and then again at how perfect it sounds.

Cardyn soon falls into a deep, gruffling sleep.

I'm fading in and out as Rain and Brohn compare notes about how things are going so far.

Rain sounds optimistic and says something about having a

good feeling, especially with Wisp leading the way. "And I think it's good for Manthy to get to know Olivia. Kindred spirits and all. This could be a new home for us. San Francisco, I mean. A good place for us to finally settle down, you know?"

Brohn grunts a little and sounds suddenly serious. "Let's see if we're all still feeling that way in five days. Let's see if we're still feeling anything. Right now, this is all just fun and games. Now is when everything looks like it has no choice but to go right. On Friday, it gets real. And let's face it, Rain. These kids...they may be juiced up for the *idea* of war, but they aren't anywhere ready for the reality."

In the silence that follows, I think about how long five days used to seem and how short it seems now. Wishing that Rain is right but fearing that Brohn is, I fall into a restless sleep filled with more visions—one of them of Brohn being shot and killed— I pray never even come close to coming true.

# 7

*M*ONDAY

THE NEXT MORNING, MONDAY, WE RISE, SHOWER, AND DRESS before heading to the Mess Hall. This time, everyone is up and about, and the whole floor has the feel of a college dorm with an assortment of tired boys and girls plodding around in the hallway, passing in and out of rooms, and rubbing the sleep from their weary eyes.

Brohn and Cardyn must have really worked them hard yesterday. All the hustle and bustle I saw on my visit upstairs has given way to a kind of sloth-y fatigue. Two girls are doing slow stretches against the wall. Another girl, probably not more than twelve or thirteen years old, is sitting, eyes closed and cross-legged, on the floor. Three older boys, one of them with red splotches and dry skin on his face, are passing a green comb between them and running it, one boy at a time, through their oily black hair. Just down the hall from them, a cluster of boys and girls, also older—maybe in their late teens or even early twenties—are complaining about their aching muscles. A lanky boy with loopy curls of reddish-brown hair is slowly wrapping a strip of cloth around what looks like a series of cuts on his knuckles.

Brohn gestures toward the boy with a tip of his head. "That's Ethan. Good skills but gets frustrated easily."

"Did he do that in your combat training yesterday?" I ask, pointing to the boy's red knuckles.

Brohn shakes his head. "Got mad when he lost a sparring match with his buddy over there and punched a hole in the wall."

"Great," I say. "A hot-head."

"He'll be okay. He learns fast, and there's a lot on the line. A few more days'll be enough to get him ready."

I know Brohn is trying to convince himself as much as he's trying to convince me. I give a quick glance behind us to where Cardyn, Rain, and Manthy are walking along, taking in this bustle of early morning stirrings. "I'm not sure a few days are enough to even get *us* ready," I tell Brohn. "And we already have a ton of experience and a full arsenal of survival skills."

Ethan looks up at us as we pass but then slips back into his room with two other boys and three girls like a school of fish fleeing from a great white shark swimming by. Other than that quick visit upstairs to check in on Brohn and Cardyn, this is my first time seeing so many of these rebel Insubordinates together in one place. Dressed mostly in military surplus army-green cargo pants and an assortment of pastel-colored compression t-shirts and tank-tops, they seem to be content milling around, chatting and comparing notes about their first two days of training. Their cackling overlap of conversations and their shuffling movements give the wide hallway the feel of an impromptu cocktail party. Like Ethan and his skittish friends, they all get quiet as we pass.

They may be shy, but it's nice to know people, especially people our age, care enough and are willing to risk so much to oppose Krug and his Patriot Army. Unfortunately, it also highlights how much trouble we're in. As I'm looking around more carefully, it occurs to me that these are still just kids, and I wonder if the entire rebellion is in the hands of a bunch of immature and ill-prepared children who are about to get spanked.

"Are there more to the Insubordinates than this?" I ask Wisp.

"There are older members," she explains, talking over the murmur from the parting crowd around us. "A few families are here with us in the Style. Most of the Insubordinates live in their own places, their own apartments in their own neighborhoods. They have to be careful. It's not the kind of situation where you want to be out on the street with an "I Hate the Patriot Army" picket sign. Not if you want to wake up alive the next morning. Being against the Patriots means being against Krug, and being against Krug, for Krug anyway, is the ultimate sacrilege. The Insubordinates you see here are mostly the castoffs and runaways, the ones with nothing to lose and nowhere else to go. We take care of them as best we can."

The "castoffs" continue to step to either side of the hallway as we pass. One of them, a sad-eyed girl with a transparent synth-cast on her right arm, offers a daring, "Hello" to me. I say, "Good morning" back, and she smiles and averts her eyes. I honestly can't tell if we're royalty, celebrities, aliens, ticking time-bombs, or a line-up of circus side-show freaks.

"What's up with them?" I ask.

Wisp waves good morning to a cluster of shaggy-haired pimply-skinned boys who stare awkwardly as we walk by. "They're not sure if you're real."

"Me or all of us?"

"Mostly you."

"What is she?" Cardyn asks, leaning over Wisp's shoulder. "A ghost?"

"Kind of."

"Kind of?" I ask through an incredulous squint.

A shirtless boy with a towel slung over one shoulder steps up and hands Wisp an info-pad. She scans it, nods, and presses her thumb to the identification plate. The boy says, "Thanks" and scuttles off into a nearby dorm room.

Wisp tosses an amused look in his direction. "Imagine if you heard that the one thing that could restore freedom and order to the world was a teenage girl who talks to birds. Then imagine seeing her walking past your bedroom. That's kind of what this is."

"Bird," I correct her. "It's just Render. I can't talk to all birds."

"The day's young," Wisp says through a cryptic smile.

"And I'm certainly nobody's savior," I grunt.

"The day is *very* young," Wisp says.

Before I can respond, a tall girl with nervous, darting eyes says, "Good morning, Major" to Wisp and asks her if a delivery is still on for later today. Wisp tells her "Yes" and instructs her and her team to be at the back door at sixteen-hundred sharp. The girl salutes and trots off to join a bunch of other kids who are milling around in an open dorm room doorway.

"What was that all about?" Card asks. "Weapons delivery?"

Wisp shakes her head. "Toiletries. You wouldn't believe how stinky some of these kids can get."

Several of the Insubordinates creep forward toward Brohn and Cardyn and tell them how much they're enjoying the training so far.

"We're really learning a lot, Sir," a slender boy with the faintest blond hint of a moustache tells Brohn as he pads along, puppy-like, beside him. "This is already the best week of my life."

"Jerald, right?" Brohn asks.

The boy beams broadly. "Yes, Sir!"

Brohn stops walking. "There is no 'best' about any of this, Jerald. I'm glad you're having a good week so far. I really am. But if we don't do this right, it'll be our last."

The boy called Jerald hangs his head and takes a step back as Brohn and the rest of us pass by.

"Sir?" Rain chuckles out of the side of her mouth.

"I didn't tell them to call us that," Brohn protests.

Rain answers Brohn with a drawn-out, "Riiiight" and gives him a playful punch to the shoulder.

Brohn blushes. "We have a big job to do here. Nothing wrong with getting a little respect along the way."

"No, Sir," Rain giggles. "No, Sir. There's certainly not. Sir."

With Brohn trying unsuccessfully to hold back a smile, we walk uninterrupted the rest of the way down the corridor. Stepping into the Mess Hall, Wisp enters a series of codes into the input panel on the wall, and nearly instantly, plates of steaming vegetables and tofu appear through openings all along the table tops.

"I don't suppose there's any deer?" Cardyn asks. "Not that Chef Angelique's many spinach, bean, and tofu recipes haven't been delightful."

Wisp grimaces at Cardyn.

"I know we had to eat meat for survival back in the Valta. But here, we adhere to a strict vegetarian diet. As humans, we've done enough damage to the planet and to our fellow sentient Earth-dwellers."

"Is this one of those 'thou shalt not kill' things?" Cardyn whines.

"If you're referring to the biblical rule," I remind him, "the more accurate translation is 'thou shalt not *murder*.' Exodus. Chapter 20. Verse 13 of the King James Bible. Killing is justified for any number of reasons. War, self-defense. Stuff like that."

"And we need to kill to live," Wisp says as she slides into her seat. "Just try breathing without slaughtering bacteria. But we don't need to engage in deliberate slaughter, especially at the expense of animals and the land."

The rest of us slide into our seats as we begin to eat and, as Wisp explains more about how her dietary philosophy intertwines with her work with the Insubordinates and against Krug and his Patriot Army, the rest of the Insubordinates file slowly into the Mess Hall.

They fill the room, and we all eat military style with the Insubordinates gathered along the rows of long rectangular tables. A quick head-count tells me there are forty-eight Insubordinates in all. That's an assortment of forty-eight freedom fighters, who, according to Brohn, range from those with some military training to those who have never been in so much as a thumb-wrestling contest.

Down on the far end of the room, there's actually a family of four: a hetero couple with two teenage boys about our age. Another family sitting across from them has a grandmother, a mother, and her four children. That's three generations of rebels under one roof. Still, as Wisp pointed out, the vast majority are kids about our age, some a few years older, some a few years younger, all of them wide-eyed, inexperienced, and very bad at hiding how nervous they are about what's to come. They remind me of a slightly cleaner and better dressed version of the kids we stayed with at Adric and Celia's camp before making our way here. Absently, I tap my jacket to feel the thin bundle of papers I keep folded up in the inside pocket. A girl named Chace drew a bunch of pictures of us when we stayed with them for a few days in their mountain camp. She had a real gift as an artist, as a tracker, and also as a kind and very caring human being. I keep her drawings with me at all times as a reminder that we're not in this alone, and we're not in it for ourselves. We mean something to the people who need us.

In the Mess Hall, the restrained and groggy chattering from the hallway a few minutes ago has descended into a strange graveyard silence. The Insubordinates are sitting shoulder to shoulder, crammed into the bench seats with a buffer of empty spaces between us and them. Rain looks up from her breakfast and notices dozens of eyes on us.

"Why do they keep looking at us?" she asks Wisp. "Kress here may be some kind of ghost to them, but they're acting like we're all going to leap at them and chew their faces off."

Wisp offers a scoffing chuckle at this just as one of the kids, an older-looking girl who introduces herself as Triella, tells us from down at the far end of the table that she heard about our time in the Processor. "You've got to tell us about it," she insists. "Please?"

I have to admit, I'm slightly annoyed at her enthusiasm at what was, for us, several months of radically intense physical and emotional trauma. But then I remember what Wisp said, and I realize we're not really real to them yet. Just a collection of walking myths.

Brohn and I exchange a look, and I tell him to go ahead. Triella and her friends scooch forward and lean in, their mouths hanging open as Brohn begins to tell them about the Recruitment.

"I know you've been curious about it," he begins. "And about us. I give you credit for going two whole days without asking about it. Okay. Every November first, the government gathered up the new Seventeens and took them away, leaving the rest of us to fend for ourselves for another year. In the Valta, it was just us kids. The last of the adults died trying to protect us in one of the drone strikes. We taught ourselves and each other how to read, write, learn, live, and survive, and we tried to forget about the next first of November when the Recruiters would come to take away the new Cohort of Seventeens."

With a frantic wave of her hand, Triella calls a bunch of other kids over, and before we know it, Manthy has quietly slipped away, leaving the rest of us to regale the throng with stories of training and torture and life on the run. Overlapping with each other and interjecting to add details or to correct errors in memories about events or chronologies, Brohn, Cardyn, Rain, and I fill the Insubordinates in on the reality of our mythology. We tell them some more details about growing up in the Valta with no adults around and having to fend for ourselves after the waves of bombings when we were still just little kids. We tell them about being recruited and being taken away to the Processor with the big silver Halo rotating above it. We go into detail about the physical and psychological tests, the Escape Rooms, the outdoor training in the huge Agora with its multiple configurations, the eight Cubes where we risked our lives, and the final getaway where two of our friends—Terk and Karmine— lost theirs. Cardyn finds a way to amuse the eager listeners with stories of what it was like being on the run and near death for all those weeks after our escape. Rain takes over when we get to the part about meeting Adric and Celia in the mountains. I tell them about meeting Vail and Roland and acquiring the truck that got us here, and then Brohn finishes off with only slightly exaggerated stories about our time in Salt Lake City and our adventures in Reno.

The Insubordinates, their mouths open and their eyes wide, hang on our every word.

"And the Eastern Order?" Triella asks, although I'm sure she and everyone else in this room already know the answer.

"That's the real myth," Brohn explains. "And like all myths, it can be more powerful than any reality. Myths feed on ignorance, laziness, and fear."

"Well, there's none of those here!" a small boy sitting next to Triella proclaims with a fist to his heart.

"Good," Brohn says rather sternly while suppressing an amused grin. "Because any one of them can get us all killed."

Finally, Wisp jumps in to remind us why we're here, how much work we have left to do, and how little time we have to do it in. "We're falling behind," she warns. "Every minute not gathering intel or training for combat is another minute that the Patriot Army has an advantage."

Granden is the first to push himself up from his seat at the bench table. He tells us that Wisp is right and that we'd better get moving. Although he's sincere about agreeing with Wisp and seems genuinely eager to get upstairs and back to work, I get the sense that he's also been a little squeamish about sitting here listening to us talking about our past and especially about the Processor. He was part trainer, part prison guard. He had a job to do, and he did it well. But it can't be a time of fond memories for him. He was living two lives: one as the son of President Krug, who had assigned him the task of turning us into his personal slaves, and one as the human being determined to save us from that fate.

Still twittering back and forth about our stories, the Insubordinates follow Brohn, Cardyn, and Granden down the hall and through the metal door where they begin to file upstairs for their next day of combat training while I get ready to head downstairs with Manthy and Rain to join Wisp and Olivia once again in the Intel Room.

Brohn holds me back on the landing while the others go their separate ways.

"I feel like I haven't seen you in years," he says. He runs his hands along my shoulders and down my arms.

"It's nice remembering the old times," I say, tilting my head back toward the Mess Hall. "Well, not all of them. But being together instead of being dead. That part's definitely nice."

"It's going to be another long day," Brohn sighs.

"Another long day apart."

He gives me a pleasant surprise by asking me how things are going with Render.

"I've never been connected to him for as long as I was yesterday," I say, relieved to be able to talk openly with Brohn about some of the bizarre turns my relationship with Render have been taking. "We used to be two beings with a common bond. Like siblings or good friends. Then, we were partners. Yesterday, we were beyond that. Like identical twins or soul-mates or something. I almost feel like..."

"Like?"

"Like I'm going to get stuck in his head someday."

"Yeah. Don't do that. If you do, I won't be able to do this."

With the two of us alone on the landing, Brohn tips my head back and kisses me.

"Well," I sigh, licking my lips as we draw apart. "If Render and I do eventually merge, you'll still be able to do that. But I have to warn you, you might wind up with a mouthful of black feathers."

Brohn laughs and kisses me again. He cups his hand against my cheek with his fingers curled gently just behind my ear. He tells me how much he's going to miss me, and I watch as he heads upstairs, taking the steps two at a time with powerful strides. When I hear the fifth-floor door click shut behind him, I head downstairs to continue planning with Wisp for the upcoming battle. I lick my lips again. I can tell it's going to be hard to focus today.

## 8

WITH THE TASTE OF BROHN'S BREATH STILL MINGLING SWEETLY with my own, I walk down the single flight of stairs to the third floor and over to the Intel Room.

I'm somehow wide awake but kind of tired at the same time. I don't know why I thought that being stable for a change instead of on the run like we've been for the past couple of months would be somehow easier or more relaxing. Instead of rest, we're already working as hard as we ever have before. Sure, it's nice to have a bed to sleep in and proper meals to eat, but the idea of death being just around the corner is as exhausting and stressful as it is terrifying. Since escaping from the Processor, I've been in a constant state of worry, wondering if some enemy or another was going to leap out from around the next corner and kill us all. There is little comfort in having that worry suddenly replaced by cold certainty.

Once inside Olivia's Intel Room, I join back up with Rain, Manthy, and Wisp at the long oval table where Wisp is already flicking and spinning schematic images, scrolling through floating lines of text and code, and building on our battle plans from the day before. Olivia greets me with a wave of her jelly-fish-like array of multicolored tendrils and laughs at my reaction.

"I'm sorry," she says through a tinny giggle. "I know how odd I must look to you, but I can't help myself. The look on your face is priceless." She laughs like she's told a real thigh-slapper despite the fact that she doesn't have thighs, let alone hands to slap them with.

I laugh along with her and at my own ignorant sense of shock. "I don't think 'odd' does you justice," I tell her as I slip into my seat next to Manthy. "'Amazing' might be more like it."

Olivia gives me an appreciative smile before rotating back around to face the semi-circle of consoles and gadgets that comprise her workstation at the head of the table.

"We need to get back inside the Armory," Wisp calls out to us. I guess she can read the fear in my eyes because she calls me over to the side of the table where she and Rain are sitting. "I know yesterday was tough. Scary even. I wouldn't ask you to do this if I didn't think you could. You're the only person I know, maybe the only person in the world who can get us what we need."

"I'm not doubting my abilities," I say at last. "Or my role. I get it. I'd rather not be the lynchpin holding this whole thing together. But then again, there are a lot of things I'd rather not be."

Wisp puts her hand on my forearm. "Then it's Render, isn't it?"

I nod. "Other people see him as a pet. Or even just a bird I happen to be able to connect with in a way they don't totally understand."

"And he's more than that, isn't he?"

I nod again, and Rain tells Wisp, "He's more like Kress's friend."

This time I almost agree, but then I stop. "Well, No. That's not exactly it either, Rain. I think…I mean, I wonder sometimes…"

"What is it?" Wisp asks, her voice a soothing wave of reassurance.

"I think he might be me."

The words sound strange even as I say them, and they don't convey exactly what it is I mean. Even on the stairwell landing with Brohn a few minutes ago, I couldn't really get my head around what seems to be happening. Render has his own way of doing things. His own way of thinking. He has his own character, feelings, emotions, moods, and temperament. But lately, I feel like they're all mine, too. Like we're a deck of personality cards someone riffled together. And now I'm starting to have trouble knowing where I begin and where he ends. What's worse, I don't know if I'm supposed to deal myself out of the deck to preserve who I am as an individual or if I'm supposed to keep things mixed up and hope I don't get lost in the shuffle.

I don't know if Wisp and Rain get it, but they both offer their understanding and support, which I guess has to be enough for now.

Sitting there in my chair next to Manthy, a wave of adrenalin surges through me. I feel strengthened by Wisp's confidence in me but also by a powerful sense of purpose. It takes me a second, but I realize what it is: I'm vital here. I'm part of something, a connection bigger in scope and in importance than I've ever experienced. There's a thread running from Render, through me, across to Manthy, and over to Olivia. Wisp and Rain pick up the thread and turn it into a true lifeline that could lead us to victory and save us all. Until now, my life has been defined by danger and by the potential for great pain, loss, sorrow, and, ultimately death. None of that has changed. What has changed is my ability to do something about it. I'm not just a bystander or a victim or even a simple participant anymore. This time, I'm bringing something to the table no one else can, and I can do things no one else here can do. It's an empowering feeling but kind of scary, too. I wonder how people like Wisp and Brohn and Rain deal with the pressure of walking around every day knowing everyone is looking up to them as some sort of infallible leader.

Taking a deep breath, I swipe my fingers along the tattoos on my forearm. It's a gesture I've done dozens, maybe hundreds of times, in my life. Although I've experienced varying degrees of success, failure, discomfort, and even pain, for the most part, it always works the same way: A slide of my index and middle fingers along the main black curve running in an arc from my elbow to my wrist followed by a specific pattern of quick taps with my thumb and ring finger on the series of button-sized black dots sprinkled around the longer curve. If I do it in the right way, exactly like my father taught me, I'm able to enter Render's mind. This time, everything works the way it always has. With one exception: The connection happens before I've completed the motions. This has only kind of happened before, and it shouldn't be possible to this degree now, but my fingers are hovering above the final part of the pattern when Render's mind and mine overlap, intersect, and intertwine like a gently tied shoelace.

I think maybe I'm imagining it. Maybe I completed the pattern without realizing it. I didn't sleep well, and I'm tired down to my bones. I don't have time to think about it, though. And even if I did have time, I wouldn't want to. Some moments are too perfect, too symmetrical to waste on overanalyzing. This is one of those moments. It's harmonious and light, and, at the same time, it's one of the most exhilarating and powerful feelings I've ever had in my life.

Once Render and I are connected, he's able to infiltrate the Armory again. This time, he's much more wary. After being shot at yesterday, he's now intimately aware of how high the stakes are. As a predator without a lot of natural enemies and having grown up with us in the isolation of the Valta, Render isn't used to the concept of fear. Nevertheless, he approaches the building cautiously.

Before he heads in, he spends some time circling the massive structure. Perched on tree branches, window sills, balconies, and any other spots that offer a good view, he sends back intricately-detailed images. Like yesterday, we form an organic-techno-conduit with Render feeding images to me, which Manthy interprets and passes along to Olivia who turns it all into detailed 3-D images, which Rain and Wisp then use to flesh out the rest of their battle plan. Manthy stays in physical contact with me and occasionally gives my arm a comforting squeeze.

For the most part, I can't see what's going on in the Intel Room. Right now, my vision is Render's. But occasionally, I get snippets and snatches of what's going on around me: Manthy's hand on my wrist. Wisp standing up to stretch and pace. Rain pointing out details on the large, 3-D schematics hovering above the table. Olivia, her tendrils in overdrive, connecting all of us to each other. The images are shadowy and out of focus, like I'm looking at them out of the corner of my eye through a fractured pane of wet glass.

I shake the images out of my head and re-focus on the task at hand.

Out in the city, Render banks and soars counter-clockwise around the imposing Armory, which occupies an entire city block. The wind flicking against his extended directional feathers and his wedge-shaped tail feels real, as if it's whisking over my own arms and across the backs of my hands.

The part of the Armory with the four turrets at each corner appears as a mass of grayish-orange brick punctuated with rows of tall, narrow windows. The main door is a plain-looking rectangle of reddish wood and is guarded by two men, boys really, with huge guns retro-fitted with laser scopes and grenade-launchers heaved onto their shoulders. Decked out in red, white, and blue army camo gear with big black boots laced up to the top, they look annoyed and uncomfortable but appear committed to fulfilling their duty. They keep their heads on a swivel, scanning the area for anyone or anything out of the ordinary. Naturally, they don't pay any attention to the large, black, and barely-visible bird minding his own business on a branch high up in a tree just across the street.

Like this door, the others—three pedestrian-doors along the east and west sides of the building and two towering vehicle doors on the north and south sides—are guarded by more young men in patriotic military apparel. Although the pedestrian-doors appear to be the old-style wooden fortress kind complete with black, cast iron handles and hinges, Render's vision detects unusual heat signatures coming off of some of them, which means there must be a system of security circuitry running through them. I relay this information to the others, and Wisp adds it to her notations on the meticulously detailed schematic.

Satisfied that he's seen all we need to see on this side of the block, Render lifts off and soars skyward. Around back, he lands on top of a tall fence and scans the building's rear entrance. Hovering security cameras, each with a single red eye, zip back and forth along the rear wall. If this is one of Wisp's infiltration access points, we're in a lot of trouble. I don't think any person could get within a hundred yards of this building without being spotted. Render relays this information to me. Manthy extracts it from me and turns it over to Olivia who continues to populate Wisp's diagrams, charts, schematics, and scrolling lines of computer code over the middle of the table.

"Keep it coming," Wisp calls out to me gleefully. "This is exactly what we need!"

I mutter to her that I'll do my best. Meanwhile, Render flutters from his position on the fence up into a nearby tree whose branches hang over the sidewalk. The whoosh of something mechanical in motion catches his attention, and he swings around to see the two towering double doors at the back of the building lurch open. He watches as a squadron of gas-powered military jeeps grumbles out, coughing exhaust fumes into the air. Render wants to fly away from the noise and from the offensive pollution belching into the trees around him, but I ask him to stay.

*We need all the information we can get. We need to get back inside.*

A fizz of static interrupts my connection with him. He's pulling his mind away from mine. I can't blame him for being reluctant. After all, he's the one inhaling the clouds of toxic smoke. He's the one who got shot at yesterday. Unfortunately, he's also the only one who can get us the information we'll need when we try to take over this intimidating and well-guarded citadel in a few days.

Following Wisp's advice, I try to merge more seamlessly with Render, to look at the world, not just from his point of view, but also from his points of feeling and experience.

Render relaxes and soars up to the roof of the domed part of the Armory. Like before, he's able to slip into an open exhaust vent and make his way into the massive interior of the building.

He is even more stealthy than I ever realized. I've known him to kick up dust and make a deafening racket with his wings. He's great at creating distractions when called upon. When he wants to, he can cry out in a range of guttural, human-sounding shrieks. He's even been known to imitate a screaming baby. But now, in hunting mode, he glides silently along the support struts in the top of the dome, his black form a perfect camouflage among the crisscross of black steel beams and the intricate dark shadows high above the polished concrete floor of the drill court far below. It makes me wonder how many times I've been followed and watched by him or by some other raven without my knowledge.

Down below, more vehicles follow the others out of the big double doors.

"A lot of them are leaving," I say to Wisp, my voice sounding strange in my own ears as I continue to focus through Render's eyes on the interior details of the Armory.

"They go on patrol like this from time to time," Wisp informs me. Her voice sounds as odd as mine, like it's coming from underwater, and I have to concentrate to understand what she's saying. "Don't worry," she reassures me. "This is good. More of them on patrol means less of them in the Armory…"

"…which means fewer of them to shoot at us," I finish.

"Just get what you can, and get out," Wisp advises. "No risks. Not yet."

I agree and adjust myself in my seat, digging deep into my mind for every bit of strength and focus I can muster. For the next several hours, Render hops, banks, weaves, and soars through the facility. In one of the far corners, he's able to land on the Armory floor behind a cluster of small military jeeps, one of them up on jack-supports for maintenance. Four soldiers sitting at a nearby table are playing cards and telling dirty jokes back and forth before switching topics and comparing notes about the arrests and "quiet kills" they've been making in the city over the past few weeks. Two of the men tell a story about how they shot a bunch of homeless women and girls in a park over on Church Street. "Bunch of useless tumors," one of the men says. "Might as well use 'em for target practice." They cover their choking laughter with their hands like they don't want to draw attention to their moment of goofing off. Like it's their indolence and not their casual cruelty they're ashamed of.

With one look, Render floods me with information about the four men: Their names embroidered on the breast pocket of their shirts, their approximate ages, the build of their bodies, their eye color, their clothing, and their weapons. He can even sense their relative health: breathing patterns, heartbeat irregularities, things like that. I'm nearly overwhelmed by it all, but it's a thrilling feeling to have instant access to so much information I could never otherwise hope to have, and I'm looking forward to the time when the other rebels and I can take these men down. I'm finding myself imbued with Render's predatory instincts, which are beyond anything I could have imagined. He's hard-wired to probe for weaknesses in potential prey. Tapped into his senses, I can tell that the first man at the table is dehydrated. The second man is allergic to certain grasses and pollens. The third man is sick with some kind of flu-like virus. He's the weakest of the four. The fourth man is nervous, probably about the prospect of a superior officer coming by while he's busy joking around with his buddies.

Quietly, invisibly, Render analyzes a hundred more men like this throughout the busy and cluttered main floor of the Armory.

Then, with a whoosh that's barely more than an exhalation of breath, Render is off again, exploring more of the space. He navigates through access corridors, construction scaffolding, heating ducts, and up and down a network of unused stairwells snaking through the facility. When a closed door or a dead end prevents him from proceeding, he gets resourceful and finds ways around, either through alternate access corridors, pedestrian walkways, ventilation and power conduits, or even by flying back outside and re-entering through an open window.

Render takes in everything. When he senses eyes about to be on him, he goes into full stealth mode, gliding to an invisible halt in the rafters or on top of one of the many silver ventilation ducts crisscrossing the huge space. His instincts are uncanny, and I'm amazed at how quickly they're becoming my instincts as well. We work in tandem, our minds and intentions overlapping, sometimes fusing into one, as we soak up more and more details.

Ravens largely feed on carrion, but they are also formidable hunters, and I'm starting to get a glimpse into some of the evolutionary advantages they have in the wild. Render's black feathers are perfect for keeping himself concealed. From most angles in this place, he probably looks like just another shadow. His feathers also keep him quiet as the air flows effortlessly over his streamlined body. His vision is far beyond the best human sight and even rivals some of the high-tech scopes and surveillance gear I've seen and used. Plus, he's smart. He's not just absorbing random information in this place. He's being stealthy and systematic about it. Starting from the ground floor, he works his way first down to the basement level and then methodically back up toward the domed roof. Along the way, he identifies every vehicle, stock room, workstation, communications port, input panel, staircase, grav-lift, emergency exit, supply closet, and storage locker. The main floor is lined with glass-walled offices around the perimeter. There are four mag-jeeps and seven gas-powered jeeps parked in the northwest corner by a large garage door. Nearby, a long bank of tall green lockers contains everything from extra uniforms and weapons to food and first-aid supplies. Overlooking all that is the mezzanine, which is basically a giant steel-railed balcony encircling the entire interior of the Armory's second level. It's lined with offices. Some are empty. Some are filled with stacks of wooden crates and plastic totes. Others house men seated behind large desks. People walk back and forth throughout the facility, carrying on with their daily duties in the service of what will be Krug's final takeover of one of the last major free cities in the country. Unless we can stop them first.

The mezzanine level of the Armory houses the Command Headquarters. It's from here that Ekker appears to run the show.

Dressed in a crisp military uniform with the red and white camouflage colors of the Patriot Army, he strides from his office to a larger room just down the walkway. This room is labeled "Communications Center," and it will be one of our primary targets when we storm this place on Friday night.

I relay this new information to Wisp who instructs me to

gather as much detail as I can about this large room within the Armory.

With the Communications Center and Command Head-quarters located, identified, and scouted, Render and I move on to the Munitions Depot, which is housed, along with the military barracks, in the large castle-like section of the domed Armory.

Render easily infiltrates this part of the building, and, with not as many people around, he gets through it with blazing speed and efficiency.

Cruising through the air ducts, access tunnels, and interior fire escape routes throughout the building, Render makes his way down to the basement where he finds a series of locked doors. They appear to be some kind of brig or holding cells, but there's no way to get in so Render flies the length of the dark corridor, up through a large aluminum duct, and, finally, back out into the open air.

I admit, part of me feels like a bit of a cheater, like I'm getting all the answers before I even sit down to take the big test. I laugh to myself at the ignorance of Ekker and his Patriot Army. Here they are, going about their business as if a teenage girl and a raven aren't in the middle of stealing all their secrets.

I don't know about love, but all is definitely fair in war.

Bursting into the sky from the top of the Armory, Render gives a few powerful beats of his wings before gliding back across town toward the Style. I ease back into my chair, enjoying the freedom of flight and congratulating myself and Render on a job well done.

I'm about to disconnect from him and go over everything we've learned with Wisp, Rain, Manthy, and Olivia when I sense a message burbling up in my brain:

*We are going to experience terrible things.*

It's Render's voice in my head. It's a warning. A lot of times in the past, he's demonstrated a keen sense of playfulness and humor. Right now, though, he's dead serious. I can tell he's scared, although I can't tell if it's for me or for himself.

*It's for us.*

*Because of the battle?* I ask the voice.

*Because we will hang in helplessness, and we will be reunited with death.*

## 9

---

I'M SHAKING WHEN I FINALLY DISCONNECT FROM RENDER, AND Manthy is there, quiet as always, with a comforting hand on my arm.

"What happened?" Rain asks from across the table where she's been working with Wisp.

"I don't know," I answer as a small shudder wriggles its way from my neck and all the way down my back before finally disappearing somewhere in my lower legs. "It's Render. He's worried. I think he thinks…"

"…What?" Rain finally asks as my voice trails off.

I rub my temples, but the pressure remains. "I think he thinks we're going to die."

"Who's going to die?" Wisp asks.

"I don't know. He said 'we.' It could mean me and him. Or all of us. The Insubordinates. Whatever it is, he's not optimistic at the moment."

Dropping the intensity, Wisp relaxes back into her seat. "Okay. So it's just a feeling. He's not a fortune-teller, right?" Wisp gives a little laugh, but I have to stop her.

"I'm not sure what he is, Wisp. Or what he's capable of."

"You told us there's more to us than we think," Rain chimes in. "Maybe there's more to Render as well."

"He's shown me visions of things that aren't there anymore. Or that maybe haven't been there yet," I tell Wisp. "When we were still on the run, we found an old military base. He showed me images of soldiers and a girl inside—all dead. But when we actually went inside, they weren't there anymore."

"Or yet," Rain adds.

I expect Wisp to be dismissive, but it's the opposite. She leans toward me again, her arms crossed in front of her on the black glass tabletop. She looks like she wants to say something, to pass along some kind of information. Her lips start to move, but nothing comes out.

"What is it?" I ask.

Wisp shakes her head. "Maybe nothing. Maybe everything. I think we should stop for tonight."

"Wait," Rain snaps. "If you have information we should have… something that might help us…"

Wisp stands up and walks around the table to where Olivia is still fiddling away at her bank of consoles and monitors. "Unfortunately, Rain, I don't have information or anything that can help. Just conjecture. I'd rather not base anything on partial information if I can help it. You guys head upstairs to the Dorm. It's late, and we have another long day ahead of us tomorrow."

"But Render…" I start to say.

Wisp shakes her head. "Let me consult with Olivia and Granden. I'll tell you what I know when I know it and not when it's just guesswork," she promises with a sympathetic smile.

Rain looks like she's about to argue, but Manthy shakes her head, and Rain stops.

"You've been cooped up in this room for days now and cooped up in Render's head for even longer. You need to decompress. All of you."

"And how do you propose we do that?" I ask.

"We need you to go and do some on-the-ground recon of your own. Kind of a field trip. Tomorrow is Tuesday. Rain and I will meet with Cardyn and Manthy to start combining what we know with the battle tactics the Insubordinates are learning. While we're doing that, you and Brohn get to go outside and see the city."

I try not to smile at this prospect, but I can't help it. The thought of it fills me up like too much water in a glass, and I feel like I might overflow with pleasure. I'm sure Wisp notices my reaction, but she's gracious and shrugs it off like it's no big deal. "We need you to get out of here for a while. Relax. You're no good to the cause if you're too stressed out and stir-crazy to function. Makes sense, right?"

"Yes," I say, still straining to sound professional and to repress my smile. "Perfect sense."

"Then it's settled," Wisp says in that strange tone that fills her tiny frame with the air of authority. "Tomorrow, you and Brohn are on reconnaissance duty in the streets of San Francisco. Now get out of here, please. Olivia and I have work to do!"

With me and Rain walking side by side and Manthy trudging along behind, we make our way upstairs to the next level where the last of the Insubordinates are milling around, yawning, and getting ready for bed. A couple of them offer us hesitant half-waves of greeting as if they're still not sure how much they're allowed to talk to us. I smile at two girls who look like they're at least a few years older than us. They start to smile back but then seem to think better of it and, instead, avert their eyes as we pass. A young man, probably in his early twenties, looks like he's about to say something to me, but, like the two girls, he seems to have second thoughts and decides to turn back to the whispered conversation he's having with his friend in the doorway of one of the dorm rooms. I was hoping that talking with the Insubordinates this morning about our past would normalize us. Instead, I think it's made us even more odd in their eyes.

"I think they're talking about us," I suggest to Rain and Manthy.

"I don't think so," Rain says. "I think they're talking about *you*."

I don't care what Wisp said before or what Rain thinks now. This is still an absurd suggestion. In the Valta, I was the girl in the background. Not quite as invisible as Manthy, but I certainly wasn't ever the center of quiet, awed attention that I seem to be at this very moment. And I certainly was never the girl who others spoke about in hushed, reverential whispers.

Now, curious eyes peek out from the open doorways as we continue to walk along the dark hallway toward our own room at the far end. I feel like I'm hiking through a shadowy forbidden forest in some super old fairy tale with the eyes of a hundred hiding elves following my every move.

"This is so weird," I say.

Rain gives a dismissive snort. "No weirder than being able to see through the eyes of a bird."

"Come on. Let's get to our room. This is creeping me out."

Suppressing a fit of the giggles and with Manthy in tow, Rain and I grab each other's hands and sprint the rest of the way down the long hallway to our room.

We burst through the door, and close it behind us. Laughing, we have our hands on our knees as we pant and chuckle at our sudden release of anxiety and exhaustion.

Brohn and Cardyn are already sitting on their beds waiting for us.

"Tough day at work, Honey?" Brohn jokes through a breathy yawn.

I release a very satisfying full-on laugh and walk over to give him a peck on the cheek. "It was a rough one all right, Dear."

Brohn heaves himself out of his bed with a grunt and throws his arms around me. "I feel like I haven't seen you in a week."

I return his hug, and he asks me what's so funny.

"Nothing," I say. "Everything."

"She's not used to being stared at," Rain offers from just inside the bathroom where she's splashing cold water on her face from one of the sinks.

I plop down on my bed and kick off my boots. "I just don't feel like I know who I am anymore," I sigh. "Not in a bad way. More like I feel like I'm turning into someone else. Or something else."

Brohn sits down on his bed across from me and gives my knee a little squeeze. "Well, whatever happens in these next few days, whatever or whoever you find yourself turning into, you'll always be you to me."

"Brohn," I say, dropping onto my back and staring up at the ceiling, "I think that's probably the weirdest and nicest thing anyone's ever said to me."

Dabbing her face dry with a fuzzy yellow towel, Rain comes back into the room and joins us in our little Conspiracy circle at the foot of our beds.

As Rain and I start filling Brohn and Cardyn in on our day, Manthy burrows herself into her bed until even her wild tangle of brown-hued hair disappears into the folds of her white sheets and crisp, green army blanket.

Cardyn rolls his eyes and reaches over to pat the pile of Manthy-shaped bedding. She squirms and moans but stays firmly ensconced.

The rest of us sit facing each other on the edges of our beds. Brohn leans forward with his arms draped over his legs. He winces a little as he flexes his shoulders and forearms. "This training stuff is exhausting," he says. "But kind of fun."

"Sure," Cardyn grumbles. "If you consider being one day closer to an unwinnable war as fun."

"Don't be such a pessimist," Brohn tells him. "I saw you upstairs. Barking out orders. Teaching those kids how to slap a magazine into a Sig Sauer. Giving them tips on proper hand position for optimal accuracy in firing. And the lessons in hand-to-hand, close-quarters combat. Admit it. You were enjoying every second of it."

Leaning back on his bed, Cardyn gives Brohn a dismissive wave. "I just like having something to do. Beats walking through the desert waiting to get killed or starve to death." He sits up, leans forward, and gives my knee a playful swat. "How about you, Kress? I feel like I haven't seen you in a year. How's our resident superstar?"

"Give me a break."

"Aw. You're blushing!"

"No, I'm not," I protest with my fingertips pressed to my cheeks. "This is my tomato impersonation."

"It's uncanny."

"We've been getting really good intel thanks to Render. Detailed stuff. Very helpful. But these Insubordinates..."

"What about them?"

"I've been getting some strange looks. The other day when I came upstairs to visit you guys. This morning at breakfast when we were telling our stories. Then again just now when we were walking down the hall."

"You really don't know?" Cardyn asks.

I shake my head and offer up a deep sigh of slightly annoyed resignation. "Let me guess, they've heard about my connection with Render, and they think I'm some kind of freak."

"Actually, I wasn't kidding about you being a superstar. Yes, they've heard about your connection with Render. But they don't think you're a freak. I think they think you're some kind of savior."

As tired as I am, I can't help but laugh out loud at this suggestion. "You're kidding."

"No. Even before we got here, word was going around. About all of us, really. But especially about you. They call you the *Kakari Isutse*." Apparently, it's from an old Costanoan language."

"Costanoan?"

"One of the Insubordinates explained it to us. The Costanoans were an indigenous group of people who lived here before the settlers hundreds of years ago. They called themselves the Ohlone. 'Costanoan' is the name the Spanish colonizers gave them. It means 'from the coast.' A few of the Insubordinates trace their ancestry to them."

"And this thing they're calling me?"

"*Kakari Isutse*. It means something like 'The girl who dreams in raven.' Or just, 'the Raven Dreamer.' They said it makes you our protector."

The way Card says this, all serious and mysterious, gives me another case of the giggles. Chuckling, I wipe the tears of incredulity from my eyes. "They know I'm not a superhero, right?"

"To them, you are. Well, maybe not the skin-tight costume and fluttering cape-wearing kind. But yes, they think you can save them, save all of us, from this life they're being forced to live and from the very bad things that are about to happen if Krug gets his way."

I flick away this suggestion. "I just spent the last eighteen hours gathering information. I can tell you every detail about half the buildings in the city and about every person and square inch inside the Armory and the Barracks building attached to it. There's hardly anything superheroic about that."

"Explain to me again how that works," Cardyn says, lying back, his voice now made nearly inaudible by the fluffy white pillow covering his face. "How are you able to get so much information?"

"It's not complicated. Render relays what he sees to me. Manthy uses her powers—"

"They're not powers," Manthy objects from deep under her covers.

"Sorry. Manthy uses her abilities—"

"It's not abilities, either," her muffled voice complains.

"Then what is it?" I ask, turning toward her and feeling slightly exasperated.

Manthy pushes the covers away from her face and sits up. "It's a curse."

"It's not a curse," Cardyn says.

"Is too."

"If you could speak a second language," Cardyn snaps, "would *that* be a curse? Or if you could juggle. Or play the piano. Or write plays like Shakespeare or do physics like Einstein. Being different enough to be able to help others is a gift, not a curse."

Sitting up all the way now, Manthy crosses her arms and frowns in a pout so powerful it's practically audible.

"Hey!" Cardyn exclaims into the silence that follows. "I just won an argument with Manthy!"

Manthy rewards him for his victory with a hastily-swung pillow to his face. Cardyn shrieks like he's been shot and falls in an exaggerated tumble off of his bed and lands with a thump onto the floor.

"Give me a break," Brohn says, reaching out a hand to help Cardyn to his feet and back onto the bed.

Cardyn offers a hearty "Thanks" like Brohn's just saved him from falling into a pool of molten lava.

"If you're done…" I say, feeling like an overburdened mother and desperate to change the subject, "I'd like to hear how things are going upstairs."

"Yeah," Rain says. "How's the babysitting going?"

Brohn gets suddenly serious. "Honestly, not as well as we'd hoped."

"How do mean?" I ask. "I was up there yesterday. You looked like you had everyone whipped into shape already."

"We have the *floor* whipped into shape. The rooms, the supplies, the training plans…it's mostly all in place. But the Insubordinates are inexperienced. There are too few of them,"

Brohn groans. He shakes his head and taps his temple. "They're too…I don't know…scattered."

"More like scared," Cardyn says.

"That's normal, right?" Rain asks. "I mean, they're not like we were. We had to struggle our entire lives just to survive. We lost so much so early. I think maybe that gave us a certain strength, an edge. Kind of like a 'what do we have to lose?' attitude."

Brohn thinks about that for a second before nodding his agreement. "I think you're right, Rain. They want to help. They really do. They want to be part of something big, something important. But they have families out there. A lot of them do, anyway. They have friends and schools and hobbies. Some of the older ones even have jobs. That's a lot to lose."

"It's an odd combo," Cardyn explains. "They're excited, eager, desperate, hopeful—"

"And scared out of their minds," Brohn finishes.

Talking back and forth like the partners and almost-brothers they've become, Brohn and Card continue to fill us in on life up on the fifth floor.

"Some of them actually have military training," Cardyn explains. "The older ones know a bit about tactics and weapons. A lot of them are just kids, though. Most of their parents hate Krug and the Patriot Army, but they don't know what to do about any of it. Underneath the eagerness and bravado, there's kind of a numb helplessness about it all."

"They've been to rallies and protests. The older ones and their parents have tried voting for different politicians. They complain to anyone who'll listen."

"Well, they used to," Cardyn informs us.

"Right. Turns out there's all kinds of censorship and surveillance systems in place. People who get too vocal in their opposition tend to disappear."

"Or die."

"There're no secrets anymore," Brohn says. "No anonymity. As it turns out, if you have an opinion these days, you'd better be willing to die for it. Because if it's against Krug, you probably will."

Cardyn rubs his eyes as he nods his agreement. "One of the younger Insubordinates told us his parents both got arrested along with hundreds of others in one of the recent protests. No one's heard anything from them in weeks."

"Not even where they are?" I ask.

Brohn says, "No. The local police don't like the Patriot Army being here, but they can't do much about it. Technically, the Patriot Army is run by Krug, and his orders take priority over local law enforcement."

Cardyn rubs his eyes again and sighs. "But there are plenty of police out there who are sick of all this. They may even be ready to help the Insubordinates drive out the Patriot Army."

"Or at least not get in our way," Brohn adds.

Rain sits up in her bed. "What about retaliation? Even if we pull this off, won't Krug just send in more troops to take back the city?"

"I asked Granden the same thing," Brohn says.

"And?"

"And Krug doesn't have as much power, pull, or personnel as he wants everyone to believe. Granden says a lot people are sick of this endless war against the Eastern Order, and some are starting to suspect the truth."

"You mean about the Order being fake?" I ask.

"Among other things. Wisp wasn't kidding. A lot of people really do seem to know about us, what we've been through. You heard those kids this morning. They're hungry for anything other than what Krug's been feeding them. People are still scared. They're just sick of being scared, especially about an enemy they've been asked more and more often to believe in on faith. A lot of people are ready to get back to their lives."

"Well," I sigh as I my eyelids flutter, and I feel sleep taking me over. "Their lives are worth fighting for."

I lie back in my bed, and I'm fading off to sleep when Brohn stretches his arm out and rests his hand on my forearm. His hand feels big and warm like the world's best security blanket.

Since our time in the Processor, Brohn has always slept next to me like this, always in the adjacent bed, always within arm's reach. Remembering Render's ominous thought from before—part feeling, part warning—I start to worry that, this time, proximity alone might not be enough to save us all.

# 10

I'M DEEP INTO A DREAM ABOUT MANTHY GETTING UP IN THE middle of the night and sneaking out of our dorm room to go downstairs to be with the Modifieds when the sound of shuffling bedding next to me wakes me up.

In the dark, I can just make out Manthy's ghostly figure as she disentangles herself from her sheets and blanket and slips into her black cargo pants and army-green compression top. Barefoot, she tiptoes toward the door, which eases open. Without looking back, she slips out into the corridor, quietly clicking the door shut behind her.

Wondering if I'm still dreaming, I untangle myself from my own covers and sheets, throw on a robe, and follow her, completely unsurprised to find that she's heading downstairs to the second floor to where we first encountered the heartbreaking group of lost souls known as the Modifieds.

Olivia may consider herself one of them, but in reality, she's a whole other world away. The people we met down here a couple of days ago barely register as people. They're more like the spirits of people entombed in cold bodies of flesh, metal, and code. I don't judge them. I wouldn't even if I could. I don't know them. I don't know their hopes, fears, circumstances, and I certainly have no idea what led them—voluntarily or under duress—down this path toward what people today are calling the "post-human." Personally, I think we, as a species, ought to figure out what it means to be human before we start jumping into being post-anything. But that's just me. If these people want to modify their genetic makeup, tinker with their synaptic networks, and swap out their organic parts for something mechanical, that's their choice. I don't begrudge them that right. I don't necessarily agree with it, but, then again, I don't totally understand it either. That leaves me ignorant and in no position to rain moral judgement down on people I met once and whom I don't know at all.

Still half-immersed in the fog of sleep, I shake my head to separate the dream I was having from the reality I'm living.

From the creepy quiet of the corridor outside the room, I hear Manthy talking with Caldwell, caretaker for the Modifieds. He seemed like a nice enough man when we met him that first night in the Style, but we don't know him well enough to be careless. Manthy's tone, however, is relaxed, and he sounds genuinely happy about her unannounced, middle-of-the-night visit.

I shouldn't be able to hear them this clearly, but it's like their voices are traveling through a vacuum instead of through the thick night air, and I'm wondering if Render is around. Maybe he's feeding me intel like he did at the Armory. Or maybe, like Wisp claims, there's more to him, more to all of this, and more to me than meets the eye. Either way, I hear every word, breath, and whisper as clearly as if they were coming from inside my own head.

"What am I?" Manthy asks from deep inside the room.

Caldwell clears his throat. "Are you asking if you're one of them?"

"Yes. I guess."

"You're not. It's possible to do what you do without being what they are."

Manthy doesn't say anything, and I can only imagine that she must be looking around at the nearly-neglected half-human, half-machine people under Caldwell's care. I hear her footsteps on the tiled floor inside the room.

"There are always freaks," she says.

Caldwell doesn't answer. Maybe he's nodding. Maybe he didn't hear her. Their voices continue to slip into my mind on something other than vibrations in the air. I stand with my back to the wall in the quiet corridor and continue to take it all in.

"Krug isn't the problem," Caldwell says at last. "It's in here. It's in our heads. And our hearts. We want to have stability and still be on the move all at once." I hear what must be the sound of him patting the breast pocket of his lab coat. "In here, we want to belong, but we're taught to keep others out."

"Seems like everyone wants to be alone. But no one wants to be lonely."

Caldwell agrees. He says Manthy is wise. "So much better than being smart," he adds.

Manthy's voice sounds so sad when she says, "We can't escape our own defects."

"Did you think I could help you?"

"Maybe."

"Why?"

"Because you seem to know people. And you seem to know the Modifieds. And I think maybe I'm somewhere in the middle."

"And you don't want to be?"

"Who does?"

"I think I can help."

"You can?"

"Sure. Here's my help: You don't need any help."

"I don't fit in."

"Manthy, do you really *want* to fit in?"

Manthy pauses before saying, "Sometimes."

"You know how the Eastern Order is all just a big trick?"

"Yes."

"I'll let you in on a secret. That's not the only trick being played on you. Like the rest of us, you've been tricked into thinking you need help when really it's the rest of the world that's just too ignorant, lazy, and afraid to have you walking around being yourself."

"Ignorance, laziness, and fear," Manthy mutters. "There seems to be a lot of that going around these days."

"It's been going around for as long as there've been people. Unfortunately, those things tend to be the driving force behind most of what people do. The secret is to not let those things be the driving force behind you."

In the brief silence that follows, the guilt about eavesdropping is finally too much for me to bear, and I give a gentle knock. The sound of my knuckles on the old wooden door sounds thunderous in the graveyard silence of the empty hallway.

The door swings open.

Standing toward the back of the main room, her head down, Manthy looks embarrassed, but Caldwell invites me in with a welcoming and unsurprised smile like he's used to entertaining stray visitors in the middle of the night.

"Did you hear...I mean, how long have you been out there?" Manthy asks from behind his shoulder.

"Just for a second," I lie. "I didn't hear anything," I lie again. "I heard you get up, and I was worried about you."

That part's the truth.

"Come in," Caldwell says as he steps aside. I enter the room, and he closes the door quietly behind me. He plunges his plump little hands into the pockets of his white lab coat and looks at me sheepishly. "Couldn't sleep?"

I nod and have a long look around. Two of the Modifieds we

met the other day are in mag-chairs like Olivia's and are plugged nearly lifelessly into a charging port on the far wall by the window between two other Modifieds lying just as lifelessly in adjacent hospital beds.

"Marcelo and Retta, right?"

"Yes. Good memory."

"Thanks."

Caldwell told us about these two. A husband and wife who basically fried their brains trying to be whatever comes next after human.

"Why?" Manthy asks. When Caldwell and I just stare at her, waiting for her to finish, she wipes her eyes. "What were they hoping would happen?"

Caldwell pushes his square-framed glasses up from where they've slipped down on his nose. "There are too many answers to that. But, if I had to sum it up, I'd say they were hoping you would happen."

"Us?" I ask.

"Both of you. Yes. They wanted it all. The warm blood of a human being and the calculating coldness and lightning-fast processing speed of a computer."

"That's not us," Manthy objects.

"No. It's not. And I'm not saying it is. Only that it's what some people misunderstood you to be."

"We're not anything," Manthy says. "No one should try to be us."

"Actually, from what I hear, the two of you are far too important to what happens next to be down here in the middle of the night talking with me."

"I think talking with you might be exactly what helps us to accomplish what happens next," I tell him.

When we talk about the upcoming encounter with the Patriot Army, I notice we don't say "battle," "fight," "war," or "rebellion." It's like saying it out loud might make it happen faster, make it more real. Or maybe saying it out loud will prevent it from happening at all. It's still an abstraction, this thing we're about to do. Something days away whose costs haven't yet been calculated.

Caldwell invites us to walk with him though an interconnected series of rooms. "It's time for me to make my rounds, anyway."

"Are you the only person who works with the Modifieds?" I ask.

He chortles an, "Oh no" and tells us about volunteer support-workers from a place called Haven House before explaining that the Major, the girl the rest of us know as Wisp, is the real person in charge. "She's made it her mission to find the Modifieds out there and to bring them here for the kind of help they can't get anywhere else. Especially with the Patriot Army here now. Krug wanted to weaponize the Modifieds. When that mostly failed, he discarded them. That's where the Major steps in." Caldwell folds his arms across his chest and grins appreciatively like he's surveying a room full of beautiful artwork. "Without the Major, these folks would be scrap. Homeless. Possibly dead."

We follow him as he makes his way around the main room where he tends to six of the Modifieds, including Marcelo and Retta. Part doctor, part mechanic, part digital technician, he examines their pupil dilation, inspects the scrolling red holo-notes floating in the air above and around each bed, and he tends to a variety of ailments from bed sores to misfiring circuits in the neuro-chips some of the Modifieds have embedded in their brains or fused to the base of their necks.

Then we go into a second room, just off the first, to find a dozen more Modifieds—some seated, some standing—lined up around the perimeter of the room. They're all leaning against a long horizontal strip of blue light running like glowing wain-scoting along the wall behind them.

Some of them I recognize from the other day when we first

arrived. Others are new to me. One of them, a woman, I think, stares at me and Manthy as we walk past. Her exposed titanium jaw hangs open like she's trying to greet us, but the only sound that comes out is a horrifying crackle of static. Another woman, the entire top half of her face replaced by a pane of black glass, tilts her head in our direction. A flickering series of green computer code I can't read fills the mirrored glass.

"That's Tyressa," Caldwell tells us. "She's trying to scan you. But her neural network's been so badly compromised over the years, she's essentially locked into a cyclical computer diagnostic running inside her head." Caldwell shakes his head and makes a little "tsk" sound with his mouth. "Must be maddening."

He sets about explaining little bits and pieces about the other Modifieds in this room as he squints at the red holo-notes hovering over each one like a halo. Caldwell taps at the scrolling text of diagnostics, skimming through some, lingering for a few seconds on others and making "hmmm" and "ahhh" noises as he goes. A couple of the Modifieds acknowledge us. One of them, a man with a patchwork of circuitry covering most of his fragmented body, even manages to ask us how we're doing. I'm just telling him I'm fine when his eyes flicker like a glitchy viz-screen and then glaze over white.

"Don't take it personally," Caldwell says without looking away from the holo-notes of his current patient. "Vasco fazes in and out like that. He was part of a military-led experiment designed to integrate neurotypical brain patterns with stochastic algorithmic learning optimizers. He spends half his life inside his own head trying to find patterns in the pattern-less. The ultimate introspection."

"Sounds like hell," I say.

Caldwell gives me a sideways glance as he taps out code on the display in front of him. "I can only imagine."

By the time we get to the third room and another collection of Modifieds—some immobilized on floating gurneys, others limping aimlessly around the sparsely furnished space—I'm struggling not to cry. Once we pass through there, Caldwell leads us through one more door to his office, an enormous and well-lit room packed floor to ceiling and wall to wall with shelves, work-tables, storage lockers, and an array of cubbies, all labeled with the complex names of a wide assortment of surgical equipment, computer parts, and mechanical tools. There wasn't a lot of need for me to study mechanics back in the Valta, but the little I learned comes flooding back to me as I scan the names on the boxes and drawers: camshaft bearing, cylinder bore, torque wrench, vacuum modulator, diagnostic scanner. Mixed in with those are the names of an assortment of medical tools including harmonic scalpels, retractors, distractors, microsurgical needles. On top of that, Caldwell's office is dotted with specialized work-stations and is hip-deep in computer-repair tools: copper tape, motherboards, mounting plates, couplers, multimode optical fibers. It's a lot to take in, and I'm impressed that one man has learned how to do so much to help so many.

"Have a seat," Caldwell says grandly, as he drops down onto a hovering stool in front of the largest of the six silver work-benches in the room.

Manthy and I sit in the two hovering mag-chairs in front of him.

For a few minutes, the three of us discuss the tragedy of the Modifieds, the hopelessness. Unsure how to phrase it and less sure I should even bring it up, I finally ask Caldwell if any of the Modifieds ever ask to be put out of their misery.

"Suicide," Caldwell says, his head down, his eyes wet. "Euthanasia. Sure. It's a moral dilemma we all live with every day. Well, *they* live with it. I can always just go home and turn that conversation over to the clerics, the lawyers, and the philosophers."

"Euthanasia," Manthy says to the floor. "It means 'good death.'"

Caldwell looks over at her and nods but doesn't say anything.

Finally, Manthy raises her head and asks if she can walk around, and Caldwell assures her that it's okay. "Just be careful."

"Are they dangerous?" I ask, looking toward the doorway.

I expect Caldwell to laugh this off. After all, the majority of the people in these rooms around us can barely move or talk. But Caldwell looks up at the ceiling like he's seriously considering my question. "Some of them are in a lot of pain," he says. "It's hard to communicate with them, even for me. They may not react well to an unknown person milling around. I don't think any of them will react poorly to you. But I can't say for sure at any given time how they'll react to their pain. Pain's a funny thing. If we can't get at it directly, we tend to lash out at whatever else is handy. I don't want that handy thing to be you."

Manthy stands in the doorway of the lab, quietly looking at Caldwell through the tops of her eyes until he finally gives her his full assurance that it's okay.

"She can be a little odd," I tell Caldwell after she's disappeared back the way we came. In my own ears, it sounds more like an apology than an explanation.

"She's amazing," he gushes. "Does she know what she is?"

"Does she know what who is?"

"What she is."

"Why? What is she?"

"She's a miracle of human evolution."

"Manthy? She's got an ability."

"I know. I know about you from Granden and the Major. But I never knew the extent. Never met one of you in real life."

"What extent? And why can't we get a straight answer out of anyone?"

I frown at Caldwell's chuckle, but he promises he's not teasing me. "You can't get a straight answer because no one has one. I've probably got more experience working with the Modifieds than anyone, and even I don't know what motivated them in the first place or what makes them tick today."

"I'm not a Modified."

"That's true. You're an Emergent. You didn't choose to be who you are. But then again, none of us did. I didn't choose to be short. Or bald. Or allergic to eggs." He taps his temple with his chubby finger. "I also didn't choose to be able to visualize the intricate details of pretty much any complex machine, even the ones we call 'human beings.' But I choose to focus on what I can do instead of what I can't do."

"It sounds like a pretty easy choice to make."

"Don't be too sure. Do you have any idea how many people, when given the choice between pursuing their strengths or their weaknesses, choose the latter? Selfishness is a weakness. So are pride, ignorance, narcissism, racism, sexism, ageism, ableism. And yet countless people follow those impulses at the expense of the *real* strengths—honesty, generosity, curiosity, selflessness— they've been conditioned to repress."

Caldwell takes off his glasses and rubs the lenses with the corner of his white lab coat. He looks around at his well-stocked lab and sighs.

"We better get back upstairs," I say after a pause. "Long day ahead of us and all."

"Yes. We can't have our heroic rebels falling asleep on the battlefield." He grunts as he heaves himself out of his mag-chair, and I follow him out of his lab and through the adjacent rooms. He stops as we walk through the room with the Modifieds standing along its perimeter with the blue light that had been glowing around its edges. Only now the blue light has turned a shimmering silvery-yellow in most places. Caldwell stops in his tracks and gestures with a sweep of his hand at the lights along the wall. "How'd that—?"

"What is it?" I ask.

"The S.A.N.S. system. Sorry. It's the name of the diagnostic system: Synaptic Autogenetic Neuro Synthesis. The light running around the room. It's a spectral systems monitor. Keeps track of what the Modifieds need and how they're doing. Everything from identifying neuron depletion to molecular density stress-levels in their purely mechanical parts. Since most of them can't really communicate what they're feeling and because their neurology is so intertwined with their nano-tech, the system also helps register their pain levels. Blue indicates their usual pain level. It's pretty high. That's what it's almost always at, unfortunately. Green means no pain or limited pain. Yellow, like this, actually indicates an experience of pleasure. Peace even."

"So it's good that most of it's yellow now, right?"

"It's amazing. Only…"

"What?"

"Well, it's never been yellow before."

Arriving back at the door to the main room, Caldwell gives Manthy an odd look, but he doesn't say anything. She doesn't seem to notice and instead tugs me by the arm and starts heading down the hallway toward the stairs.

I call out "Goodnight" back to Caldwell, and he raises his hand in a kind of stunned wave.

"I know how good you are with tech," I whisper into the dark as Manthy and I trudge on tired legs back up the two flights to the fourth floor Dorm. "But on second thought, I think maybe your super power is being kind to people who need kindness," I say to her back.

"Being kind to people in need shouldn't require a second thought," she mumbles without turning around.

## 11

WHEN WE GET TO OUR FLOOR, WE SEE THE SILHOUETTE WAY DOWN the hall of someone standing just outside our bedroom door. Looking at each other for a second, Manthy and I walk the length of the dead-quiet hallway until the dark figure comes into focus.

"What are you doing up?" I ask Brohn.

"Can't sleep," he says, leaning, arms crossed, against the wall just outside of our dorm room. He covers a yawn with his hand. "You?"

"No."

"Hi, Brohn," Manthy says as she nudges past him and into our room without making eye contact.

"What's with her?"

"Couldn't sleep. I kept her company."

"Where'd the two of you just come from?"

"Downstairs."

Thrusting his hands deep into his pockets, Brohn looks surprised and suddenly awake. He looks up at the gentle purple glow of the strip-lights running along the walls of the empty hall-way. "You visited the Modifieds?"

"Yes."

"How are things down there?"

"Sad," I say. "But also...revealing. They're people. Human beings. They have feelings, fears, pain, everything. It's like the world is too small and restrictive to accommodate them, but we've somehow made that their fault instead of ours."

Brohn opens his mouth like he's going to ask me to say more, but he doesn't. Instead, he leans back against the wall and crosses his arms again. Our voices are quiet, just above a whisper. "Worried?" he asks.

"Yes."

He nods and looks down the empty hallway to the left and to the right. "We've lived through a lot."

"True. But nothing quite like this. Not with this much at stake. In the Processor, if we failed, whatever consequences there were happened to us alone. Here, if we fail, it could mean slavery, poverty, the death of thousands. According to your sister, it could also mean the death of an entire way of life."

Brohn looks down at his boots. "I really wish she were exaggerating."

"But she's not."

"No. She's not." Brohn looks up at me, and I'm surprised to see a coy smile tugging at the corners of his mouth. "Take a walk?"

"What?"

"I was about to sneak out for a walk. Since you're already up and about anyway, I thought maybe you'd like to join me while I head upstairs to make sure everything's set up for the next round of training."

"What about sleep?"

"We can sleep after we've saved the world."

"You never stop working, do you?" I ask in a whispery laugh.

Brohn eases himself away from the wall and extends a hand out to me. "I never stop thinking about you," he says in a voice so quiet I have to perform a double-check in my head to make sure I heard him right.

I take Brohn's hand. His fingers curl around mine, and he gives a tender squeeze. With a finger to his lips, he leads me down the corridor back the way Manthy and I just came.

Under the gentle purple glow, we walk to the door at the end of the hallway. Brohn leads me through and up the stairs to the fifth floor where he and Cardyn have been working so hard with Granden these last couple of days. Our footsteps sound hollow against the concrete steps of the wide staircase.

Brohn tells me how Cardyn has really thrown himself into his role as a trainer. I'm proud of Card for that, and I'm happy he's happy. But I miss him. Growing up in the Valta, Cardyn was my go-to guy, my best friend who was always magically there when I needed him. Other than the time I spent alone or with Render, Cardyn made up a big chunk of my very limited social life. I know we've only been apart for a couple of days here in the Style, that we're only two floors away from each other at any given time during the day, and that we still have a few hours together at night. But it's more distance than I'm used to.

I'll give him credit, though. Brohn, too. The fifth floor looks incredible. It's even more set up than before with long tables full of weapons and other gear lining the wide hallway. I recognize a lot of the weapons from my own training: a row of Magpul FMG-9s, FN F2020 Assault Rifles, Sig Sauers. There's even an older version of the sniper-rifle that Kella got so good at so fast during our time in the Processor. Boxes of ammo are labeled and lined up tidily on a long table between two open doorways. I peek inside another open doorway to find a fully-furnished boxing and martial arts studio complete with blue mats, hanging heavy bags, jump-ropes, and even a *mu ren zhuang*, one of the wooden dummies I remember so well from our Wing Chun and Jeet Kune Do training in the Processor. I'm startled for a second by a glint of light and a hint of movement on the far wall of the dark room until I realize it's just my reflection in a bank of mirrors the guys have set up. Brohn laughs when he sees me jump, and I give him a playful whack on the bicep with the back of my hand.

Leading me from room to room, Brohn finally stops at the end of the long hallway. This is the room directly above the Mess Hall where we eat. Pushing the door open, he shows me where they've been doing target-practice with bullet-ridden disks of nano-plasticine set up at the far end of the long room. It's pretty dark in here with only a thin courtesy light-strip casting a misty purple glow into the expansive space.

"It's bigger than I thought it'd be," I say as I take in the cathedral ceilings and look down the length of the long room into the darkness at the far end.

"I think it used to be two or maybe even three conference rooms or maybe something they converted into a lecture hall," Brohn says, pointing up to a long metal rail that must have once held a floor-to-ceiling divider of some kind. "It's still not a ton of space, but it's enough to get this firing range set up. Since we can't very well practice outside, this is the next best thing."

"And how are they doing? Any Kella-level marksmen in the bunch?"

"Nothing quite like that. But they're coming along," Brohn assures me, although from here, squinting into the distance, it doesn't look like the bullseyes on the targets have seen much action. "I wonder how she's doing. Kella, I mean."

"I'm sure she's fine. Probably running Adric and Celia's whole operation by now."

Brohn and I share a chuckle over the very real possibility that Kella may currently be out there as the leader of a band of forest-dwelling orphans. She was always talented in so many ways. To see her fall apart so completely after Karmine's death left me worried about her ability to survive at all, let alone up in the mountains and on the run. But I have to give her credit. No matter how weak or sad she got, she never once gave up during our time on the road.

Still thinking fondly about the best dead-eye shot in our Cohort, I walk over to the bank of windows on the far side of the room. They've been covered over with some kind of shimmering black, rubbery-looking tarp that Brohn explains are noise and light-reducers. "We're five floors up, but there are some tall buildings around here, and Granden wants to make sure we stay as invisible as possible."

"I can see why. Last thing we need is for the neighbors to hear gunfire and get the local police or worse, the Patriot Army, involved."

"Exactly. According to Wisp, there's no back-up plan. No second band of Insubordinates waiting in the wings. If we're discovered here, that's the end of the entire operation."

Doubling back along the side of the room, I push aside some of the handguns and bins of ammo and hop up onto the big table near the door where we first came in.

Brohn walks over to stand in front of me with my legs on either side of his hips. I look up at him through the tops of my eyes. I remember when we were the same height. On November first about five years ago, we were all gathered in the clearing at the top of the road watching the newest Cohort getting taken away from the Valta by the Recruiters. The next year, we were all in the same clearing watching the next Cohort disappear down the road in the Recruiters' trucks, only this time, Brohn was a full head taller than me. Today, looking powerful from this angle, he towers over me. The scruff on his jawline and the bulge of muscles in his shoulders and rippling twist of tendons in his forearms are a world away from the slender, ropey-muscled boy I knew growing up.

With all my reminiscing about the past and anxiety about the future, I completely forgot there's a present right here in front of me.

Brohn leans in to kiss me, and the boy he once was disappears completely, leaving me alone in this dark and quiet room with this tall, confident, and authoritative man.

I return Brohn's kiss and sling my arms around his neck, pulling him closer.

Last night, I connected with Render without completing the scanning process on my tattoos. It felt strange. This feels like that, like Brohn and I are somehow more complete once we've surrendered a part of ourselves to each other.

I've had a lot of strange sensations these past few days: fear, hope, and everything in between. I've met the Modifieds, and I've felt their pain and admired their courage. I've soared through the skies with Render. Or is it *as* Render? Or is it *both*? Either way, I've experienced the terror and the thrill of living in two worlds at once. So many odd and unexpected moments. And now, this. I'm safe in the arms of someone I've known nearly all my life but hardly talked to until it was nearly too late, and now we're getting ready to risk our lives to save our world.

It occurs to me, as Brohn kisses me again, that just because something is strange doesn't mean it's not perfect.

12
───────────

W ᴇ ʜ ᴇ ɴ  Bʀᴏʜɴ  ᴀɴᴅ  I  ᴇᴠᴇɴᴛᴜᴀʟʟʏ  ᴛɪᴘ-ᴛᴏᴇ  ʙᴀᴄᴋ  ɪɴᴛᴏ  ᴏᴜʀ  ʀᴏᴏᴍ, the others are still in a deep sleep even as slivers of pinkish morning light start to appear at the corners of the shaded windows.

I'm feeling giggly and guilty but also oddly energized. Far more than I should be at this hour and without any sleep.

Brohn and I ease into our beds with the sound of Rain's and Manthy's gentle breathing and Cardyn's chainsaw snoring filling the room around us.

With our heads adjacent in the center of our spoked-wheel pattern of beds, Brohn and I don't even bother to sleep. We wouldn't get much anyway before it was time to get up. Instead, we lie there for the few minutes of the night we have left, holding hands across the space between us, lying on our sides, and occasionally looking into each other's eyes and smiling. I'm torn in a dozen different directions. Part of me wants to leap over and curl up in Brohn's bed with him. Part of me wants to step up the timetable and conduct our raid of the Armory right now.

In the end, I'm shaken from my dilemma by Rain who is the first one to start stirring. I've already resigned myself to a long day of being tired. After spending the first half of the night downstairs with Manthy and the Modifieds and the second half upstairs with Brohn, I should definitely be wiped out. But thinking about it all seems to have given me a second wind. I'm not sure how long it'll last, but I vow to take full advantage of the energy I have while I still have it.

After showers and a quick breakfast in the Mess Hall among some of the other early risers, the five of us make our way down to the Intel Room. As we walk downstairs, I'm filled with a renewed sense of purpose and belonging. It's a familiar scene: Brohn leading the way followed closely by Rain with me and Cardyn just behind her, and Manthy, as she's done so often, bringing up the rear. The five of us haven't really been together like this in a few days. Walking through the fourth-floor hallway door and down to the Intel Room feels great and right and like this is exactly the way it should be. This is our line of soldiers, our five-person army of Emergents. Our Conspiracy. If we still had Kella, Karmine, and Terk with us, and if we weren't all about to face almost-certain death in a few days, it'd be yet another almost perfect moment.

But the reality of our situation comes flooding back as we enter the Intel Room single-file to find Wisp and Granden already hard at work, coordinating intel and battle plans with Olivia. Olivia rotates in her chair to offer us a welcoming smile and a surreal wave of the dozens of animated tendrils curling and twisting from the ends of her wrists.

For her part, Wisp offers us a cursory greeting before rattling off our instructions for the day.

"Things are going about as well as expected," she informs us from the table near Olivia where she's busy flicking through the scrolling text and lines of code of a neon-red holo-display. "But we're getting close to Friday, and there are still some pieces we need to put into place. Granden tells me training is going well."

Brohn and Card assure her it's going as well as can be

expected. Wisp looks up and gives them both a curt nod of thanks before turning back to her displays. "Our supply runs have been successful. Surprisingly so, actually. I don't think local law enforcement would get in our way even if they knew what we were planning. We've been able to transport all kinds of weapons through various checkpoints right under their noses. Either they've suddenly become as dangerously incompetent as the Patriot Army or else they've decided to look the other way."

"I'm making progress with local law enforcement," Granden says.

"What about personnel?" Brohn asks. "We have forty-eight Insubordinates we've been working with upstairs. Most of them are coming along quickly and trying really hard. But in reality, with the limited time we have, only about thirty of them will be truly useful in a major infiltration and combat mission like we're talking about."

"Thirty, *tops*," Card adds, and Brohn nods his reluctant agreement.

Wisp looks from Brohn to Card and then gestures all of us over to seats around the oval table where we sit down. Dropping into my chair, I catch a glimpse of my reflection in the polished, black glass tabletop. I've got a strange expression of determination and confidence in my eyes. I also look worn-out and battle-weary, far too rough and weathered for a seventeen-year-old girl. Brohn glances over and catches me staring at my reflection. Somehow reading my mind, he puts his hand on my forearm and whispers a reassuring, "You look beautiful" as he sits down next to me.

With Olivia, as always, in her seat at the head of the table and surrounded by her tech, Brohn and Cardyn inform Wisp and Granden that they'll definitely need more troops and more time.

Wisp says she can help with the first but not with the second. "We don't have control over the timetable. But there are more Insubordinates scattered throughout the city."

"I was able to get confirmation on Krug's travel plans," Olivia adds, her voice sounding like wind chimes. "He's definitely on his way."

"All the more reason to gather as much help as we can."

Pointing one at a time at highlighted portions of Olivia's projected images of the city, Granden tells us about places on the San Francisco map where smaller Insubordinate cells are hiding out. In his proper military cadence, he counts them off one at a time. "There is a small group here at Fisherman's Wharf. Another here at an arts plaza in West Portal. There is another underground stationed here at Pier 50. The more freedoms the Patriot Army takes away, the more we hear about people wanting to join the cause. But they can't be too vocal about that, and we don't have time to chase down rumors. We need to stick with what we know and leave the speculation for another time when the stakes aren't quite so high."

"Since you've already found them," Rain offers, "it sounds like the rest is just a matter of unifying and incorporating them into our existing plans."

"Agreed," Granden says. "Part of today's mission is exactly that. There are potential fellow rebels out there, but they won't do us or themselves any good sitting on the sidelines. They need us as much as we need them."

"So what's the plan, Boss?" Cardyn asks Wisp.

Wisp stands and paces. She doesn't seem nervous or anxious or anything. It's more like she feels the need to be on the move. It's a feeling I can relate to. We finally stumbled upon a city where the air is clean, the people aren't starving and killing each other, and the buildings are all intact—for now, at least—but I still have to be cooped up in this Intel Room for eighteen hours a day. It's one of the things no one ever tells you about rebellions: it's not all battles and glory. Behind the scenes, there's a lot of planning, waiting, and a whole lot of worried pacing.

Still walking around the table, Wisp pushes up the sleeves of her hoodie. "Cardyn, you and Granden will take over training for today. It's got to be serious and intense."

"It always is," Cardyn mumbles with what sounds like slightly hurt feelings.

Wisp stops her pacing and apologizes to Cardyn. "You're right. From what I've heard from the Insubordinates and from what I've seen with my own eyes, you've done more for them in a few days than most military training programs could accomplish in a month." After Cardyn has finished blushing, Wisp continues with her instructions. "Make sure we save enough ammo for Friday. Kress and Render have gotten us some excellent intel. Manthy, I need for you and Olivia to see what you can do about hacking the Patriots' system to get us the rest of the way inside."

"I've tried," Olivia says. "I don't think I can do it."

"I don't think you can either. Not alone. The two of you together, though…I don't think there's much you can't accomplish. Rain, you'll stay here with me. I'm okay setting things up and directing traffic, but I don't have your gift for strategy. I'm not sure if anyone in the world does, actually. I need you to help me arrange the timing, initiate the waves of initial attacks, anticipate counter-attacks, and teach me how to expect the unexpected. Thanks to Kress and Render, we've got great structural and logistical details and a good start on a battle plan. Unfortunately, good isn't good enough. For this little rebellion of ours, we'll either be perfect or dead."

Rain sits up tall in her seat, clearly proud to have her gifts publicly recognized even if the implication is nearly certain death in less than four days.

"What about us," I ask, flicking a thumb between me and Brohn. "You said something about us taking a field trip?"

"Yes. The other day, I mentioned I'd need you outside of the Style at some point. Today just became 'some point.' Those little pockets of Insubordinates and Insubordinate wannabees scattered throughout the city Granden was pointing out? We've discovered that one of those pockets is actually pretty well-organized, partially-trained, and is chomping at the bit for something to do. Your job is to track them down, find out if they're serious about helping, and determine if they're actually able to contribute, or if they're just going to get in the way."

"How will we know where to find them?"

Wisp says, "Light it up" to Olivia.

Olivia swivels in her floating chair and wriggles her tendrils in front of us. She says, "Initiated," and the floating hologram of the city zooms in on a church. "Grace Cathedral," Olivia says. It's one of the major hubs of potential rebels we showed you on your first day here."

"Start there," Wisp says. "See where that leads you."

Cardyn claps his hands together and then pats Granden hard on the shoulder. "Well, by now there are a few dozen Insubordinates milling around up on the fifth floor just waiting to get some more intensive training. I guess I better head upstairs and show Granden here how it's done. What do you say, Granden? Up for tagging along?"

"Of course, Cardyn. How else will I learn?" Granden jokes, and we all have a unanimous chuckle at this stern soldier's rare moment of humor.

Together, Cardyn and Granden head out of the room to make their way up the two flights to the fifth-floor where Brohn and I were hanging out not more than a couple of hours ago.

"You should get going, too," Wisp instructs me and Brohn.

Standing up, Brohn and I say goodbye to Wisp, Manthy, Rain, and Olivia. We're just stepping out the door and into the corridor when Manthy rushes up to me and puts a hand on my shoulder. "Please be careful."

I assure her I will and turn to go, but she pulls me back toward her and leans in to whisper in my ear. "I can't be me without you." Her voice is so soft. She's practically crying, and I don't know where this sudden bout of raw emotion is coming from, but I know Manthy well enough now not to question it. She doesn't talk much, but when she does talk, it's to say what she means.

After giving Manthy my full reassurance and a peck of appreciation on the cheek, I head down the hall with Brohn. He and I practically skip over to the stairs and jog down the three flights to the basement level where we navigate our way down the long twisting corridor leading to the rear door of the building. We push the door open, walk up the short flight of outdoor basement steps up to street level, and step into the cluttered alley out back. Hand in hand, we walk down the cool, shaded space between the Style and the tall brick building next door and out into the bright light of the bustling city.

Brohn cranes his neck up to take in the tall buildings and then turns slowly in place to marvel at the colors, sounds, and at the hundreds of people already up and about and getting into their daily routines.

"Amazing," he gushes.

"The people?"

"Yes."

"And the buildings?"

"All of it," Brohn sighs. "The roads. The mag-cars. The shops. The houses and trees. All of it intact."

"Do you think they know how close they are to having it taken over or else taken down?"

Brohn points to the two Patriot Army soldiers, machine guns as big as canons on their shoulders, standing ominously on the corner. "I think they have some idea. It's a nice city, but like Wisp and Granden pointed out, they're being slowly enslaved right under their own noses."

I have to agree. There is something shocking about places like Oakland where pointless poverty and a sense of resigned helplessness have been woven into the fabric of daily life. Or places like Reno where violence is the default setting. There is something nearly as shocking and, in some ways, even more upsetting, about a place like this where the violence, divisiveness, and discord Krug cherishes so much are lurking under its lively, clean, and colorful surface. I want to shout to these people: "Wake up! You're about to be the next victims of Krug's wrecking ball!" But even though I've been out here in this world for only a short time, I still know how hard it is sometimes for good people to see bad things percolating right in front of them.

I hook my arm into Brohn's and sigh. "We haven't had a lot of 'intact' in our lives, have we?"

"No. We've had plenty of 'broken,' though."

"Too bad everyone can't live here," I say, my thoughts on the wrecked mess of extreme wealth and poverty the rest of our country has turned into over the years.

Brohn points down the road to where three more Patriot soldiers, dressed in their red, white, and blue camo, are pointing guns at a mother and her two little kids and laughing as the poor woman tries to lead her children on their way. "It's not exactly heaven."

"No," I reply. "But it's not exactly hell either. For now, at least."

I'm tempted to dash over and intervene on the woman's behalf, but the laughing soldiers seem to have had their fun, and they send the woman scurrying off down the steeply slanted street.

"How about if we start by getting our bearings?" Brohn suggests.

"Render?"

"Render."

I swipe my tattoos and enter Render's mind. I melt into his senses and consciousness. Between Olivia's detailed schematics, Render's multiple flights through the city, and my oddly-great memory, I'm confident I can get us exactly where we need to go. With the detailed road map firmly in mind, I disconnect from Render, who sends out a series of *kraas*! from where he's circling just overhead before banking off and disappearing behind a cylindrical silver and glass apartment complex.

"We'll head down Bush Street, then over to Taylor. From there, we should see Grace Cathedral. As long as we follow Render's suggested path, we should be able to avoid running into Patriots."

"You realize what's happening here, right?" Brohn asks with a wry smile as we set out.

"No. What?"

"We've become Recruiters."

The weirdness of that should send a shudder through my body, but all I can do is laugh at the irony. "All we need now is a transport truck and a few big machine guns, and we can just scoop up the straggling Insubordinates and drag them away to our very own makeshift Processor for training."

Laughing together, Brohn and I start out on our mission.

The city we walk through is strange, beautiful, and terrifying.

Not counting the nice house I lived in back east when I was little, a time I remember only in dream-like abstractions, I've lived my life from six-years-old on in the cratered ruins of the Valta and trapped in the horrifying lie of the Processor. The rest of the time, I've been on the run in the woods or passing through the bleak remoteness of the deserts and mountains, the sterility of Salt Lake City, the violence of Reno, the poverty of Oakland, and the apocalyptic hellscape of all the rest of the bombed-out towns and highways in between. It's hard to recall a time when I wasn't walking over rubble, averting my eyes from the fragments of bodies scattered on the sides of the roads, struggling to breathe in the oppressive and radioactive heat, or navigating my way around craters of fused earth from one of the countless drone strikes or incursions by the Patriot Army in their so-called battle against the imaginary Eastern Order.

San Francisco is different. The roads are wide, winding, steep, and clean. The people look like people instead of like scavengers or shoot-from-the-hip gun-slingers. They walk, talk, laugh, shop.

This is more like what I imagined a city was before the fabricated war—minus the occasional Patriot Army squadron that zips by on mag-jeeps or patrols the streets with the scowling disdain of a bunch of constipated prison-guards.

As we walk, I put my arm around Brohn's waist, and he rests his arm across my shoulders. "Do you think there are other cities out there like this one?" I ask.

"I hope so. But even if there aren't, even if this the last of them, we need to do our best to save it. This is what life should be like. Minus the Patriot Army, of course."

"Ha! I was just thinking the same thing."

Brohn gives my shoulders a squeeze. "Nice to be in synch, isn't it?"

"Definitely. And, who knows? Maybe when this is all over, and we come out victorious, Krug and his Patriots will see the error of their ways. They'll put down all their guns and learn how to enjoy a sunny day in a place where all the buildings are still standing, and the people aren't scared, divided, and trying to kill each other all the time."

"Kress, that would be wonderful."

"And impossible."

Brohn grunts an enigmatic, "Hm," and we continue on our way.

Trying not to draw attention to ourselves, we look up at the tall buildings and at the mag-trams running between them. Navigating through a park, around groups of pedestrians, and slipping in and out of alleys and small laneways, we step through holo-ads projected from many of the businesses onto the sidewalks. There are even places where the sidewalks move on their own, and we don't have to walk at all. Occasionally, I spot Render flying overhead. I'm not connected to him at the moment, but I don't need to be to feel his joy at having a morning fly-around.

Brohn and I continue on our way, and I feel more like a sight-seeing tourist than a seasoned warrior about to assemble an army and engage a deadly enemy.

At one point, we arrive at an outdoor café where people are reading scrolling texts from news feeds projected in front of their spec-displays. One woman at a small round table in the corner is actually reading from an old-style paper book like the ones I grew up on. When she licks her thumb and turns a page, I'm flooded with wonderful memories of reading, teaching, and being taught in the Valta.

Brohn must be thinking something similar because he gestures with his chin toward the woman and smiles at me as he takes my hand.

There are all kinds of people coming in and out of the café. Through the huge crystal-clear windows, we watch for a second as people inside place their orders with eye-scans at a bank of small self-service kiosks.

We're just about to move on when we hear someone call out, "Sir!"

We turn to see four teenagers sitting together at a larger round table in a shaded corner under the café awning.

Jerald, the boy we met in the hallway back in the Style, raises his hand and waves it frantically in our direction. Brohn gives him an "Us?" look, which Jerald responds to with a vigorous nod.

We wind our way through other tables of people and slide into two empty seats with the four teens.

One of them is Ethan, another boy we met before. The two girls with them look familiar, but I don't know their names. The taller one, her long blond hair tied back in a thick French braid, introduces herself as Sabine. "And this," she adds, pointing to her heavily pierced and tattooed female friend, "is Orion."

"These are some of the ones we've been working with upstairs these past few days," Brohn explains to me. "Wait," he says, turning to face the group. "Aren't you supposed to be in training back at the Style?"

They laugh in unison and tell us that the Major gave them permission to be out today. "We're technically supposed to be on a supply run," they explain. "This little detour was Sabine's idea," Ethan adds.

"Not that I heard you objecting too much," Orion teases.

Ethan smiles and asks us if we want coffee. Before we can answer one way or another, he calls up a red holo-menu and starts scrolling through its selections. "Roasted Cinnamon Ginger? Basil Green Tea? Sweet Rose Chai? Maybe a morning Mai Tai?"

"How does all this work?" I ask. I look around at the tables of people, some talking, others reading or quietly sipping various beverages and staring out at the pedestrians and the couriers on mag-bikes passing by. "Other than a few experiences with tap-coins, we don't really know how commerce works here."

The tattooed girl named Orion tilts her head back and laughs at this. "Tap-coins are so old-world," she says pleasantly but with a hint of dismissive condescension. "It's what they use out there. In here, in the city, each person has to have their retinal scan done before they turn three. Then, that info follows you throughout your life. It's attached to your bank account, the Civil Bureau, the Law Society, Department of Transportation, Judiciary Council, everything."

"Don't worry," Ethan says, poking his finger at the icons on the holo-menu to input a drink order. "I'll surprise you."

Sabine sets down her steaming cup of what she says is Ethiopian Jasmine Coffee. "You really don't know about all this? I mean, you told us about the Valta and getting here and everything, but did you know there were still cities like this left?"

Brohn shrugs, and I blush and look away.

"Like we said, we were raised...differently," Brohn says. "We knew what we taught ourselves and what we were fed on the viz-screens."

"Which was lies."

"Not the best foundation for an education," Brohn points out as our drinks appear like magic in a small dispenser in the middle of the table. Tentatively, like we're afraid we might get bitten or something, we reach out and take the warm cups.

"Bamboo," Ethan tells us. "The cups. Totally biodegradable."

Orion fiddles with the head of a silver stud protruding from her eyebrow. "So you grew up without tech?"

"We had viz-screens," I tell her. "And my dad had some pretty sophisticated equipment in his lab."

"Was he an Operator?"

"A what?"

Sabine elbows Orion. "You know. A techno-smith. Someone who does code and fixes things."

"Oh. I guess so. He was a scientist. And an engineer." I flip my hands over to expose the inside of my forearms. "He wrote the code for these. My tattoos."

Sabine says, "Dishy" and runs her finger along the black chevrons, swoops, and dots. "Do they revamp?"

"Revamp?"

"Like this," Orion says, slipping a thimble-like cap of metal onto the tip of her finger. She runs the cap along the dragon tattoo on her neck, and it morphs magically into a tiger. She swipes it again, and the tiger re-forms into a pink and white-petaled Japanese cherry tree.

"She only calls them 'tattoos,'" Brohn explains. "They're actually part of a neuro-tech integrated network that connects her to Render."

"The prophet," Jerald says, gazing up into the sky and then back at me. "And the savior." He looks solemn and serious, but then Ethan, Sabine, and Orion burst into laughter and tell him to stop being so dramatic.

"Don't worry about him," Ethan says. "He's caught up in the whole idea of the five of you being the ones who are going to save us before things get out of hand around here."

Brohn glances around at the other patrons in the café and leans in over our table, suddenly just as serious as Jerald. "And do the people here know what they're in for after Krug gets his hooks into the city? Do they know how bad things are about to get?"

Speaking in a low voice and with her eyes alert to any attention being paid to us by other customers, Sabine tells us that the Patriot Army doesn't have total control over San Francisco yet, although they're working hard in that direction. Local law enforcement tolerates them as a hybrid vigilante-government militia. But there is tension there. "We just don't know which way the pendulum will swing."

I'm amazed at how normal this all is. Four teenagers talking, having coffee, and occasionally laughing together and discussing politics. There's a dream-come-true quality to the moment with me and Brohn sitting with four new friends on a sunny day in a colorful city.

With a confidence I very nearly feel, I make a promise to Sabine and to the others: "It'll swing the right way."

---

## 13

REMINDING ME THAT WE HAVE A MISSION TO COMPLETE, BROHN tells the others we have to get going. There are handshakes and hugs all around. We thank our four new friends for telling us more about them and their city, and, under their breath, they each thank us for "saving them and their city."

"We haven't done anything yet," Brohn corrects them.

"You've inspired a lot of people and opened a lot of eyes and minds," Orion says, leaning in to whisper into our group huddle.

Saying another round of goodbyes, Brohn and I leave the café, and I feel the ridiculous sting of tears in my eyes like I'm going to start crying, which makes me feel like an idiot, which makes me feel like I'm going to start crying even more. Brohn turns to stare at me, stunned, like I'm on fire. Fortunately, that makes me chuckle, and pretty soon, we're both walking along, holding hands, and laughing in the middle of San Francisco as if we were two normal teenagers out on a date.

Straying from the specific directions supplied by Render, we explore the northeastern neighborhoods of the city. The holo-ads we walk through are impressive. Instead of being passive displays, they're designed to interact with us like a real person might. One of them looks like a transparent waiter, and it asks if we'd like to try one of their tasty breakfast specials. Brohn laughs and tells it "No thank you," but the hologram is persistent and follows us another ten feet before it fizzles away and resets back in front of the diner to annoy the next pedestrians passing by.

After that amusing little encounter, we stroll through SoMa, cross into the Tenderloin District and the East Cut. We walk hand-in-hand down Geary Street where we pop into an old bookstore and inhale the wonderful scent of paper. We get a few odd looks as we flip open book after book and run our fingers along the colorful rows of dusty paperbacks, but no one says anything or tries to shoot us, so I consider it a successful experience.

After that, we meander through Nob Hill before cutting across Stockholm Street and into Chinatown until we stumble upon a place called Little Paris with a gaudy holo-display out front advertising a Vietnamese dessert called "chè."

"Wisp mentioned this place," Brohn says. "Said chè is a must-try San Francisco treat."

I pull Brohn down to me by his shirt collar and give him a kiss just because.

He kisses me back, and we get an approving smile from an older couple passing by on the sidewalk.

Once inside the store, it occurs to us that we don't have a way to pay for anything, and, even if we did, we don't know how to work the automated serving system everyone in the place is using. As we're standing there, chuckling and immersed in our stupidity, a smiling, kind-eyed woman hops down from a bar stool by the window and offers to help us out.

"Not from around here, are you?" she says.

I'm too busy staring at the array of colorful vending machines to answer, but Brohn tells her that no, we're not from San Francisco.

The woman says, "Interesting" and looks around like she's

making sure we're not being overheard. "Because the city's been under barricade orders for over two months. So where did you two come from?"

When Brohn and I don't answer, she tugs us by our sleeves toward one of the machines currently dispensing a large cup of what looks like black-bean soup on the bottom with a thick layer of white cream on the top. The concoction is collected by a round man in a three-piece fluorescent pink business suit. When the man takes his cup and moves away, the strange woman leans in toward one of those floating retinal-scanner like Jerald and the others showed us back at the café. She says, "chè dau trang. Three," into a small grid of red lights, and, in an instant, three small glass bowls appear on the silver counter under the dispenser. She gives a bowl to me and one to Brohn, but we both just stare at her as other customers nudge past us to place their own orders. The woman gestures with us to follow her, which we do. She leads us to a tall, round table in a quiet corner away from the front door and the big window. Holding up her own bowl, she announces that this concoction is "a delicious blend of coconut milk, mung beans, basil seeds, tapioca, and pomegranate over crushed ice." She hands us each a spoon from a cup of utensils on the table. "Trust me," she says, "you'll love it."

Brohn and I exchange a look of caution before sampling the dessert.

Brohn extends a hand across the table to the woman. "Brohn," he says. "This is Kress."

The woman says, "I know."

When Brohn and I exchange another look, this time one of stunned surprise, the woman whispers for us not to worry. "I know the Major. I help her feed her crews."

"Wait," I say. "Are you Chef Angelique?"

Now it's the woman's turn to look surprised.

"We've heard of you, too," Brohn explains. "Thank you for risking so much for my sister."

Angelique shakes her head. "It's no more than what she's risking for the rest of us."

"She's been through a lot," I tell her. "We all have."

"And the Major is dedicated to sparing the rest of us from the same fate."

"We're headed to Grace Cathedral," Brohn says. "Do you know anything about it?"

Angelique looks around but doesn't answer right away. Finally, she tells us she lives there. "From time to time, anyway. It's a sanctuary for a lot of us these days." She pulls down the collar of her shirt to reveal a thick ring of reddish scar tissue around her neck. "It's where those of us who've already had a taste of what the Patriot Army is really all about gather from time to time."

Brohn manages to offer his sympathy, but Angelique shrugs it off. "Just be careful. Not everyone will rush to join you in this rebellion against divisiveness, tyranny, and inequality. In fact, there are plenty of people in the world who thrive on those things. Now, I'll leave you to your job, and I'll get back to mine." She adds, "Feeding you," before offering up a broad, matronly smile as she stands and heads toward the door.

With the woman disappearing from view, Brohn and I scarf down the last of our chè and get back to our sight-seeing before we return to our real mission of gathering troops from Grace Cathedral.

It really is a very pretty city, all things considered. There are towering buildings, but also small parks with thick, green grass. And the colors. Having grown accustomed to living in rubble or else being on the run, I forgot what it was like to see so many hues. Along one of the residential streets we wander, there are houses mixed in with small businesses of every color: flamingo pink, duckbill orange, caterpillar green, canary yellow, mountain stream blue. It's like someone detonated a box of crayons over the city.

We take Broadway down to the waterfront where, off in the distance, over the Bay, we see the thick cloud hanging over what we now know to be the slums of Oakland.

"Big difference, isn't it?" Brohn asks.

"It's like Wisp said: Krug is all about barriers and walls."

"Maybe too much togetherness scares him," Brohn suggests. "Like having everyone getting along and living on equal terms will make him irrelevant."

I ponder this idea for a minute. "Yeah, well, he's right. But he's still an idiot."

Now that we have a chance to take it all in, we get a much better sense of the tension behind the scenes. Despite the apparent day-to-day normalcy around us, the city is still under a kind of semi-martial law. There are Patriot Army troops, but there aren't many, and they're not especially well-armed or intimidating. But they *are* there, and they're just the beginning. The advanced guard. The not-so-calm before the totally destructive storm on the horizon.

Like us, most of the Patriots are teenagers or in their early twenties. They remind me of a pack of wolf puppies: They look playful, but they're one growth-spurt away from being able to kill us all.

Brohn and I walk along, laughing with contempt at the news scrolls advertising the saintliness of Krug and his government and at the viz-screen info-feeds still hailing his ongoing victories over the Eastern Order.

"If only they knew," I say.

"They know," Brohn says. "They might not know that they know. But they figure they can't do anything about it anyway, so they gripe and brainwash themselves into thinking nothing they do matters."

"Then I guess it's up to us to do something about it on their behalf."

"Might as well," Brohn grins. "We've got nothing better to do anyway."

Brohn shouts out "Hey!" when I grab him by his jacket sleeve and sling him into the alley.

"What was that for?"

With my back to the alley wall, I motion for Brohn to stay quiet as I peer out across the street. There's a man and a woman about a block away leading a six-man platoon of armed Patriot soldiers marching in our direction. The man strides along, brimming with confidence and determination. The woman is the one in the red jacket and cowl I recognize from my recon missions with Render in and around the Armory.

"What is it?" Brohn asks.

"It's Ekker."

"Ekker?"

"The Patriot Army general. The one who shot those two soldiers in the Armory. You know: the one in charge of making sure our rebellion fails and that we all die in the process."

"Are you sure it's him?"

"You never forget the face of a man who shot at you."

"Technically, he shot at Render."

"Technically, what's the difference?" I snap. "He's bad news. If he sees us, we're dead."

"But he's never seen us before, right? He won't know who we are."

"Unfortunately, that's not true. Before he shot them, Render and I saw him interrogate those two soldiers who were on guard duty when we snuck into the city a few days ago. And if what Wisp says is true, that we've become some kind of local celebrities, my guess is he'll know exactly what we look like and won't be shy about shooting first and identifying our bodies later. Remember, they were told we died escaping the Processor. If they get even a whiff of the truth, they're going to be on high alert for us."

Brohn says he's convinced and grabs my hand as we scurry deeper down the alley, push through an uncharged metal security fence, and emerge on the other side of the block.

"Do you think he saw us?" Brohn asks.

I shake my head. "He was a man on a mission. But I don't get the sense he was looking for us, specifically."

Brohn points down California Street past Huntington Park. "I think he was headed there."

"Grace Cathedral?"

"If he knows it's where people like Angelique are hiding out..."

"What should we do? We can't go charging after him and challenge him to a fight."

"Let's follow him. See what happens." I tap the comm-link behind my ear. "And then we can report back to Wisp. See if she has any ideas."

A quick tap to the comm-link returns nothing but static. I tap it again, but this time, even the static is gone, and I'm left with an empty echo bouncing around in my ear.

"Must be on the blink," I say to Brohn. "Try yours."

He does but with the same results. He tells me he's sure it's nothing to worry about and that we'd better get moving.

Brohn and I cut into Huntington Park, ducking down behind a long row of thick green hedges until we come to a kneeling halt at the park's perimeter.

"I guess it could be a coincidence," I pant. "Running into him, I mean."

"I guess."

"One way to find out."

"Render?"

"Render."

I go to swipe the pattern onto my forearm that will enable my connection, but, like before, the connection happens before I finish the input.

"He's on the job," I tell Brohn.

Render glides onto a window ledge across the street.

Out on the sidewalk, Ekker is talking to the figure in the red coat and cowl.

I relay all this to Brohn, who tells me how impressed he is. "I don't remember you being able to talk like this while you're connected."

"You can thank your sister for that."

"Wisp? What did she do?"

"A lot. She's been teaching me new ways to think about my relationship with Render."

"Can she do anything about the creepy way your eyes still go all black like that?"

I swat Brohn with the back of my hand and get back to channeling my vision through Render, but, to my surprise and shock, Ekker's Patriots are still there, but Ekker and the woman in red have vanished.

"Where'd they go?" I ask.

Brohn peers over the hedge and turns back to me with a shrug. "I don't know. But let's not stick around to find out."

Now that I've got my bearings, I disconnect from Render and join Brohn in a stooped jog. We make our way across the street and down an alley running between the church and a smaller chapel. We cut right and head for the street up ahead, but before we get to the road, a tall, shadowy figure steps into the entrance of the alleyway.

Brohn and I come to a skidding halt.

"It's Ekker," I screech. "He doubled back!"

We're just about to turn around and make a run for it back the way we came when Ekker, in a move too fast for my eyes to follow, whips out a gun and fires.

The blast explodes in a terrifying echo in the tight confines of the alley.

Right next to me, Brohn is slammed up against the alley wall.

He bounces off it and slumps to the ground, his eyes staring at the enlarging red splotch on his chest.

In a flash, I'm sliding down to the ground and kneeling at Brohn's side. Pushing away the broken pieces of an old wooden palette, I slide my hand under his neck and pull him part way up so he's lying with his head on my lap.

Leaning in close, I listen for a breath and press my fingertips to the side of his neck to feel for a pulse. When I scream out this name, Brohn moans a little and then his head lolls to the side, and he's dead still. No breath. No pulse. No nothing.

Frantically, I lower him back down, peel his jacket open, and press my hands to his chest, hoping to find a heartbeat. There's nothing. Only the ooze of blood through his shirt.

I'm shaking and saying "No" over and over under my breath. Like that will make a difference. Like that will change things. Like my will power alone is enough to bring Brohn back to life.

Through an acid sting of tears, I look up to see Ekker, his big golden handgun hoisted on his shoulder, walking slowly toward us like a victorious hunter on a mission to gather his kill. The woman in red strides along next to him. On the sidewalk behind them, six members of the Patriot Army stand guard, shooing away curious pedestrians and making sure no one else enters the alley.

Meanwhile, Ekker comes to a stop and stares down at me. "You've been looking for me," he announces without inflection, like he's telling me the time of day. He reaches back to hand his canon of a gun to the woman who takes it and lets it hang heavily at her side. Ekker turns back to me and looks around at the alleyway. I follow his gaze and realize I'm trapped. There's no way I can get past the six soldiers out there on the sidewalk. There are no doors on the side of the cathedral next to me and nowhere to go. I wouldn't leave Brohn anyway.

Sliding over to put myself between Ekker and Brohn, I shake my head and start to object. I'm planning to tell him I don't know who he is or what he's talking about, but Ekker holds up his hand and tells me not to talk.

"You've been looking for me," he says again. "Which is convenient. I've been looking for you."

"You killed him!" I shout, leaping to my feet.

"Casualty of war," Ekker says without taking a step back. "It's what you have to expect when—"

I'm in no mood to listen to his explanations. I lunge at him, lashing out with a straight right fist to his face, but he intercepts my punch, redirecting my energy just past him. I stagger a bit, but I regain my balance and take another swing at him with my left. He redirects this blow as well and guides me with his hand into the alley wall. Gasping for breath, my face hits the wall, but I'm able to absorb most of the impact with my shoulder. Half-stunned, I whip around, charging furiously at Ekker with a flurry of leg-kicks. He flicks away my attack, but he's left himself open on his right side. I step into him and thrust a heel strike up toward his chin. It turns out he baited me into a trap. What I thought was a weakness, turns out to be a deception, luring me into overcommitting. Ekker moves his head less than an inch to the side, and my heel-of-the-hand strike zips harmlessly past his face, but now I'm exposed, and Ekker takes full advantage.

Locking one fist into his open palm, he swings his elbow into my ribcage. A thunderclap of pain wracks my body, and my breath whooshes out of me all at once. I stumble backward, trying desperately to keep my balance. There's a flash of white, a dizzying swirl of Ekker's smiling face, the mystery woman in red, Brohn lying lifeless at my feet, and then there's the ground, rushing up at me, and everything goes black.

14

---

WHEN I OPEN MY EYES, BROHN AND I ARE IN A BUBBLE. AND NOT A metaphorical one. This is an actual clear sphere, and we're suspended, dangling and weightless, in the middle of it.

From within the sphere in the middle of a nearly all-white room. I call over to Brohn, but he doesn't answer. We're face to face, and I call out to him again, my voice cracking and tears welling up in my eyes as I beg him to say something, to say anything, to be okay. But his head and limbs sag down lifelessly, his once-strong shoulders hanging low, his chin against his unmoving chest. The front of his shirt is stained nearly black with his blood. Drops of that blood have pooled at the bottom of his shirt with dark red streaks staining the belt-line of his pants.

I cry out Brohn's name, over and over. My voice bounces around in this strange transparent orb and comes back to my ears in a dying echo. I stretch out to try to touch him, but he's out of arm's reach.

Looking around me and at my own long, distorted reflection

in the curved glass, I twist and turn, but I can't move much. I may not be tied up, but I'm clearly a captive. I'm able to move my arms and legs, and I thrash for a second, whipping around to see what's behind me. But I can't turn my body more than a few degrees either way. It's like I'm treading water in mid-air and about to drown in the frustration at being so unshackled and yet so immobilized.

Continuing to strain against the invisible force holding me in place, I investigate the room as best I can. There's not much to it. There's an array of thermal sensors and molecular identifiers up near the ceiling. The pin-hole portals in the corners are probably surveillance cameras. Otherwise, the room is a near complete sterile white. The only thing standing out is the red outline of an input panel on the wall next to the faint seam of an automatic door. The floor below the orb is one black square pad surrounded by an empty expanse of glistening white tiles. Even the ceiling with no vents, pipes, or access ports, is a smooth, hopeless white.

Looking back across at Brohn, tears of sorrow mix with my tears of anger, and my body shakes violently. In the dark, early hours of this very morning, Brohn and I shared a moment alone. Less than an hour ago, we shared the day with new friends and walked around and felt nearly normal. Now, with one wrong turn down one wrong road, everything we've been working toward and fighting for is over. Facing Brohn's dead body, I'm helpless in this infuriating torture chamber as we float gently in the air like two slowly-dancing astronauts in space.

My despair is crushing, pressing down on me like a solid weight I can no longer bear. I whisper Brohn's name across the space between us, praying for some sign of life, but I know now —even with him right across from me—I'm all alone. I don't know if this is what Render feared. Is this the death he warned me about? Was I wrong not to take the warning more seriously? Should I have been more cautious? Maybe I should have advised

Wisp that going out on this recruiting mission might not be the best idea. And now, it's too late, and I have no one to blame but myself. I got caught up in the fantasy of freedom, imagining that Brohn and I could lead normal lives—just two teenagers skipping school to enjoy a sunny afternoon running into friends at random and having a coffee while we're all out on the town. I shouldn't have been so careless. Shouldn't have ever let my guard down. I don't know what might have happened between me and Brohn. I don't know if my abilities as an Emergent would have been too much for either of us to handle and we'd wind up going our separate ways, drift apart. I don't know if our Conspiracy would have survived or if Brohn and I might have splintered off to try to make our own life with each other. I don't know if we would have been together forever, carried out this rebellion, and lived happily ever after. So many things I wonder about now, so many things I don't and will probably never know.

But I do know one thing: when I get out of here—and I *will* get out of here—I'm going to kill General Ekker.

The fury rises in my gut until I feel like I'm going to be ripped apart down the middle by an explosion of pure, white-hot anger. The cords of tendons in my neck tighten. My teeth clench. My fists ball up, and a knot of pure, apocalyptic outrage seethes like a coiled snake behind my eyes.

I try thrashing around again, but it's useless, and now the pain in my side from where Ekker hit me has turned into an excruciating throb to match the pulsing ache in the side of my head from when I must have hit the ground.

Suddenly, just past Brohn's body, the door whooshes open, and General Ekker himself—decked out in his red and white camo jacket and blue pants—strides in. His thick-soled black boots pound like thunderclaps on the white tiled floor. As he comes toward me, I get a quick glimpse of the hallway outside before the door closes behind him. I recognize it from my recon mission with Render. We're in the basement level of the barracks

143

in the Armory. The good news is at least I know where I am in the world. The bad news is, I'm still a prisoner, Brohn is gone, and I can't do anything about any of it.

Ekker says something I can't hear into a comm-link behind his ear before stepping over to stand just to the right side of me.

"Nice to see you awake, Kress." Now that he's closer, his voice is surprisingly audible through the clear surface of this spherical prison cell.

Turning my head toward him, I growl like a caged animal, which I guess I kind of am. I don't care, though. I've got a rush of adrenalin surging through me, and I try to thrust myself at him, but I can't escape from whatever force is holding me here, suspended and helpless.

Ekker walks in a slow, methodical circle around the sphere. With my body immobilized, I'm not able to turn around, but I follow him as far as I can with my head and my eyes before he's behind me, and I lose sight of him. I whip my head around as he finishes his circuit and stops just to my right again, so I have to look partway over my shoulder to see him.

"Questions?" he asks.

A snarl forming at the corner of my mouth, I stare at him, willing him to drop dead on the spot.

"No? That's okay. You're in what's technically called a Mag-Grav Suspension Cell. We call it the 'Marble.'"

I stare some more, this time hoping he'll be dumb enough to let me out of here—even if it's just long enough to take another shot at him. I don't even care if he knocks me out again. I just need him to know I'm not going to give up. Ever.

"You're suspended by a carefully calibrated gravity field. The room doubles as a kind of Faraday Cage, so don't imagine anyone is out there tracking you through any type of electromagnetic means."

I glare daggers at him.

"I'm General Ekker. Although I get the feeling you already knew that."

When I still don't respond, he looks a little uncomfortable but then smiles. "Not much of a talker? That's okay. I get it. This is all really strange and scary. You've been trained to handle anything, and yet, here you are, Kress."

When I look surprised that he knows my name, he pauses and scans the ceiling before turning his attention back at me. "I've known you for a long time. Since you were a little girl living back East with your mother and father…"

"My mother and father? How do you know my mother and father?"

Ekker waves away my question like it's nothing more than an annoying gnat buzzing around his head. "It used to be a big world out there, Kress. A big world run by a small man. Krug is dedicated to recreating it in his image. He wants a world, like him, filled with anger and fear, plagued by insecurity, divided, and small. I was one of the ones assigned to help make that happen. And you were my key to success. I'm not sure if you know this, but I was part of a team that ran the Recruiters. I even consulted on the design and program of the very Processor you got to know so well. I once worked for Hiller. Now, I'm in charge of San Francisco. I used to be one of the Deenays," he says, running his hands along the sleeves of his red and white jacket. "Don't let this obnoxious military costume of mine fool you. I spent half my life in a lab."

"Let me guess," I say with a sneer. "You were a rat."

"Cute."

"And now you're one of Krug's stooges," I hiss. "A cold-blooded killer."

Ekker chuckles. "Granted. I'm cold-blooded. And I'm a killer. But Krug? He only *thinks* I work for him. In reality, he's nothing more than a convenient means to an end."

"What end?"

"The Emergents, naturally. You're why Krug is coming here, and you're why I intend to get what I need from you before he gets here and ruins what could be the best gift nature has ever bestowed upon humanity."

"You talk like you're the good guy here," I snap, feeling far braver than I probably should considering the circumstances. "But you're a liar. And you're just as evil and power-hungry as Krug."

Ekker shakes his head like I've offended him. "Krug only knows one thing: head down and full-speed ahead to get what he wants. And he's good at that, I'll grant you. The best. But he's a wrecking-ball. He's a baby. And you don't negotiate with a wrecking-ball or with a baby. No. You have to be more clever. Survive and stay one step ahead. Let them whip themselves around and wear themselves out doing their damage. Only then can you step in and take control."

I try to even my breathing out, slow my pulse so my anger and fear don't overwhelm me into senselessness or more mistakes. "I have an idea," I say to Ekker, tears soaking my cheeks as I look from him to Brohn's lifeless body. "You could just leave us alone."

Ekker says, "Hm" and glances up toward the ceiling like he's actually contemplating this possibility. Then he shakes his head and says, "No. I don't think so. Kress, do you know how many people like you there are out there?"

When I don't answer, he says, "Not many. A couple dozen or so, tops." Ekker laughs like we're sharing a joke. "In the entire *world*. We've identified a few in Spain. One in Sardinia. A few in places like Ankara and Beijing. And, of course, a few more like you here in other cities and mountain towns across the country, others who just didn't quite reach their potential. Many more who died along the way."

"Were killed, you mean."

Ekker pauses before going on. "The point is, you're rare. And like all rare things, you're coveted. You see, humans have gone around making enemies of each other since time began. But those enemies were all fabricated. Illusions."

"Like the Eastern Order."

"Yes. Like the Eastern Order. But do you know what the real enemy has been all this time? No? I'll tell you. It's stasis. It's immobility. We're hard-wired to move, grow, change, adapt, overcome. You know it as evolution. I call it survival. Look at the Modifieds. Not content with being human, they bought into the idea of the post-human."

"That's not the same," I say. "Krug used them."

Ekker runs a hand through his thick waves of blondish-brown hair. "No. He used their fears and insecurities, their desires, and their dreams for his own benefit. The Modifieds are simply victims of their own overwhelming drive to evolve. It's a drive we all share. They just took the wrong path to get to the right place. You, Kress, you and your friends...you're the right path. And I plan on following you all the way to the very immortality Krug so desperately craves."

"Then you're just another Krug."

"No. Krug would've tortured you first and then killed you whether he got what he wanted or not. I'll only kill you if I can't figure out how to use you."

"How comforting."

"Relax. If things go as planned, it won't ever come to that. Krug gets here in two days. You and I will be gone long before that along with the rest of your Emergent crew. I was hoping to gather you up all at once, but whoever is hiding you has done a good job of keeping you off the grid. So you'll just have to double as my prize and, forgive me, but also serve as a bit of bait."

I glare at Ekker through the tops of my eyes, hoping to stare a few more flaming daggers into his smug face. But he doesn't seem to notice. He's as casual and composed as if we were chatting over afternoon tea.

"It's not what you think, Kress. I'm not some cartoon super villain who's sitting around twisting his moustache and plotting the end of the world. In fact, it's the opposite. With your help, I'll be plotting the beginning of a *new* world. A better world." Ekker runs a finger along his upper lip. "And, as you can see, I don't even have a moustache."

He probably thinks his toothy smile is charming, but I feel like throwing up right before I drive the heel of my combat boot smack into his arrogant face.

"You think I'm going to cooperate with you?" I growl. Then, through a wave of choked tears I can't hold back, I shout, "You killed Brohn!" I'm trembling with rage, and my throat feels like sandpaper on fire.

Squinting, Ekker seems confused for a second before a glinting look of realization illuminates his eyes. "Oh. I didn't kill him, Kress. I just shot him. It was only ten or twelve armor-piercing bullets to the chest. One of the most lethal projectiles in our military arsenal. Nothing a tough guy like Brohn can't handle."

"You murdering piece of shi—"

My fury gives way to startled relief at the gasp I hear across from me. It's Brohn. He's lifting his head up and choking himself into consciousness like an exhausted deep-sea swimmer finally coming up for air.

"What the—?"

"I'll leave you two alone," Ekker says as he heads toward the door, an annoying sparkle of amusement in his eye. "I get the feeling you two kids have a lot to talk about."

---

"Brohn?"

With a groan, Brohn lifts his head. He looks across at me, then turns his attention to his blood-stained chest.

"You're okay!" I squeal.

Brohn looks up at me again and forces a frail smile. "I'm alive. I think. But I wouldn't call what I'm feeling 'okay.'"

"But...you got, you know...shot."

"Oh. That would explain the blood. And the pain."

"It hurts?"

Brohn moans, "Uh-huh. A lot, now that you mention it."

At the moment, I'm too immersed in a combination of laughing and crying to sympathize. "Forget that," I yelp. "You're alive!"

Brohn wriggles his fingers and then lifts his hands, turning them back and forth in front of his face like he's inspecting them. "I'm alive. Not sure how." He slips a hand under his shirt and skims his fingers across his chest. "Great," he says. "I'm dented."

"What?"

Brohn pulls up his shirt to reveal a cluster of shallow, red-rimmed pits in his muscular abs and pecs. "I'm dented. I've got dents in my chest. I feel like a golf ball." He withdraws his hand and inspects his fingertips. "Blood. But I don't think there are any actual wounds."

"How is that—?"

"I think they healed. How long have I been out?" Brohn takes a good look around: at me, at the empty white room, at the transparent globe we're floating in. "How long have we been in...this thing?"

"It's some kind of grav-cell. They call it 'the Marble.' And we haven't been in here long enough for you to heal from a dozen bullet wounds to the chest."

"Did you...were you conscious this whole time?"

"No," I admit. "But it doesn't feel like it could be more than a couple of hours or so since Ekker cornered us in that alley. The blood on your shirt doesn't even look like it's all the way dry yet."

"Then we have a mystery on our hands."

"More than one."

"What do you mean?"

"Ekker was in here."

"The Patriot general who shot me?"

"That's the one."

Frowning, Brohn rubs a hand across his chest. "Remind me to have a chat with him about that sometime."

"He's going to take us somewhere. Do something to us. I'm not sure what. But it doesn't sound like it's for our own good."

Brohn looks around. "We're floating."

"It's some kind of gravitational cocoon."

Brohn kicks his legs back and forth a little. "Neat," he says, his amused grin dropping quickly into an irritated frown. "But kind of awful at the same time."

Something occurs to me, and I share the memory with Brohn. "Render sent me a thought the other day," I say. "Something about being 'suspended in helplessness.'"

Brohn looks around at our floating bubble of a prison. "I'd say this counts."

"He also said something about 'rediscovering death.'"

"Hm. Not the most cheerful prophecy. Any guesses about what it means?"

"No. And I'm not exactly looking forward to figuring it out."

"What about Krug?"

"Ekker says Krug doesn't matter. He's turning on him. Says he's taking us away before Krug even gets here."

"Great. So instead of being Krug's slaves, we're going to be this guy Ekker's?"

"That sounds like his plan."

"Then we need to get out of here."

"I'm all for escaping," I say. "But in case you haven't noticed, we're a little on the powerless side at the moment. Ekker took our comm-links and everything." I know this is supposed to be a tense situation, and I'm supposed to be scared and desperate to be free from this floating prison cell, but the fact that Brohn is suddenly and inexplicably back from the dead has given me a weird case of the giggles.

Chuckling himself, Brohn tells me not to worry. "We'll figure this out."

Then, turning serious, he tries rotating his body around. When that doesn't work, he thrashes side to side, but, like me, his ability to move from the center of the orb is limited to nearly nothing. It's like there's an invisible hand clamping onto our bodies and making it impossible to do much more than turn our heads and move our arms and legs in place. Clearly frustrated but also exhausted and still reeling from having been shot, Brohn settles down and reaches across to me. I reach back, and our fingertips nearly touch.

"So close," Brohn says, dropping his hand to his side in temporary resignation. "Wait. Ekker was here?"

"Yes."

"What's he like?"

"Oh. Totally great guy," I say with a sarcastic smile. "Excellent host. One heckuva human being."

Brohn laughs and rubs his chest again. "Wonderful. Can't wait to thank him for all these lovely new craters he put into me."

"If you don't mind a personal question…?" I ask.

"Sure."

"How come you're not dead?"

Brohn rubs his chest again and winces. "Ekker must've shot me with impact slugs."

"He says it was armor-piercers. And impact slugs wouldn't explain the blood."

"And the mystery deepens."

"Seriously, Brohn. What's happening to us?"

"Not sure. But whatever it is, it's enhancing your connection with Render, and it's keeping me alive after getting shot point-blank in an alley, so I'm not about to start complaining."

"I'm not complaining, either," I sigh. "But it'd be nice to know what's going on."

"They say ignorance is bliss."

"Well, *they're* wrong. Ignorance is infuriating."

"Maybe your pal Ekker will have some answers."

As if on cue, the doors whoosh open, and Ekker comes strolling back in and immediately starts his slow walk again around our sphere-cell. Brohn, a menacing scowl wrinkled into the space between his eyes, glares hot lasers at him.

"Nice to see you up and about, Brohn. Well, *up* anyway. As you can see, you can't really go anywhere."

"Is this the part where you tell us your evil plan?" Brohn asks. "If so, we're not interested."

"Kress and I have already had a very pleasant conversation about my plan. And there's nothing evil about it. This is about necessity. You're Emergents. If we hadn't discovered you, someone else out there, some other government would have. And then it'd be them trying to tap into your talents for some selfish plot to control the world."

"And what about you?" I ask. "I suppose your motives are purely altruistic? Kidnapping a bunch of kids for the good of humanity and all."

Ekker belts out a long, very loud laugh. "You grew up in a tiny world of terror, Kress. I can't imagine what that must've been like. Me? I grew up in a much larger and much more terrifying world. A world of wars and walls. A world where ignorance was valued over intellect, where everyone was a potential enemy, and where guns outnumbered people ten-to-one. Not exactly a recipe for harmonious and peaceful co-existence. Trust me. I'm on the right side of history. Well, I'm about to be anyway."

"And you think you can weaponize us to bring peace?" I ask.

"People are still violent," Brohn points out. "We've seen the results of the world you're talking about. People are still killing each other."

"True."

"And it's Krug's fault."

"Also true. But this time, at least it's the right people killing each other. With the Arcologies, the good people of the world can finally be separated from the animals."

"You're still an animal," Brohn says. "An animal with guns and a lot of self-delusion. But you're still just a mindless predator pure and simple."

"Don't knock predators," Ekker says defensively, his eyes narrowing into an annoyed squint. "We were born to be predators. All of us. We're just really bad at it." Hands clasped behind his back, he returns to pacing around the perimeter of the orb. "We have these close-set eyes on the front of our faces like all predators. But our vision is limited. Can't even see at night. Our sense of smell is worthless. The sharp fangs we used to possess have devolved into these flat, grinding stubs." He holds his hand up and rotates it slowly in front of his face. "Weak fingernails. A poor substitute for the powerful claws we once boasted. Even our minds—the most powerful in the entire animal kingdom—just keep getting in the way of our ability and our right to rule the world. Until you."

Brohn and I exchange a look across the space between us.

"Didn't you ever wonder who was the first humanoid to walk upright? In our evolutionary lineage, who was the first to use language to communicate? Who was the very first to use a weapon, tell a lie, fabricate an enemy? I don't mean in general, and it's not a rhetorical question. There had to be someone, right? A single, conscious individual who broke through the genetic restraints of the time to emerge as something new. Something better. As Emergents yourselves, you are today's version of that pioneer. The first of your kind. The end of what came before and the beginning of a long future yet to come. Surely that must excite you?"

"Actually," I say, "what would really excite me is to twist your stupid head off. Plus, a bathroom would be nice. I really have to pee."

Ekker stops in his tracks and presses his hand against the clear surface of our floating prison. "Kress, you have grown every bit as amazing as I've heard."

"I would have been happy with just average. I guess I overshot. Now, about that bathroom break…"

"And you, Brohn. Brimming with confidence. A natural leader. And still, more special than you ever realized."

Suddenly curious, Brohn looks over at Ekker. "You said 'evolutionary.' Is that why I seem to be…bullet-proof?"

"You're hardly bullet-proof. More like bullet-*resistant*. To be honest, it's why I shot you." Ekker makes punching motions in the air with his fists. "Sure, I could have just taken you down the old-fashioned way. After all, it's only your outer shell that's evolved. Underneath, you're all organs and vulnerability like the rest of us. Think about a piece of sheet metal covering a sack of eggs. Hit the metal, you hurt your hand. Hit it hard enough, you can break the eggs underneath. Honestly, I just needed to know for sure what you were capable of. Don't look so surprised. Is it really that hard to believe? I'm just an average, flesh-and-blood human being. And yet, my skin is strong enough to resist all kinds of impact. Sticks. Rocks. Hailstones. A variety of fist-strikes and kicks. A tumble down the stairs. There are plenty of forces in the world my skin is strong enough to withstand. Of course, taking a batch of bullets to the chest like I gave you would kill me. But you? You're something else entirely. You're beyond me. Beyond anyone who's come before. Don't worry. You're no superhero, and no one is counting on you to save the world. You're just the next step in an evolutionary trajectory. All of you. Just a bunch of kids from a small mountain town no one's ever heard of. The amazing thing is that you lived together all this time and never knew what you were or what you had the potential to become."

"Apparently, we've become freaks that an even bigger freak is trying to take advantage of," I tell him. "We're just a means to your twisted end."

"Don't be so limited in your thinking, Kress. It's beneath you. As the first true Emergents, you're more than just yourselves, more than just your abilities. You represent an evolution in us as individual human beings but also as a kind of…collective consciousness. We've been conditioned, by our genes and by our own culture, to think of ourselves as these little specks of solitary matter, just muddling along all alone in the world, occasionally bumping into other specks but never really connecting. The fact is, we come from the same originary source and are connected in ways we not only don't realize but have somehow learned to resist with all our might. Yes. Your abilities are your own. But they are also each other's. Haven't you noticed that your powers grow and develop the more you stick together? It's why we kept you isolated all those years. Isolated from the world but united with each other. The closer you get, the stronger you are. Something in your genes, in your DNA, in your neurology…something has rewired you. The results? Harmony. Synchronization. The ability to connect—with animals, with digital technologies, with your own skin, muscles, and bones. And with each other. That's what I'm after. The ability to connect, to tap into what's been closed off to us for all these eons."

As he talks, Ekker runs his fingers through his hair. He fidgets with the cuffs of his shirt and with the buckle on his belt, and it occurs to me that, strange as it may sound, he may be as nervous as we are. He's scared of something. I can sense it as sure as if I heard him say the words out loud. Is he afraid of Krug? Of betraying him? Or could it be something else? He seems to notice me noticing him, and he pauses outside the orb between me and Brohn.

"Seriously," Ekker says, tapping his finger on the glass. "Don't worry. And don't get too comfortable. We're going to gather up the rest of your crew. We're going to find them and ferret them out. And then we'll be out of this city and on the road before you know it. Oh, and if you're thinking of escaping, don't bother. You're in a maximum security grav-cell in a room of solid synth-steel with a dozen eyes on you at all times. We're too close to the end, and you are far too important for me to get sloppy now."

"We're flattered," Brohn says.

"Excellent. I know it's hard to believe, but this really is the greatest compliment you could ever be paid. You're the future of humanity."

Ekker circles back around behind Brohn and steps out of the room. Just before the door whooshes shut behind him, I catch a glimpse of the woman in the hooded red jacket joining him. Her face is obscured in shadow, but there's something familiar about her. I don't have time to contemplate it in any great detail, though. If what Ekker says is true—that we don't have any hope of escape—then the only option we have is to prove him wrong.

"Time to get out of this thing," Brohn says.

"What do you suggest?" I ask as I look around again at this no-win situation we've found ourselves suspended in. I don't know this technology. Mag-systems have been in place for years now. But there are still a lot of gas-powered vehicles, wooden doors, and iron bars in the world. Because we've been isolated for so long, the world outside the Valta is still new with a surprise around every corner. But this one is beyond me.

Like me, Brohn is also looking around. "Where's Manthy when we need her?" He suddenly whips around to face me. "What about Render? Could you connect with him? Somehow get a message to Wisp and the others?"

"Sure," I nod. "I can try."

I swipe my tattoos, but nothing happens. I try again. Still nothing.

Before he disappeared, my dad taught me dozens of combinations he promised would enable me to continue to develop my techno-neuro connection with Render.

Now, I try every pattern and permutation I can recall. I swipe the longest curved swoop that runs from my left elbow around to my thumb followed by a succession of quick taps to the three black dots on my wrist. Nothing. I run the tip of my index and middle fingers along the crisp black chevrons on my inner right forearm and trace a series of circles around the cluster of spots speckled on the back of my right hand. Nothing. Desperate, I tap out the reset pattern Dad showed me: six quick taps on the larger circle on my left arm followed by six quick taps to the smallest circle on my right. Still nothing. Not only that, I don't get even a glimmer of a connection. It's not even like my implants have been fried. More like they never even existed.

"I can't connect." I try to say it in a matter-of-fact way, kind of like someone might say, "Honey, the toaster's not working." But the rush of emotion involved overwhelms me, and I choke on the words. It's not simply the physical sensation that's gone. The thought that all the emotions, joys, challenges, and experiences I've had with Render have vanished sends my mind to a dark, lonely place.

"It's this cell," I mumble, rubbing my eyes with the heels of my hands to staunch the distracting trickle of tears. "I can't feel Render. I can't connect with him."

"It's okay, Kress. We'll be okay." Brohn is trying to sound calming, but it's not working. I can hear the tremor in his voice. He's as scared, frustrated, and as worried as I am.

I shake my head hard and look across at him, my vision blurry from the effort and from the feeling of disconnectedness and failure. "I feel like I'm missing a part of myself. Like if you lost Wisp. Or if I lost you."

Despite the pain in my heart and the sting of tears in my eyes, Brohn gives me a look that says more than a whole page full of words. It's a look that really sees me. That feels me and that supports and understands me to my core. It's a look that sympathizes with me without feeling sorry for me and that surrounds me without smothering me. I don't feel complete, exactly. But I do feel better. His look is a lifeline offering one thin strand of hope.

"Back in the Style…you said something about being able to connect without your implants."

"That's true," I tell him. "The last couple of times, Render and I linked up before I had finished scanning the code onto my arm. It happened again when we were trying to spy on Ekker. I thought maybe I was imagining it, but it seems to be the case."

"Then maybe you can connect without even inputting the code at all."

I shake my head. "It's not possible. I don't care what anyone's said in the past. Without Dad's tech, there's no connection." I turn my hands palms-out and show Brohn my arms. "These are all I've got. Ekker's blocking them somehow. Without them, I'm just a girl, and Render's just a bird."

Brohn's voice drops an octave. "Kress. I've known you since we were six years old. You're not 'just' an anything. You're the best and most important person I've ever met."

"I know," I moan with a sigh and an eye-roll. "I'm the *Kakari Isutse*. Some kind of super savior…"

Brohn shakes his head. "I'm not talking about your importance to the rebellion. I mean us. You and me. I somehow get shot full-force in the chest, and I'm still here, alive and mostly well, talking with you. I'm going to go out on a limb here and point out that you and I are redefining what's possible pretty much on a daily basis."

"And you think it's possible for me to—"

"Connect with Render without any of your dad's tech? Yes. I really do. In fact, I think that might be only the beginning of what's possible for you to do."

"I don't know, Brohn."

"If you don't believe me, believe Ekker."

"Ekker?"

"Kress, he didn't bring you here and keep you alive on a whim. He believes in you." Brohn gives me a playful smile. "Okay, not in the same way I do. But two powerful and dangerous men —Krug and Ekker—are out there right now plotting their supremacy over the future of our entire species, and they're both looking at you like you're the key to it all."

"*Us*," I remind Brohn. "It's not just me. Ekker kept you alive, too."

"See?" Brohn jokes. "We have so much in common. Too much to waste on getting killed in this stupid cell. So what do you say? How about if you see what you can do to get us out of here? After all, we have a rebellion to start and a fight to finish."

## 16

I GIVE BROHN A FEEBLE THUMBS UP. SUSPENDED IN THE AIR JUST across from me, he returns the gesture and tries to turn around to see the door behind him. "I have a feeling Ekker won't be leaving us alone in here for long. We should hurry."

"Stop," I say with a broad smile. "You'll make me nervous, and I'm likely to miss Render and accidentally connect with a baby parakeet or something."

"Okay," Brohn laughs. "Relax. Take your time. Take all the time in the world. Just please go super-fast while you're doing it!"

I tell Brohn, "I'm on it," and close my eyes. It takes a minute, but I hear, no...I *feel* a voice in my head. It doesn't talk to me or engage in back-and-forth conversation. Instead, it intertwines with my own. It's a voice that's part me, part someone else. It's not Render's voice, though.

*Focus on the space between... exist more completely in both worlds at once.*

It's Wisp. It's something she said to me back in the Intel Room. But this isn't a memory. It's her voice again. It's in my head and kind of all around me at once, and it's as clear and as close as if she's whispering it in my ear. Am I doing this? Am I hearing the past? Have I connected with Wisp? Or has she somehow connected with me?

Before I have a chance to figure it out one way or another, her voice morphs into Caldwell's: *We want to belong, but we're taught to keep others out.*

It's another memory. Kind of. But it's also something more. Caldwell said these very words to Manthy back in his lab while I was listening in from the hallway. So what are his words doing here in my head? I try to shake them out, but they're embedded and immovable.

While I'm contemplating this strange turn of events, Caldwell's voice is replaced by a third one: *They call you the* Kakari Isutse...*the girl who dreams in raven...They think you can save them, save all of us.*

It's Cardyn this time. It's a voice I've known since I was six. A voice I know as well as my own.

And then it turns into Rain's: *It's just another way of being in the world.*

Which transforms into Manthy's: *I can't be me without you.*

A fist-sized knot forms at the base of my skull as I try to sort out what I'm hearing, what's happening to me, and why. These aren't just repeats of things I've heard before. The voices are here right now, in my ears and in my mind, and they're talking to me, talking urgently, like they aren't casual comments anymore, like they want me to pay careful attention to them and listen with all my heart to what they have to say.

The voices overlap for a second and swarm around inside my head, carrying with them each person's intentions, feelings, and consciousness. It's a surprisingly beautiful buzz, and I think my mind must be the hive.

The buzz is interrupted by Brohn's voice cutting through the static. He's calling my name, louder and louder.

Snapping out of whatever daze I've been in, I blink myself back into full focus mode to find Brohn still hovering across from me, only now he's wide-eyed and looking at me like he hasn't seen me in ten years.

"Kress," he gasps, and I get the sense he's been holding his breath.

"I'm okay."

"What happened?" Brohn asks. "You were out for a long time."

"I was?"

"Hours."

"Hours? How many?"

"I don't know. It's not like Ekker's got a clock hanging on the wall. Maybe eight hours. or ten."

"Ten hours?"

"Give or take."

"It felt like a minute, tops. A very strange minute."

"I guarantee you—It wasn't a minute. So, what happened? Did you connect with Render?"

"I-I don't think so. But maybe more than that. Something different than that."

Brohn tilts his head.

"I think maybe I connected with *everybody*."

Before I have a chance to explain further, the door whooshes open. I'm expecting Ekker. Maybe his mysterious female sidekick with the red coat. Or maybe just some anonymous soldier skulking around on guard duty who's been sent to check on us.

It's not any of these.

The person standing in the open doorway was once the painfully shy, constantly-disheveled girl I grew up with back in the Valta. Now, it's my enigmatic, empathetic, and suddenly very heroic friend, Manthy.

I gasp her name, and Brohn twists his head as far around as he can. "Manthy?"

After whispering for us to be quiet, she places one hand on the input panel on the wall by the door and slides the other under her hair and behind her neck like she's trying to keep her head steady as she concentrates. As gently as an autumn leaf dropping from a tree, the sphere-cell floats down onto the small black landing pad on the floor, and Brohn and I drop down with it, our boots landing with a thud that sounds frighteningly loud from in this hollow white box of a room.

A vertical sliver of yellowish-white light appears around the sphere, and the transparent orb splits quietly open like a carefully-cracked egg.

Over by the input panel, Manthy's eyes roll back, and she starts to stumble to the floor. In a flash, I leap out of the orb and skid to a stop just in time to catch her, my arms hooked under hers. Brohn is right on my heels and is just reaching out to help me with Manthy when none other than Wisp, her trademark fluorescent green hoodie replaced by a sleek black one, comes bolting into the room. She slides to a stop and goes slamming right into Brohn's chest. He winces as his little sister gives him the world's biggest hug.

"Wisp!" he cries out. "How—?"

"We have time to talk or time to run. Take your pick!"

Brohn holds Wisp by her shoulders and gives a fast look around before offering up a chirpy laugh and saying, "Let's get out of here!"

With Manthy wobbly but sticking with me, I follow Wisp and Brohn out of the room. As we cross the threshold out into the corridor, I can feel Render in my head, and I feel myself in his. I breathe a sigh of relief. It's the first normal breath I've taken since waking up in this cell.

"We don't have much time," Wisp urges. "Olivia found out what happened, and Render helped create a distraction to get us inside. He and a squad of Insubordinates are over on Julian Avenue right now kicking up a major fuss. Ekker will be back here any second. With reinforcements."

Together, the four of us bolt down a long hallway, around a corner, through a metal door, and clamber up five flights of narrow stairs. Wisp leads us through another door, and we find ourselves on the top floor of the Armory. I recognize where we are from Render's aerial reconnaissance missions. From here, it's a quick scamper up a black metal-runged access ladder to the roof.

Brohn takes the lead and scrambles up into the dark. We hear a dragging screech of metal on metal, and Brohn calls down, "Got it!" The access door opens, the shaft is flooded with light, and we scurry up the ladder and step out onto the flat roof.

Crouching down, we skitter along the perimeter of the roof. Far below, Patriot Army soldiers are racing around. Some are checking out the commotion over on Julian Avenue where Render is circling overhead with a rag-tag group of Insubordinates kicking up a ruckus below.

I look over the side and count the number of floors. "It's got to be fifty feet down."

"At least," Brohn adds. "Where to now?"

Agitated, Wisp spins in a quick circle, scanning the expanse of the Armory's roof. "The intel you gave us said there's supposed to be a garbage tube of some kind around here."

"A yellow waste disposal chute!" I cry out. "But it's on the east side of the building!"

"Come on, then! This way!"

Wisp bolts. She's a blur, and, as small as she is, it's hard for the rest of us to keep up with her.

Sprinting along the outer edge of the rooftop, Wisp finally comes to a stop by a low metal railing around the large, jointed yellow construction tube I remember so well from my scouting mission with Render.

One at a time, the four of us plunge feet-first into the chute and slide down to the ground level. The riveted joints of the long chute are a literal pain in the butt. But I'm more than happy to pay the price for being free. Landing with a painful crash in a deep bin of discarded rebar, synth-steel scraps, broken roof tiles, coils of frayed wires, and heavy sacks of assorted debris, we clamber out of the large blue garbage container and land in the shadows behind a lumbering yellow and black mag-loader floating idly on its parking pad.

Peering around the back corner of the massive machine, we look out across the field toward the street where a group of soldiers is milling around with their backs to us. The young men, armed to the teeth, appear to be confused. They're engaged in an argument of some kind, probably about what they should do in the middle of the gunfire zinging through the air around us and the large, predatory black bird circling menacingly overhead.

Taking full advantage of their confusion and of the chaos around us, we run as fast as we can back around the Armory and sprint down a small side street where we find Cardyn and Rain, fully armed and decked out in black and gray military gear.

"Talk about a sight for sore eyes!" I cry out. Cardyn and Brohn exchange a hard, back-slapping hug.

"Great job!" Wisp tells Cardyn and Rain. "No problems with the Insubordinates?"

"They performed like pros," Cardyn brags. "If this is a preview of Friday, we might actually stand a chance."

"Which way?"

"This way!"

As we run, I swipe my tattoos to connect with Render.

"Uh oh."

"What is it?" Brohn asks over the clomping of our boots on the polished pavement.

"It's Ekker. I can see him through Render. He's figured out what's happening! He's got a dozen soldiers with him. They're in mag-jeeps."

Wisp calls us all to a halt, and we come to a skidding stop, almost colliding with a San Francisco police officer who looks less than amused when we cause him to nearly spill his coffee, but he doesn't say anything.

"This way!" Wisp cries.

We sprint again, and I'm far too terrified to pay attention to the soreness in my legs or to the burning in my chest as I try to suck in air to soothe my burning lungs. If what Brohn says is true —and I have no reason to doubt him—he and I might have been immobilized for as much as half a day. That's a long time to go without the supporting presence of gravity.

Zipping down one alleyway, out across a street, and down a small access road between two towering buildings, Wisp slides to a stop and turns in quick circles, analyzing our position. "Where are they?" she asks me.

I concentrate for a second to orient myself to what Render is seeing. "That way!" I shout, pointing back the way we came. We start to run again, dodging around pedestrians and weaving between mag-cars as we bound frantically across street after street. We're just turning a corner when Render sends me another image. "Wait!" I call out to Wisp who has gotten far ahead of the rest of us. "They're up ahead, too!"

"You're sure?" she asks, calling back to me over her shoulder.

I point behind us and in front of us. "Three open-top mag-jeeps that way. Two more up ahead. Gas-powered. Six soldiers on foot just crossing Van Ness right now. They're armed with sniper rifles and fully-loaded 2040s. Yes," I insist. "I'm absolutely sure."

"There's a safe house on the other side of the park," Wisp cries out. "If we can get to it, there are people who can help us get off the streets and back to the Style."

The five of us follow Wisp on a dead run. Through Render, I hear the whoosh of the mag-jeeps gaining on us. I see every detail on the face of every man with a gun trained on us. And I can see Ekker.

He's clever. He anticipated our direction and is about to cut us off.

We dive into a nearby all-night bakery with Manthy flinging the door shut behind us.

Ignoring the stunned customers, we dash down a corridor past a couple of washrooms and through the kitchen. Two women and a man wearing white aprons gasp as we fly past. Shouting back our apologies, Wisp leads us through another door and down a hallway lined with neat metal shelves filled with assorted breads and a colorful display of pastries.

"This way!" Wisp calls out as she leads us to yet another door, this one apparently leading to the outside. We crash to a halt behind Wisp, who grumbles about the door needing an input code for it to open.

"Manthy?"

Manthy is wide-eyed and out of breath. To her credit, she shakes off the terror and fatigue of the moment and tries to connect with whatever tech is controlling the door, but the thunderous sound of boots and the shouts from the soldiers storming into the bakery and heading our way is too much. She can't concentrate.

Brohn gestures for the rest of us to stand to the side, which we do as he runs full-tilt at the door. Leaning his shoulder into it, he knocks it nearly out of its frame. The steel door never had a chance. It hangs by a single hinge like a child's loose tooth.

Still following Wisp, we bolt down an alleyway, dodging a string of hovering organic and compost bins before emerging onto a wide sidewalk lining an even wider, tree-lined avenue.

"Not good!" Cardyn exclaims. "Nowhere to hide! Where to now?"

Dodging more mag-cars, which, thankfully, appear programmed to avoid collisions, Wisp leads us across the street.

We're just safely on the other side and getting ready to make a run for the small park Wisp is leading us to when Ekker and his men explode out of the alley we just came from. They raise their guns, and we don't stand a chance. There's nowhere left to run and no place to hide.

No shots are fired, though.

Out of nowhere, Render dive-bombs at top speed into the line of soldiers. He rakes his talons across Ekker's face as he streaks by in a flurry of black feathers.

Distracted, the other soldiers try flailing at Render with the butts and barrels of their guns, but he's far too clever for them and way too fast.

Seizing the momentary distraction, Wisp calls out, "This way!" and we follow her down the road before leaping over the low stone wall lining the perimeter of the park. We roll to a stop at the base of a small cluster of trees. All around us, people are starting to figure out that something dangerous is in the air and begin shouting and scattering in a frenzied panic.

When a shot rings out, I look back to see Ekker firing at Render. It's a repeat performance of his attempt back in the Armory the other day.

Only this time, it's no casual episode, and Ekker doesn't miss.

Struck full-force, Render looks like he's slammed into a wall. His black body stops abruptly mid-flight, and he hurtles toward the ground.

"Wait!" I scream out to Wisp and the others. "Render's been shot! I have to go back!"

Brohn grabs my upper arm in a vice-like grip. "No, Kress! If you go back, you'll get killed, too."

I'm shaking and crying from rage and indecision. Brohn's right, of course. Ekker and his men, already confident in their first kill of the day, are turning toward us, weapons raised, as they prepare to take us down, too.

But I can't just leave Render.

Sobbing, I let Brohn lead me by the hand as we bolt down the road, across another street, down a sidewalk, and into a store-front that turns out to be a small church.

Wisp talks fast with the man, who was in the middle of mopping the lobby floor when we burst in. He waves us over frantically and hustles us one by one to a broom closet and urges us through a small hatch in the floor, down a rope ladder, and into a poorly-lit tunnel.

"This'll get us back to the Style," Wisp promises, leaping to the ground from the make-shift ladder. We start to jog down the tunnel when Wisp calls back, "It's a bit of a hike, but at least we'll be off the streets, and…hey! Where's Manthy?"

Wisp skids to a stop in the cold tunnel, and Brohn, Cardyn, Rain, and I plow into her, nearly knocking all of us down in the process.

Cardyn whips his head around back and forth. "Where'd she go?"

Wisp pushes past us and takes a few quick steps back the way we came.

Brohn calls out for her to wait, but Wisp starts to head back up the rope ladder we just came down.

She's halfway up when the door at the top bursts open, and Manthy's silhouetted figure appears.

She's holding Render in her arms, pressed tight against her chest, and, even in the dim light, I can see that his head is hanging low and that Manthy's shirt is wet with his blood.

## 17

I DASH OVER TO MANTHY, SCOLDING HER AND THANKING HER AT the same time for going back.

"That was a crazy and dangerous thing to do!" I gush.

Manthy gives me a slightly disappointed frown, which I can't interpret, but I'm too overwhelmed with an amalgam of disbelief, relief, and sorrow to care.

She hands Render to me, and I hug him close. He's cold to the touch. His feathers are sticky and mud-caked from where he must have fallen, and, although I can tell he's putting all his effort into it, he can barely manage to shuffle his wings or lift his head.

Although he weighs only about six pounds, he's normally a strong bird, powerful and swift. In the air, he's all strength and grace. On the ground, he's an alert, head-bobbing hunter. In my arms right now, sagging from shock and dragged down by numbness, he feels shattered and like he weighs a ton.

"He's alive," Manthy assures me.

"I can feel it," I say. "But he's confused and in pain. I think...I mean, I'm afraid he's going to give up."

"We can't let him!" Rain shouts, and her voice rings out in the tunnel like a command causing the rest of us to shake off our own shock and spring into action.

Everyone gathers around me and Render and reaches out a hand to place on his quivering body. The warmth and energy of our overlapping hands seem to give him a small boost and alleviate some of his pain and fear. He raises his head, his black beak open, as if in thanks.

"It's bad," Manthy says. "But he's alive."

"He seems stronger with us around," I cry.

"How'd you manage to get to him without getting yourself killed?" Rain asks Manthy, her panting breath, like the rest of ours, making small puffs of fog in the cold, damp tunnel.

The thin light coming from small slits in a drainage grate above our heads shrouds Manthy's face in dappled shadows. She flashes a cryptic smile at Rain from behind her hair. "Easy. I turned invisible."

Brohn, Cardyn, Rain, Wisp, and I all stand frozen, our mouths hanging open. I'm recalling what Brohn said to me back in the orb-cell about us Emergents making the impossible possible, but this—the idea of Manthy being able to turn invisible—is beyond impossible. Forget tough skin or telepathy. Those are just extensions of normal. Being able to turn invisible is as abnormal and, frankly, as impossible as you can get.

Cardyn is the first to shake off his stunned reaction. "You're kidding, right? Invisible?"

Brohn raises an eyebrow. "This is life," he insists. "Not a comic book."

"How?" I ask, anxiously nodding my agreement. "It's not possible—"

Manthy puts up a hand, and a mischievous smile spreads across her face under a playful sparkle in her lively brown eyes. "Don't worry, guys. I didn't *actually* turn invisible. I just ducked down and hid behind stuff when the Patriots started to look my way. Then, when they weren't paying attention, I found Render, grabbed him, and ran. Nothing superheroic about it."

Looking only slightly less confused and a little relieved, Cardyn lets go of the breath he's been holding. "So your new superpower is…"

"That I'm not an idiot," Manthy says with a flirty grin and a frisky slap to Cardyn's shoulder.

The fact that Manthy seems so lighthearted gives me hope.

We all share a quick laugh as she slips out of her jacket, scoops Render out of my arms, and bundles him snuggly into a makeshift baby sling before handing him back to me. Brohn stands behind me and rigs his own jacket into a second sling, which he slips over my shoulders so, combined with Manthy's cradle contraption, I can carry Render hands-free.

Wisp flicks her thumb up toward the tunnel's ceiling and reminds us that we have an enemy just above our heads and a wounded soldier in our arms to tend to.

With Wisp back in the lead and with Render cradled in my arms, we race along the tunnel, hop down a few steps to another tunnel, zig and zag for what must be several city blocks, clamber up a small steel ladder and race down the tracks of what Wisp calls out to us is a long-abandoned subway line.

"I know this tunnel," I say to Wisp as we scurry along. "Render flew down here the other day."

"Right. It's part of one of our supply lines now," she explains. "It's how we got across town to you without being detected, and it'll lead us back to the Style."

As Brohn and the others form a tight, protective clump around me, we arrive at a chipped metal ladder bolted to the surface of a clammy, rocky wall. Wisp asks Brohn to lead the way, which he does.

"It's locked," he calls back down to us from the top of the ladder.

Wisp taps the comm-link behind her ear. When nothing

happens, she taps it again. "I'm trying to reach Granden, but he's not answering. Must still be out with the Insubordinates. Let me see if I can reach Sabine. She's supposed to be on door duty."

When Wisp still isn't able to get a response, Cardyn starts dancing around in place and looking down the tunnel the way we came. "What if—?"

"Don't worry," I assure him. "We're not being followed."

"Link's down," Wisp says. "I'm worried Ekker might have found a way to block our comm system."

"Then how are we going to get out of here?" Rain asks, looking unsuccessfully around for an alternate way out.

At the same time, Wisp and I look up at Brohn.

"Brohn?" Wisp calls up.

His voice drops down from above our heads. "I'll see what I can do."

At the top of the narrow shaft, he presses hard with his forearm against the heavy bronze-colored cover.

"Won't open?" Cardyn calls out frantically from just behind me.

"Oh, it'll open," Brohn promises.

Render has stopped moving, but the crack of Brohn's shoulder and upper back ringing down through the dark shaft startles him awake, and he lets out a guttural series of hacking barks.

Up above us, yielding to Brohn's incredible strength and refusal to surrender, the cover flies off the top of the shaft, and light beams down on us. We clamber up the cold metal ladder and emerge in the alleyway behind the Style. By the time I get to the top of the ladder with Render still swaddled against my chest, Wisp has already scanned open the back door and is rushing us along into the building.

Together, we sprint up the two flights to the room where Manthy and I were talking with Caldwell about the Modifieds. Technically, that was this morning. Or was it yesterday? After the night I spent awake with Manthy and then with Brohn and then having blacked out in Ekker's prison globe for I don't know how long, I've completely lost track of time.

Clearly surprised to see six wheezing teenagers storm in through the doorway, Caldwell leaps up from where he's been tending to one of the Modifieds. His eyes are wide at the sight of us: We're haggard, panting like a pack of wild dogs, covered in sweat from our run, and caked in mud from the tunnels. Plus, Brohn's shirt is still decorated with a giant patch of dried blood. After a quick explanation, Wisp instructs me to hand Render over to Caldwell, which I do. I don't even have to think twice about it. I've spoken with Caldwell. I've seen all the good he does for so many who have it so bad. Plus, I've heard his voice in my head, so I trust him with my life, and, more importantly at the moment, I trust him with Render's.

I beg him to help Render, and he swears he'll do what he can.

"Birds aren't exactly my specialty, though," he warns as he cradles the barely-moving black raven in his arms.

"Maybe not," I remind him. "But healing is."

Nodding his assent, Caldwell leads us all through the first two rooms of Modifieds and into his large, fully-stocked lab.

With Manthy's help, Caldwell unwraps Render from the make-shift sling of jackets. Taking great care, he places him onto a shallow glass tray underneath a bank of lights and various surgical and mechanical tools connected to a group of slender milky-white machines suspended from the ceiling. Despite the loaded shelves and storage containers filling this room, the main lab table is remarkably pristine with a sanitized surface and small trays of delicate instruments neatly arranged in a semi-circle around the mag-chair that Caldwell plops down into.

He calls out "Diagnostics," and Render is immersed in a bath of blue light while a red scroll of graphs and notes appears on a floating read-out above the table. Caldwell tells his med-system to "Run neuro and cardio spectroscan" as he skims the complicated-looking charts and images at top speed with his finger, tapping certain icons and brushing away others in a blur of frenetic motion.

As if she's been doing this all her life, Manthy springs into action next to Caldwell. Like him, she flicks and taps at the red display and leans in close to inspect Render, who is now lying still amid the commotion around him.

Caldwell calls out the names of supplies he needs, and Manthy rushes to gather the items from the huge banks of bins and bays along the walls. She moves with efficient rapidity, giving Caldwell the instruments he's asked for practically before he's asked for them.

"How does she know what he's talking about?" Cardyn asks quietly into the air.

"I have no idea how Manthy does or knows anything," Brohn answers.

When Caldwell asks for a digi-synaptic bonder and a cingulate gyritic encoder–two items I've never heard of and that Manthy can't find in any of the dozen or so drawers she pulls open—Wisp, who is standing right next to me, taps her comm-link.

It doesn't work at first, but she tries again, clearly annoyed, and this time she's able to get through. She orders the equipment brought upstairs from a supply room in the basement. Less than a minute later, one of the Insubordinates rushes into the room to drop off the equipment in a small, clear box.

Manthy snatches the box from Wisp and runs it over to Caldwell who leans over Render and begins performing some kind of rapid operation I can't see but that terrifies me, nonetheless.

"At least the comm-system seems to be working now," Wisp grumbles to herself before turning to us. "I need to go upstairs and see if Olivia can make sure it's fully up and running and ready for Friday. Without it, we don't have a chance against Ekker and Krug."

Brohn tells her "Thanks" as she turns to go. "Thank you for coming for us."

"Saving their big brothers," Wisp calls back as she trots out of the room. "What are little sisters for?"

With Wisp gone, that leaves Brohn, Cardyn, and Rain to mill around helplessly with me at the foot of Caldwell's work table. Brohn leans against the wall, his arms folded across his chest, a deep scowl of anger etched on his face, and I know he's already thinking about all the damage he's planning to inflict on Ekker. Cardyn is chewing on the skin around his fingernails. Rain looks worried and calls over to Caldwell and Manthy to see if there's anything she can do to help, but Caldwell tells her, "Not at the moment."

We don't know what to do, and we don't know what *not* to do.

Caldwell solves our dilemma by shooing all of us away, telling us he and Manthy need space so they can work in peace, but there's no way in the world I'm leaving Render.

"He needs to know I'm here," I start to sob as the others turn toward the door. "He needs to know he's not alone."

With his arm around me Brohn says he'll stay with me, but Cardyn and Rain convince him to head upstairs with them. "We still have a lot of work to do," Rain reminds him. "A lot of training and strategy sessions to get to before we get this little rebellion of ours off the ground. And there are still a couple dozen holo-sims we need to run through with the Insubordinates. Nothing we can do here now except get in the way."

I nod my approval that it's okay for him to go. "I'll be up soon," I promise. "I just want to be here until I know...until Caldwell and Manthy tell me he's okay." I turn to Manthy. "He is going to be okay, isn't he?"

The hope I felt earlier down in the tunnel has started to fade, and Manthy's silence is all it takes to get me crying again.

While I pace on one side of the room and try not to hyperventilate, Caldwell and Manthy, hunched over and shoulder-to-shoulder, work on Render deep into the night. Eventually, I sag down into a mag-chair where I soon fall into a dark, restless sleep.

I'm roused awake by a gentle shake to my shoulder. "Go on upstairs," Manthy says. "Get some proper rest."

Having no idea how much time has passed, I blink away the stray remnants of a vague nightmare I was having and press the heels of my hands against my thumping temples. Caldwell is still at the far end of the lab table where he's fussing over Render and examining him through a diagnostic lens. Thin golden threads run from Render's body up to the sleek white and silver machines on the ceiling. "What about you?" I ask Manthy through a stifled yawn. "You must be more exhausted than I am."

Manthy shrugs and smiles. "I'll tell you a secret."

I lean forward, waiting for her to elaborate. Finally, she glides a mag-chair over and sits down next to me. "I don't sleep anymore. I don't sleep, and I don't dream."

"You mean you don't sleep through the night?"

"I mean, I don't sleep. Ever. I'm not sure why. It started a few weeks ago. I never said anything because..."

"Because?"

"Because I didn't want to seem like more of a freak than I already am."

"I don't know if I'd call you a freak," I tell her.

"Then what would you call me?"

"I think I'd call you one of the best friends I've ever had."

Manthy gives my knee a quick pat and a gentle shake. "Go on up. Spend some time with Brohn. Tell Rain not to worry. Slap Cardyn in the head for me."

I laugh, which feels like the wrong thing to do, but it feels good and necessary at the same time. "Will do." I turn back to look at Render. He seems too big for the small tray he's in. "Just please make sure..."

Just as I'm saying this, Caldwell calls Manthy over, and the fear and urgency in his voice makes my heart flutter.

Manthy gives my knee another squeeze before she jumps up to assist Caldwell. "We'll do everything possible," she calls back to me.

Remarkably, that calms me down. From anyone else, I might consider this an overly optimistic claim. But Manthy's "possible" is better than most people's certainty.

# 18

*THURSDAY*

THE NEXT MORNING, I AWAKE TO A CLUSTER OF FOUR FACES leaning into my own. I scan them all one at a time: Brohn with his perfectly-arched eyebrows and the dark shadow of stubble on his firm jaw. Cardyn's freckles and plump lips. Rain's jet-black hair, matching eyes, and flawless skin. Manthy's pale complexion and shaded, downcast eyes. I know these faces better than I know my own, but this time, there is something different about all of them. It takes me a second, but I realize what it is: Despite the horrific events from just a few hours ago, my four friends are all sporting rosy cheeks and ear-to-ear smiles. Instead of my Conspiracy being in tears and crushed comatose by terror and trauma, they look like they're in the middle of some grand holiday celebration.

Me? I feel like I've been backed over by a Patriot Army tank. Twice.

Every muscle in my body is sore, and every synapse in my brain has its own headache. Squinting and groaning myself up

179

onto one elbow, I drag an arm across my bleary eyes. "How long have I—?"

"Been asleep?" Brohn finishes for me, brushing a lock of disheveled hair from my sweaty forehead as he kneels down next to my bed. "Not long enough if you ask me."

Rain leans over Brohn's shoulder. "After what you've just been through, you deserve a month's worth of sleep."

"At *least*," Cardyn laughs. "You only got a couple of hours. Don't worry, though. We covered for you. We may not have access to Mr. Superbird, but we were able to go over some strategy ideas with Wisp, run through a bunch of sims with the Insubordinates, and get a little closer to making sure we all don't get ourselves killed on Friday."

"Friday? Superbird? Oh, right."

All at once, the events of the last few hours come flooding back: going on a mission with Brohn, getting shot at, kidnapped, rescued, and Render getting horribly wounded at the end of it all.

Wounded? Or killed?

I bolt upright. "What happened to—?"

Still smiling, Manthy steps forward and sits down on the edge of my bed. In her arms, she's holding something swaddled in a neatly-pleated white sheet. The lump inside the sheet twitches and offers up a feeble *kraa!* I can't contain my relief and joy.

"Render! It's Render!"

Kind of. I peel back the soft white cocoon he's enveloped in and am shocked at the sight.

Over much of his body, on top of his sleek purplish-black feathers, he's outfitted with a patchwork of what looks like thin layers of gold-leaf body armor. A gilded breast-plate expands across his breast. Some of his longer primary wing-feathers as well as his shorter secondary ones are lined with some kind of slender optical fibers. Most of the small feathers on his back are covered with triangles of tiny overlapping chain-mail that glitter and sparkle like the scales of a goldfish. A band of micro-filaments runs along his sides from the base of his head to near the tip of his tail like racing stripes on a sports car. Another band, this one pointed at the ends, curves from just above his eyes, over his head, and partway down the back of his neck.

It's a sad but ferocious sight to see. On the one hand, he doesn't look exactly like the majestic black bird I've known for so long. On the other hand, he now resembles a Roman centurion, a gladiator prepared at all costs to vanquish his enemies in battle. Either way, he's still my partner and my connection to a world of experiences and sensory perceptions far beyond my own. To know how much pain he must be in and to see his sleek beautiful black body covered in this grid of gold armor and this network of wires is enough to break my heart.

Render looks up at me, his metallic, graphite-colored eyes now sparkling strangely with flecks of green and amber. It's the same combination I've been told dances around in my own eyes in certain types of light. I lean down and touch my forehead to the top of his round head. The partial helmet, curved and sleek as a king's crown, is cool to the touch. Render gives a little bark and ruffles his hackles, which are now partially covered by the golden breast-plate.

"What happened to him?" I ask, reaching out a hesitant finger to trace the circuit of gold fibers along the edge of his wing. "Is he okay?"

Brohn, Cardyn, and Rain all look over to Manthy, who doesn't answer. Instead, she reaches out and gives Render an affectionate pat on the head before turning around and walking away.

"Thank you!" I call out to Manthy through an embarrassing stream of grateful tears.

"Don't thank me," Manthy calls back as she pads over to one of the sinks just inside the bathroom and begins to splash water on her face. "Thank Olivia and Caldwell."

I look over to Brohn and ask, "Olivia?" but he just shrugs.

"Manthy says Olivia consulted with them remotely from her station in the Intel Room," Rain tells me.

"She's very plugged in," Brohn explains. "From what Granden told us, it takes a lot to move her from where she's integrated with all those consoles and monitors. So Caldwell and Manthy worked on Render from Caldwell's lab while Olivia linked in to offer whatever help was needed."

Rain reaches out to run her hand along Render's armored body. "Apparently, Olivia figured out how to integrate a digital patch into his synaptic neural network. Caldwell was able to repair the internal damage, suture up his wounds, and outfit him with this nice new suit. Very dashing, I must say. But it was our very own modest Manthy over there who was able to talk to the program and refine the code. Olivia and Caldwell kept him from dying. They rebuilt his body. But Manthy, she's the one who saved his life. Oh, and she was also apparently able to build on the tech your dad implanted in him."

"Build on it? How do you mean?"

"We're not a hundred percent sure yet," Cardyn chimes in, throwing his voice toward the bathroom loud enough for Manthy to hear. When she ignores him completely, Cardyn turns back to me. "Manthy says she doesn't really know what'll happen. Only that he's likely to be pretty out of it for the next few days, but he should be good as new after that."

I nod, and then something occurs to me. "Wait. A few days? Today's Thursday, right? We're supposed to raid the Armory tomorrow."

"Wisp says it's okay," Brohn tells me as he sits down on the edge of my bed. "She says you and Render already got us more intel than she and Granden know what to do with. She says thanks to you, we know more about the Patriot Army and their facilities than they do!"

"And you?" I ask. "How's life after death?"

Brohn shrugs again. "I'm not traumatized if that's what you mean. My chest is still a little numb, but otherwise—"

"Otherwise, our friend here is totally bullet-proof," Cardyn gushes. He leans over my bed to give Brohn a big hug around his neck, which Brohn gags at before pushing Cardyn away.

"Now, if only I was Cardyn-proof," Brohn grumbles, rubbing his neck where our enthusiastic friend nearly choked him out.

"They know?" I ask.

"Unfortunately."

Rain gives Brohn a pretend scowl, crosses her arms, and stomps her foot. "'Unfortunately?' We've known each other all these years, and it never occurred to you to mention that you were indestructible?"

"I'm hardly indestructible," Brohn objects as Rain tries to contain the grin pulling at the corners of her mouth. "Getting shot like that hurt like hell. Besides, I didn't know for sure myself until Ekker shot me point-blank in the chest and knocked me out cold. Not exactly the most pleasant way to go about learning something new about yourself."

"I didn't get a chance to ask before," I say, looking over to Rain. "How'd you all find us anyway? Olivia?"

Rain squints and gives the tiniest shake of her head. "We didn't know you were missing at first. Wisp discovered the comm-link was down. She and Granden were trying to get it back up so they could reach you. And Olivia can't access most of the Patriot security protocols anyway."

"So how—?"

"A bunch of us heard you in our heads." Cardyn nods at this bit of information and taps his fingertip to his temple while offering up a wry smile as Rain continues to explain. "Wisp thought she was imagining it. Cardyn here thought maybe he was going crazy."

"Not a long trip," Brohn quips.

Cardyn says, "Hey!" and Brohn offers up an exaggerated apology before Rain goes on.

"Manthy was the one who figured out what was happening. She said this telempathy thing you have is...well, it's growing."

"She called it a spider web," Cardyn adds.

"Right," Rain says. "'Intricate, delicate, powerful, and a great conveyor of information to and from its source.' Those are her words, not mine. I'm not sure how it happened, but I don't think we found you at all. I think maybe somehow you reached out and found us."

Cardyn makes a creepy, wriggly spider-like motion with his fingers. "We were just responding to vibrations from your web."

Rain gives him a sisterly whack with the back of her hand. "Get serious. This could have turned out a lot worse."

"What about this stuff?" I ask, running my finger along the cold metallic plates and filaments covering much of Render's body. "He won't be able to fly."

"The body armor is super-lightweight," Rain explains. "It's a synth-titanium, carbon, and polished glass alloy with a specially-enhanced tungsten polymer. Light as a spider web. Similar to the material viz-screens and holo-displays are coated with. Only Caldwell says it's even better."

"His own invention," Cardyn adds.

Rain nods her agreement as she continues to pet Render, who coos appreciatively. "It won't stop bullets or anything like Brohn here, but, in time, he might be able to fly in it. As for the rest, like Cardyn says, Manthy's been kind of tight-lipped about how the new tech will work with the stuff he already had."

"So, they turned him into a Modified," I point out.

"I suppose so," Rain says slowly. "But as Olivia will be the first to tell you, being a Modified isn't always a curse. And it doesn't mean Render's life is lost. Being a Modified is just another way of being in the world."

"Why don't you try connecting with him?" Brohn suggests.

I tell Brohn that he read my mind. Placing Render gently at the foot of the bed, I sit up all the way, kick my covers off, and swing my feet down to the floor. Brohn stands up first, and, with a grunt, I follow. I roll up my sleeves and say, "Okay. Let's give it a try," as I swipe my tattoos to initiate the connection. It's hard at first, like Render is sleeping or resisting me. After a few seconds, though, the connection engages, and our minds and perceptions intertwine.

The pain that rips through me is so intense it almost feels like pleasure. But it's not. A bolt of lightning burrows into my neck just below my skull and shoots down my back and into both legs. I gasp and start to fall over, but Brohn catches me. He says, "Whoa" as I fall into his arms, grateful he's so strong.

Cardyn and Rain rush to my side as well. It takes me a second, but I'm able to keep my balance and work through the blurry haze that's flooded the room as the pain passes and settles into a kind of dull ache I can feel in my bones.

"Are you okay?" Cardyn asks.

I tell him I am as he and Brohn guide me back down to my bed next to Render, who's sitting there as warm and still as a loaf of black bread. When I put my arm around him, he offers a whimpering *kraa* of gratitude.

Over in the doorway to the bathroom, Manthy is looking on, but when she sees me catching a glimpse of her, she quickly averts her eyes.

Brohn puts a comforting hand on my shoulder. "Cardyn and I are about to meet Granden upstairs to conduct another round of training. We don't have much time left, and we need to be sure everyone knows the plan and how to play their part. We're going to conduct a few practice runs, take them through a few more simulations, give them some last-minute target practice. Besides, not all of us can afford to lie around all day, you know. Are you ready to go?"

185

"I'm not sure I can do this," I tell the others. "I'm glad Render's going to be okay, but without him..."

"You're not without him," Brohn says. "You're *with* him."

"According to Manthy," Cardyn adds, "you might even be more with him than before."

I look over to Manthy, who has now walked back into our main sleeping area and is easing herself into her bed. She moans with the effort, and I know how much doing what she did for Render must have exhausted her. "Manthy," I call over to her. "Is that true?"

She gives me a dismissive shrug before turning her back to us and curling herself into a ball under the white sheet and green army blanket covering her bed.

"What's wrong?" Brohn asks me. "And don't say it's just Render. I can tell you're worried about more than him. Is it the mission coming up?"

I tell him, "Kind of" and slump forward, my arms dangling loosely over my knees. "I don't know. I mean, you nearly got killed. I thought you *were* killed. Then Render gets shot and nearly killed. There's no telling what would've happened to you and me if the others hadn't broken us out of there. And here we are, happy and treating this situation like it's normal while we're talking about preparing a bunch of kids to take on an army."

"It's just a little army," Cardyn reassures me.

"Thanks. That's helpful."

"I know what Kress means," Rain says. "We're about to do something that's equal parts brave, important, and stupid. We're only seventeen years old. A lot of the Insubordinates are our age or even younger."

"Well," Brohn says in what's turning into his trademark baritone drawl. "We can give up, or we can grow up."

"We've never given up before," Cardyn reminds us. He drops down to his knees with his elbows on my bed and reaches over to give Render's head a gentle pat. "Even when we probably should have."

I tell Cardyn "Thanks," and then I thank the others as well. "Seriously. I can't imagine a better family to have. Or a better bunch of warriors to fight alongside of."

With Manthy still curled up under her bedding, the others join me in a deep group hug at the edge of my bed.

The camaraderie of the moment is destroyed, however, as Wisp bursts into the room with Granden hot on her heels.

Startled, we all look up to see her looking frantic and anxious.

"Render's okay," Brohn tells her.

"Glad to hear it," she calls out, "but we can't celebrate just yet."

"What is it?"

"Right after she finished helping with Render, Olivia tapped into an unscrambled communiqué over an unsecured network. It's Ekker. He tracked us down. And he's on his way here."

"ON HIS WAY HERE?" BROHN ECHOES HIS LITTLE SISTER. "BUT HOW did he find us?"

"We can figure that out another time. Right now, we're going on Full Eclipse!"

"Full Eclipse?"

"Lockdown. Concealment Mode. Total camouflage. Come on!"

Beckoning frantically, Wisp and Granden cry out for us to follow them from our dorm room out into the hall, which we do in a rush with even Manthy flinging off her sheets and sprinting along.

I scoop Render up from my bed and cradle him in my arms baby-style and try not to jostle him too much as I run. I wince, and in a flash, even without being connected through the tech in my arms, I'm feeling his pain and his fear through our telempathic link. I don't know if he's sensing my own distress, reacting to Wisp's and Granden's feverish anxiety, or if his heightened senses have alerted him to something else entirely, but he's overwhelmed by his near-death experience and by the life-saving surgery he just went through.

"Take it easy," I whisper down to him as we burst into the hallway. "Everything's going to be okay."

Wisp and Granden bolt down the hall, banging on each dorm room door along the way. Wisp slaps her hand against an input panel on the wall between two of the rooms toward the middle of the hall, and the purplish ceiling lights turn into a silently strobing red.

"Everyone follow us downstairs to the Intel Room!" Wisp and Granden cry out as the Insubordinates bound out of their rooms, stumbling over each other like puppies in a panic.

With us right behind them and with the confused Insubordinates right behind us, Wisp and Granden race one flight down on thundering feet to the fourth floor and straight to Olivia's Intel Room, where Wisp pauses at the door to usher all of us in.

Once inside, Rain looks baffled and doesn't answer when Cardyn, shuffling around on nervous feet, keeps asking her what's happening. Likewise, the Insubordinates are abuzz with questions, none of which gets answered, and Brohn and I have to explain that we're as in the dark as they are.

With more than fifty us now crammed into the Intel Room, Granden sprints over to an input panel on the far wall near where Olivia still sits at her console, somehow relaxed and unshaken amid the chaos of the moment. Granden's fingers are a flurry on the scrolling red holo-code projected from the panel into the air just in front of it.

"Full Eclipse!" he barks out to Olivia over the buzz and hum of the rest of us who are milling around, shoulder to shoulder, scared and very much on edge.

Olivia says, "Initiated," and, immediately, a square of light appears toward the bottom of the wall behind her. Before our eyes, a panel slides open to reveal a small, square-shaped crawl-space, not more than four feet high and four feet across.

Wisp leaps up onto the black glass conference table in the middle of the room, cups her hands on either side of her mouth, and shouts for everyone to follow Granden into the low, dark duct. "We're about to be raided," she cries. "Ekker and the Patriot Army are on their way here right now!"

"How'd they find us?" one of the Insubordinates calls out.

"We don't know. And we don't have time to find out or to get out of the Style."

"Then what—?"

"We have passageways in this building," Wisp says pointing to the small opening behind Olivia. "Granden will lead you to our Safe Rooms!"

"In there?" Cardyn asks, coming to a complete stop even as the Insubordinates surge past him on Wisp's orders and begin to duck one at a time into the shadowy crawlspace. "We're supposed to go in there? It looks like a hot air vent to Hell."

"Just go!" Wisp barks.

Thinning out from a crunched-together herd to a single-file line, the Insubordinates continue to follow Granden and each other into the opening.

With Render in one hand and with Brohn holding my other hand, I start to head toward the opening along with Manthy, Cardyn, and Rain but Wisp stops Manthy with a hand on her upper arm.

"I may need you here," she says to Manthy. "For help with surveillance."

Manthy pauses for a second then shakes her head and starts to follow the jostling, stooped-down line of Insubordinates.

"Please?" Wisp calls to her, and Manthy stops in her tracks. "We'll be safe here. But we need to see what's happening outside, and our surveillance systems keep going on and off-line."

Manthy looks from Wisp to me and back before finally saying, "Okay. But I want Kress to stay with me."

Wisp hesitates but finally agrees.

"And I need Brohn with me," I say.

"And if Ekker's really coming here, I've got a score to settle with him," Brohn snarls.

"We're not going in there without them," Rain insists as she gestures over to where the last of the Insubordinates are disappearing into the opening. "We've been split apart too much lately, and we don't work without each other."

"Plus, it looks really scary," Cardyn quips.

Wisp frowns and insists there won't be room for all of us in the Intel Room after it's converted.

"Not enough space?" I ask, looking around at the large room, now liberated from the throng of the nearly fifty people who were just in here.

"Converted?" Rain asks.

"I'll show you." As the doorway to the small portal zips seamlessly shut, Wisp bounds over to the end of the table where Olivia has her monitoring station. With Olivia's help, she activates a series of high-tech security protocols as a detailed holo-schematic of the Style materializes in shimmering red and yellow above the black mirrored table.

"This isn't just any old building," Wisp tells me. "We've had it outfitted with some special tricks in case we ever get discovered and can't get everyone out in time. Top-secret. Even the Insubordinates don't know about it. Although they're about to find out. We're all going for a little ride."

As she's talking, the floating image of the Style begins to shift and transform before our eyes. We all look around as we pick up a sound coming from behind the walls and seemingly from within the ceilings and floors, themselves. It's a hum of gears and machinery in motion. The sound is powerful but smooth, and I imagine a benevolent giant breathing evenly in his sleep behind the walls. It reminds me of the Agora in the middle of the Processor and the way Granden and Trench used to reconfigure the huge field into battlefield simulations, war games obstacles, firing ranges, martial arts combat facilities, or whatever was needed for our training at any given time.

Wisp explains to us how Olivia controls some impressive tech buried in the walls of the old building. "She's integrated into this place like any system. Plumbing. Electrical. Communication. Cybernetic. But she's a lot more important and much easier to talk to than any of those."

"I'm more than just a pretty face," Olivia jokes, her slender tendrils dancing along her monitors and slipping into the three spheres floating around her head.

Olivia explains that she's hiding our heat signatures and activating ambient noise dampeners while reconfiguring the interior of the very building itself to conceal certain rooms.

We're all riveted to the glowing red and yellow image above the reflective black glass, and I'm vaguely aware I have my mouth hanging open. I've never seen anything like this. The transformation is miraculous. On the detailed schematic, walls drop down, floors slide over, whole rooms rotate and realign, and the collection of cube-shaped rooms making up the interior of the building turns and shuffles and reconfigures. The outside of the building is still the same boxy, five-story rectangle. But inside, the rooms, hallways, and stairways, have all been changed and shifted around.

Here in the Intel Room, walls descend around Olivia's monitors and the glass table, and the ceiling drops down to just above our heads to form a smaller room, a closet really, with the seven of us, plus Render, packed in tight, our bodies pressed against the edges of the oval table.

Instinctively and with my stomach in a knot, I reach out for Brohn's arm as the room trembles and begins to slide sideways and then down. Brohn puts his hand on mine as Cardyn and Rain grab onto each other and onto the edge of the table.

"Where are the others in all this?" I ask, my attention still focused on the shifting image of the Style while I concentrate on not throwing up.

Wisp points to three cube-shaped rooms currently on the move. "Those are the three Safe Rooms. They're locked, stocked, and shielded from scans."

One of the rooms is shifting from the third floor up to the fifth. Another is sliding down to the second floor. The third room does a zig-zag before settling between another room and an exterior wall on the first floor. As each room moves, it's replaced by an identical but completely empty one.

More than just cleaned and cleared out, Olivia has reconfigured the entire building like a giant version of the sliding transfer-conversion puzzle I used to play with in my dad's lab when I was little. Only that puzzle turned from a boat into a robot and into a dragon from its original shape, which my dad explained was a "sixty-two-faced truncated icosidodecahedron." The Style has turned into an empty version of itself. There are rooms where none were before, and other rooms are being flipped around and hidden from view throughout the bowels of the building.

Wisp points at the schematic as the building completes its final transformation. "Everyone's divided up among these three rooms. The Modifieds. The Insubordinates. Everyone. They're Safe Rooms. Like panic rooms. Like us, Granden and the others will be tucked away behind empty dummy rooms and concealed from scanners while we monitor the situation from here."

Wisp nudges past me to lean in over one of the monitors. "Now let's see what we're dealing with, exactly. Olivia, can you give us externals on Pacific Avenue?"

"Initiated." In the now-cramped and very dark fragment of the Intel Room, Olivia calls up a display showing the outside of the Style and now adding the surrounding area within a few blocks. Things look normal. Except for the line of Patriot military vehicles rumbling this way. Wisp is just leaning in to get a closer look at the approaching enemy when the images pixilate away.

"With Render out of commission, that's all I've got," Olivia apologizes. "Their surveillance systems are still too secure for me to infiltrate totally. But as you saw, they're definitely headed in our direction."

"Can you at least access the surveillance system from the lobby?"

Olivia says, "Initiated," and the lobby of the Style pixilates into a slightly fuzzy focus. And then Olivia's monitors flicker and go dead white.

"I'm sorry," she says. "Their firewalls are too strong, and their network paths are constantly being reconfigured."

"That's what I was afraid of."

"What?" I ask.

"The communication problems we've been having. The interference with the comm-links. Our inability to communicate with you and Brohn when you were out in the city. The partial and sometimes plain wrong intel we were getting before you and Render got us the good stuff. The fact that we can't even access our own monitoring systems. Ekker is tracking our frequencies somehow. He's patched into the code that operates our surveillance." Wisp turns to Manthy. "This is why I needed you. We need to see what's happening. Can you help Olivia get our eyes back?"

Working with Olivia in the cramped space, Manthy is able to circumvent Ekker's security overrides to do what the security cameras downstairs can't: show us the men who are pulling up outside the building to kill us.

As we watch the monitor in front of Olivia, a squad of twenty angry-looking soldiers leaps down from military mag-jeeps and accompanies Ekker and the mystery woman in red up to the front of the building. At the same time, another group circles around back.

Ekker and his men enter through the building's front doors and go storming into the lobby.

To our surprise, we see three people we don't know scrambling for cover as the Patriot troops follow Ekker inside. They run full-tilt toward a door on the far side of the lobby only to be met by more soldiers. They slide to a stop, turn, and run back the way they came, but it's too late. They're surrounded in the middle of the lobby with no way out.

"Damn it!" Wisp says, slamming her fist down on the table. "No one's supposed to be down there!"

"Who are they?" I ask. "Insubordinates?" The two men and the one woman on the image appear older than most of the Insubordinates we've met so far and don't look familiar.

"They're not Insubordinates," Wisp informs us without taking her eyes off the monitors. "Not exactly. They're from Haven House. They sometimes help Caldwell take care of the Modifieds. Damn!"

As we watch helplessly, Ekker interrogates them.

With Manthy's help, we can see and hear everything that's happening.

Ekker paces around the men and the woman and accuses them of being Insubordinates.

They deny it, except for the middle-aged man with glasses and a salt-and-pepper beard. He tells Ekker that he is, in reality, the leader of the Insubordinates. "They call me the Major," he declares through a choked-back laugh. Forced by the Patriot soldiers onto their knees, the man's two partners stifle laughs of their own.

Ekker steps forward, grabs the chuckling man by the scruff of his neck, and shoots him right through the eye. The back of the man's head bursts open, and we all step back, shocked at the sight of the uncalled-for execution played out on the holo-display in front of us.

Leaping to their feet, the other man and the woman scream

and tear themselves away from the grip of the Patriots. They run across the lobby and dash up the stairs where they disappear from view.

Ekker turns to the woman in red. She taps a comm-link behind her ear and makes a circular motion in the air with her finger. Instantly, the Ekker's soldiers go bounding through the lobby and up the stairs after the man and woman, firing at them as they flee.

What we're seeing is shocking. The slaughter of the man and woman is as barbaric as it is complete. The parts we hear are every bit as horrifying as the parts we see.

Ekker stands and watches, his arms folded across his chest, as his soldiers drag the man and woman down the stairs, back into view, and up to his feet like dogs returning a stick to their master.

Cardyn turns away, not wanting or needing to see or hear anything else.

The rest of us watch on Olivia's holo-display as Ekker says something we can't hear to the woman in red. Like before, she taps her comm-link. This time, she points around the lobby and up the stairs with both hands, and the squadron of soldiers marches forward. The soldiers unclip some kind of scanning or monitoring devices from their belts and call up infra-red displays that appear in front of their faces.

"They're going floor by floor," Olivia says. "They'll kill anyone they find."

"They won't find anyone," Wisp says.

From the safety of the Intel Room, we watch as the Patriot troops march down the long hallway of each floor, kicking some doors open and shooting through others before shouldering their way in.

In each case, exactly as Wisp promised, they find nothing. Just empty rooms.

Terrified, we watch for a full twenty minutes as the invasion continues until Ekker, the woman in red, and the other soldiers finally give up and reunite in the lobby.

Ekker turns to the woman in red. "You said they'd be here. You swore this was the place."

In a voice largely muffled by her hood, the woman in red says something about recognizing a black raven and following him.

Ekker pauses, clearly suspicious, but there's simply nothing here. Cursing, he leaves with his men and with the woman in red.

"Do you think he'll be back?" I ask.

Wisp shakes her head. "Doesn't matter. By this time tomorrow, we'll either be celebrating or else Ekker will be dancing on our graves."

Olivia plugs back into the system she used to hide us and transforms the building back to its original configuration. Shuddering and then gliding along, our room reverses its path from before. The walls drop back into place, the ceiling slides up, and the Intel Room returns to its normal size and shape.

A minute later, the small door opens in the wall, and Granden, crouched low, shuffles his way out with the Insubordinates right behind him.

Granden stands and brushes his hands on the thighs of his pants as he walks over to Wisp. "It's pretty cramped in the access shafts," he exclaims. "And dirty. But at least the Safe Rooms are all in good shape."

Wisp gives him a sad smile and tells him "Thanks. Thanks for taking care of everyone."

With the last of the Insubordinates emerging from the dark crawlspace into the once-again crowded Intel Room, Wisp hops up onto a mag-chair and announces the all-clear to everyone in the overcrowded room.

"Ekker and the Patriots are gone, but not before they did their damage."

"What damage?" one of the Insubordinates asks above the hum of the crowd. "Granden said we were all accounted for."

"Except for the six Insubordinates who are out on supply runs," Granden adds, tapping his ear. "And I haven't been able to contact them."

Wisp lowers her head. When she looks up, her eyes are wet and red. "Xander, Jerred, and Annalisa. The ones who help Caldwell with the Modifieds. They were in the lobby...They didn't make it into a Safe Room in time, and Ekker...Ekker caught them before they could slip out the back."

Someone in the crowd screams out, "No!" and several Insubordinates put their arms around a young girl whose body is wracked with spasms of grief.

"Jerred was her father," one of the Insubordinates standing next to me explains.

The hum around us turns into a dead silence and then a disgruntled rumble. There's no need for Wisp to describe what we saw. Everyone in this room knows what the Patriot Army is capable of, what they live for, and what they kill for.

As the anger in the room threatens to seethe over, Wisp hops down from the table and orders the Insubordinates to follow Granden, Brohn, and Cardyn upstairs for their last round of battle preparation. As Cardyn is walking past me, Wisp clutches his arm and draws him aside.

"That's Alessandra," she says, nodding toward the girl whose agonizing cries of grief ring out in the somber quiet of the Intel Room. "Can you take care of her?"

Cardyn nods his response without looking at Wisp and walks over to where Alessandra is being consoled by the other Insubordinates. The crowd parts for him as he approaches and then watches through tears as he puts his arm around the sobbing girl and guides her toward the door.

Wisp turns toward me. "They drew first blood," she says through a fierce scowl. "Let's make sure we draw last."

## 20

BROHN, CARDYN, AND GRANDEN HEAD UPSTAIRS TO THE FIFTH-floor training rooms.

Watching Brohn leave makes me sad, and I'm wondering how our budding romance will ever evolve with each of us constantly going our separate ways. On top of which, we could be dead in less than twenty-four hours.

When the room has emptied out, Wisp drops heavily into a mag-chair, her head down, her arms draped over her knees.

"Kress," she says quietly. "I need you, Rain, and Manthy to help me with one final surveillance and strategy session."

Still dressed in her usual lime-green hoodie and khaki cargo pants, Wisp sounds exhausted and looks somehow different, worried, like the weight she carries on her shoulders is about one ounce away from being too much. Normally, that would make perfect sense. After all, she's a fourteen-year-old girl who was raised without parents in a tiny mountain town that was bombed out of existence, leaving her alone and on the run until she made it to San Francisco, where she assumed command of a small group of inexperienced rebels who are now a day away from staging an audacious midnight attack on the president of the country and on his trigger-happy personal army who are all stationed in and around an impenetrable fortress.

So, yes, a lot of fatigue and worry are understandable. Except this is Wisp. The Major. The survivor. The unwavering leader who commands respect with her presence, with her brilliance, and with her unshakable confidence. This is the girl who, mostly before we arrived but also before our eyes over this past week, has saturated those around her with an abundance of optimism, confidence, and ability. She's seen death before. We all have. But somehow the sight of those three people getting executed seems to have hit her especially hard.

Rain walks around the table and sits down next to Wisp. "You knew them well, didn't you?" she asks.

Wisp glances up at Rain and nods. "All three of them. From when I escaped from the Valta. They were part of the group that found me, that brought me here. They were the first ones who introduced me to the Modifieds and told me about the Emergents. They were the ones who showed me what I was capable of."

Wisp is quiet again for a minute and seems content to spin the holo-schematic in front of her and watch the multiple lines of code scrolling underneath.

"Last week when you first got here," she says at last. "I told you about being on the run after the Valta got attacked."

"We remember," I say.

"And I told you about how someone attacked me when I was on the road, threw me into the back of a truck, and basically beat the hell out of me?"

Rain and I both nod our heads.

"Well, Xander is the one who threw the bag over my head and tossed me into the truck. Annalisa is the one who beat me up. And Jerred interrogated me for a few hours before they finally figured out we were on the same side."

I don't know about Rain, but I'm not sure how to respond to

that. Finally, I clear my throat. "It sounds like a...traumatic experience."

"They were the first people I ever met outside of the Valta. They were the first ones who told me the truth about the Eastern Order. They were the ones who got me into the war and who introduced me to the reality of what the world has become."

"You're talking like getting kidnapped and assaulted is the best thing that ever happened to you," I say.

"Up until then, it was. And you know why? Because it led to the truth. And I liked it. As depressing and agonizing as it was," Wisp adds with a small, unamused laugh, looking from me to Rain to Manthy, "it was better than living a lie. And I was hooked. I got hungry for it. I started seeing things differently. Stopped taking everything at face value. There are forces at work, girls. Forces that make this world what it is. No one is rich or poor, free or enslaved, fearless or afraid by chance. Xander, Jerred, and Annalisa...they opened my eyes. And now I can see the puppeteers behind the curtain."

"It sounds...liberating," I say, still not totally sure how to react.

"It is," Wisp smiles. "But it's like our rebellion. Liberation comes at a cost. And right now, I think I'm paying it."

Wisp smiles at us and suggests we get back to work.

After that, our time in the Intel Room drags on, and Wisp returns to driving us and herself with relentless, nearly dictatorial determination. Her eyes, once filled with thoughts of justice, have smoldered into eyes brimming with vengeance.

"This isn't a game," she reminds us, her hands a blur as she whips through the countless holo-images we've assembled over the past few days. The cityscape skims above the surface of the table, the green parks and tall towers combining into a wash of color. "We can't just resign and say we didn't understand the rules." She pauses for a second, her hands suspended over a series of images outlining one of tomorrow's paths of attack. "Hm. I think we've been compromised."

"You mean because of the comm-link problems?" I ask.

"And the network glitches. And Ekker finding you and Brohn. And then him finding this building."

"One of the Insubordinates?"

"I don't think so." Wisp sighs and turns back to the schematic above the table and runs her eyes over a series of info-tags. "They're all accounted for."

"What about the ones you've been sending out on missions? Brohn and I ran into four of them in the city. You said yourself that surveillance has been a big problem, and I can't imagine you can keep total track of all these kids and their families and friends. What if one of them had a change of heart? Or if the Patriots got to them somehow?"

"I've considered that. But my gut tells me no. And trusting my gut is one of the first things Xander, Jerred, and Annalisa taught me."

Zooming in on the Armory and expanding two of its points of entry, one on the ground floor and one on the roof, Wisp flips the images, assigns some time-signatures, and tags them with a code for later reference. "This'll be a problem," she mutters under her breath.

I feel like I should ask her what's wrong, but I'm tired. It's getting late. I miss Render who's downstairs with Caldwell, and I miss Brohn who's upstairs continuing to teach fifty kids how to invade an army garrison without getting killed, and I'm in a generally rotten mood, overall. A few hours ago, the violence we're about to leap into literally showed up on our doorstep. Now, we've got Wisp's unnerving worry on top of that, which is making me worry in turn.

I figure maybe I can reassure her and set her busy, over-worked mind at ease. "We know everything we're going to know, Wisp. We've been over the plan a million times. Nothing we do at this point is going to help us or hurt us one way or another."

Wisp slows but doesn't stop her active hands, but she does sigh before telling us she has a confession to make.

"Let me guess," I say. "You're nervous about the possibility of betrayal. And about facing the Patriot Army tomorrow. We're all edgy. But even if we lose, we'll go down fighting, and if we hit them hard enough, maybe we'll expose a weakness, some flaw that others can exploit after we're gone."

Now Wisp does stop, which makes the rest of us stop, too. She's an active, multi-tasking kind of girl who is in constant motion, always planning, calling out orders, talking strategy, and accomplishing more in ten minutes than most people can manage in a day. To see her suddenly dropping her hands and sitting stone still is a little disconcerting.

"I *am* nervous," Wisp confesses. "But that's not what this is about. And it's not even really about the possibility of an infiltrator." She pauses and gives us what I think is supposed to be a reassuring smile, but it comes across as a little forced. "I know I exude confidence, but I'm not ignorant about what we're up against, and I certainly don't have a death wish."

"What then?" Rain asks.

"I can't *not* be the Major," she admits, head down now, palms flat on the table. It sounds like a confession, a statement of fact, and a regret all rolled into one very odd emotion.

"Nobody can help but be who they are," Rain assures her from across the table without looking up, her eyes, instead, scanning a bunch of running lines of communications code along with Manthy.

But Wisp shakes her head like Rain isn't understanding her at all. "That's not what I mean."

"It's okay," I say. "You can tell us anything. We're family. We have been all our lives."

"I know that," Wisp says with a genuinely appreciative smile. "I really do. But one of the drawbacks of family is that it's for life, and I can't appreciate what we all mean to each other because of who I am. What I've become."

"What have you become?" It's Manthy. She's been sitting between Olivia and Rain in silence, but now she seems invested and interested in whatever it is Wisp is trying to tell us.

"I'm one of you, I think."

"Of course, you are!" Rain laughs with relief, finally looking up from her project of the moment. "That's what Kress was trying to tell you."

Wisp shakes her head again and frowns. "No. I mean I'm an Emergent. I have an ability to lead people, to make good decisions, and to wade through all kinds of advice, obstacles, worries and still come up with the right course of action. I don't have Kress's memory or Rain's gift for military strategy. Oddly, I suck at chess. And I certainly can't come close to doing what you do, Manthy. I don't know why or where it comes from. And the truth is that sometimes it's so much responsibility...it's just...being a one-hundred percent leader doesn't leave a lot of space for enjoying being part of a family."

We don't say anything for a minute. After all, being an Emergent is new to me and Manthy, and I'm not sure if Rain even really believes in the idea of it, or of *us*, at all these days. Even after all she's seen us do, after all she's been able to do herself, and after all she's learned and heard, Rain is an analyzer, a pure scientist to the core. She holds a small part of herself in check just in case she's being duped. Probably a helpful side-effect from our many years of living in fear of a non-existent enemy. But Manthy, usually reserved to a fault, stands up and walks around the table to sit down next to Wisp.

"Why do you think being an Emergent might be a bad thing?"

I'm startled to see Wisp's eyes well up with tears that she quickly suppresses.

"I can't get close to anyone," she laments with a glance up at the ceiling. "It's like the same thing that made me able to assemble and lead these people is the same thing that's in the process of putting a thick wall up around my heart."

"But you love Brohn," I remind her. "You love us, right?"

Wisp nods, clears her throat, and sits up straight in her seat. "More than anything. More than you know."

"Then what...?"

"I don't know. Maybe it was seeing my three friends die like that. Maybe it's because our battle could be over tomorrow, but the war could last a lifetime. Something's happening to me, Kress." Wisp shakes her head like she's clearing it and gets back to the schematics and her strategic analysis.

"We really are all in this together," I assure her.

When I reach out to her, she shrugs me off. "Don't worry," she laughs. "I'll figure it out."

I start to invite her to say more, but she's already back to being Wisp: focused, poised, and steadfastly determined to succeed. All business now, she taps her comm-link and orders someone, probably one of the Insubordinates, to deliver a package to Grace Cathedral and another case of ammo to be delivered through the Mission Street tunnel to a nearby park. At the same time, she's making tiny adjustments to precise locations on the holograms in front of her to illustrate where our various strike teams are scheduled to rendezvous. Each room in the Armory lights up at her touch and rotates around as she peels back layers, exposing everything from plumbing to circuitry running through the walls. From her side of the table, Rain is doing the same, her hands whipping around almost as fast as Wisp's. The two of them make little adjustments, inputting codes as they go to help us circumvent certain parts of the security protocols and identify optimal entry and exit points. Manthy and Olivia have returned to their monitors as they continue to try to identify and repair the odd problems we've been having with our communication network.

That leaves me with little to do except sit and watch and

remember something Ekker said about us kids from the Valta all being connected. There's no doubt Wisp has some serious abilities. Practically super human. There's no doubt she's one of us, and it's clear she's stronger with us than she ever was alone. So why does she seem so lonely?

It's nothing I'm going to figure out any time soon, so I stand and stretch and ask Wisp if she needs me for anything.

"Not at the moment," she says, her eyes still glued to her schematics and screens as she calls across the table to Olivia for help with one of the Patriot Army surveillance drones she's trying to patch into.

"I'm going to pay a visit to Render," I say.

When no one says anything, I figure that's my permission, and I slip out the door and head downstairs to Caldwell's lab. I'm tempted to head upstairs to visit Brohn, but I know he'll be immersed in the most important part of their training program right now, and I don't want to be a distraction. So I walk down the single flight of stairs to the second floor where the Modifieds live.

They either ignore me as I enter the main room or else look at me through hollow eyes like they've never seen me before. From his lab two rooms over, Caldwell calls out for me to join him.

When I go through the room just before his lab, the one where the Modifieds had mysteriously been upgraded through what Caldwell explained was a Synaptic Autogenetic Neuro Synthesis monitoring system, I notice some of the indicator lights have dropped down to green. Others are back to blue, indicating the highest level of pain.

When I enter Caldwell's lab, I ask him about it as I lean over to press my cheek to Render's side in greeting.

"Manthy seems to have been able to relieve some of their pain," Caldwell explains. "But the effect, unfortunately, is temporary."

"Should I see if she can come back down and help them again?" I ask.

Caldwell plops down into the lab chair next to mine and reaches out to run his hand along Render's sleek black feathers and gold-plated armor. "I'm not sure that's a good idea. What she does for them…what she gives them…it's an amazing thing. A real gift."

"So what's the problem?"

"It's also a drug. It's artificial. It's not real."

Caldwell is a brilliant scientist and mechanic. His knowledge of the Modifieds extends from knowing everything about who they were to all that goes into helping them live as they are. Still, I feel I have to disagree with him on his last point. "I don't know if I'd be so quick to dismiss what Manthy can do," I tell him. "Yes. It seems whatever she did may have been temporary. But if she had time, I think she could give them real, permanent peace."

Caldwell picks up a toothpick-sized tool and fiddles with one of the filaments running along Render's left wing. "Can I ask you a small favor?"

"Sure."

"This is a satellite operation we're in right now. The real hub of power is back east in D.C. That's where the Deenays are stationed."

When I don't say anything right away, Caldwell continues talking, his head still bent down, his eyes glued to the flashing code in the air in front of him as he makes micro-adjustments to Render's new implants. "The Modifieds are intricately networked. It's by design. They are the recipients of and the vessels for some of the most inventive and complicated code ever written."

Caldwell looks at me, probably to see if I'm still paying attention, which I am. "You see," he continues, "if someone had the ability to wade through that code, perhaps even communicate with it…they could theoretically break into the Deenays' headquarters, infiltrate their Modifieds program, tap into and alter the existing protocols, rewrite the code, and..."

"Wait. After all this is over, you want us to recruit the Modifieds into the war against Krug? That's the small favor?"

"Okay," Caldwell admits, "the favor isn't small. But neither is the good that can come out of it. Who knows? Maybe someday, with Manthy's skills and your guidance, these Modifieds could help us win this war. They could bring about peace. Not just for us, but for themselves."

I sink down into my chair as the enormity of what Caldwell is suggesting sinks down into me. "It's funny," I say.

"What's that?"

"The idea that Emergents and Modifieds, the two biggest groups of freaks, might be the only ones who can get the world back to normal."

## 21

THE NEXT MORNING, AFTER WE'RE AWAKE AND DRESSED, WISP AND Granden join us in the Mess Hall. It's beyond early, and we're the only ones up. I promise myself, if we live through the night, I'm going to make it a top priority to curl up somewhere and sleep for three days straight.

For now, I'm resigned to running on fumes. I've got Render on my lap, and I absently stroke the feathers around the helmet on his head and run my fingers along the gold circuitry lining his new, streamlined body armor.

"It's Friday," Cardyn announces, rubbing his hands together. "Tonight's the big night."

Manthy scowls at him. "Thank you so much, oh bearer of obvious news."

Cardyn's clever retort consists of sticking his tongue out at her.

"Unfortunately, he's right," Granden says. "Krug and his entourage arrive this morning. The remainder of the Patriot

Army troops arrives tomorrow. If all of them manage to get into the city, this whole thing is over. They'll control everything here like they do everywhere else. Taking over the Armory tonight is essential. Which means it's now or never."

"Then it's definitely *now*," Wisp says. "Krug will be escorted into the city and over to the Armory. With the change of guard on Mission and another guard change on 14th Street fifteen minutes after that, they'll be at their most vulnerable. Not defenseless, mind you. Just slightly less prepared."

"So, you're saying this'll be easy," Cardyn says with an exaggerated sigh.

"Exactly," Wisp banters back. "Only just the opposite. Even with Olivia and Manthy's help, we've managed to hijack just four of their security feeds and one of their network channels."

"And how many feeds and channels are there?" Cardyn asks.

"Forty-five unique security feeds, seven separate network channels, and another batch of drone protocols we weren't able to tap into at all."

"See?" Cardyn says, his fingers interlaced around his piping hot coffee cup. "Easy."

Rain shakes her head, but I think I catch Manthy smiling.

"Was there ever any talk of taking Krug out before he even gets to the Armory?" Brohn asks. "After all, there are only so many ways into the city. If we could ambush him or something this morning..."

"We discussed it," Rain says. "But even if we managed to catch him and kill him, it would still leave the city at risk of being taken over by the Patriot Army."

"It's true," Wisp adds. "Cutting the head off of this particular monster will still leave it with lots of dangerous limbs thrashing around. No. We need to do it this way. The Munitions Depot, the Communications Center, and especially the Command Headquarters in the Armory are the key. Hit them all at once, take out the head, the heart, the whole thing. What happens tomorrow won't change much in the outside world. Even if we manage to capture or kill Krug tonight, the generals in his Patriot Army will still be in control of the country. But not of this city. And if we liberate just one city, make just one safe place, we can build a real home base and begin to finally spread the word about what Krug is really up to."

"I still can't believe they're even letting Krug into this city," I say. "They should be burning him in effigy."

"I don't know where Effigy is," Cardyn declares, his fist raised high. "But it'd be so much easier to just burn him here in San Francisco."

"You're kidding, right?" Manthy asks.

Cardyn gives her a sly smile. "You'll die wondering."

"Okay, okay," Wisp says. "Let's keep the talk of death to a minimum, shall we?" She gives me a strange look. "They're not going to welcome him."

"What do you mean?"

"The people of San Francisco. They'd even protest if they could. But, technically, they're not allowed. Too many zoning restrictions in place. The local police won't enforce them, but the Patriot Army will. And *they* make kills, not arrests." Wisp puts down her coffee cup and sits up straight like she's had an epiphany. "Do you want to see the big parade?"

"Parade?"

With an impish glint in her eye, she glances down at the thin silver band on her wrist. "According to the news feed this morning, Krug will be arriving in less than half an hour. There'll be quite the gala celebration upon his arrival. Music. Fireworks. Laser light show. Cheering crowds. The works. Want to have a look?"

"Cheering crowds?" Cardyn asks.

Brohn and I exchange a slightly terrified glance before he clears his throat and wipes the corners of his mouth with a napkin. "Last time we went out, we almost didn't make it back."

"Don't worry," Wisp laughs. "We can watch it on Olivia's monitors downstairs. It'll be broadcast all around the city. Trust me. You'll want to see this."

The five of us look around at each other and then at Wisp.

"Okay," Brohn says at last, his hand on his chest, unconsciously I'm sure, as he must be recalling the pain of getting shot and suspended in an anti-grav cell. He hasn't talked much about it, but a couple of times, including this morning, I've caught him cringing and inspecting under his shirt to check on the progress of the purplish bruises still covering his chest.

"What about them?" he asks, gesturing with a flick of his thumb toward the hall.

"I'll take care of them," Granden offers. "I have some updated sims and a few new programs to run through with them before tonight. If you're going to be downstairs, I can go ahead and wake them early and get them started." He's got his eyes on Wisp as he awaits her permission.

Wisp tells him it's a good idea and that he can go, and then she takes me, Brohn, Cardyn, Rain, and Manthy downstairs to the Intel Room.

"Is he here yet?" Wisp asks Olivia as we walk into the room. "Krug, I mean."

"Just arriving," she sings out. "He's a little ahead of schedule."

"Can you call it up for our friends here?"

"Initiated."

Cardyn rubs his hands together. "I've never seen a parade before. Sounds exciting. I wish we could go out and enjoy it in person."

Brohn and I shake our heads in unison. "Bad idea," I tell Cardyn with a hand on his shoulder. "Ekker already caught me and Brohn once, and he managed to locate the Style. We're lucky to be alive. Let's not tempt fate."

Rain tells him he's welcome to go rushing out into the streets and greet Krug in person if he really wants to.

Crossing his arms and pouting, Cardyn harrumphs his reluctant agreement that rushing out into the streets in full view of Krug, Ekker, and the Patriot Army is probably not our best course of action at the moment.

"Okay," Wisp says. "Here we go."

Above the table, a large 3-D satellite feed materializes in vivid color and detail. Just as Wisp promised, a massive parade is in full swing from the San Francisco-Oakland Bay Bridge down what Wisp tells us is Interstate-80.

"They're on their way to the Armory," she says, pointing to certain points on the display. "You can even see some of the streets and neighborhoods Kress and Brohn got to explore."

"I still don't think it's fair they got to go on a date while the rest of us had to stay here and work," Cardyn groans.

"Yeah," I say. "That was a fun day."

"We really should do it again sometime," Brohn says.

"Absolutely. I especially enjoyed getting shot at and imprisoned."

"Oh," Brohn adds, "Don't forget the fun part where we got to run for our lives."

Brohn and I share a laugh as Cardyn scowls at us.

"Hey, look," Rain exclaims, her hands on the edge of the table as she leans in for a closer look. "It's starting!"

We all sit down around the table, our eyes fixed on the images being projected in front of us.

The pageantry is incredible!

I recognize Krug's heli-barge from the images we used to see projected on our own viz-screens back in the Valta. The large, flat raft was always Krug's preferred method of making an entrance. Running on mag-boosters, it ferried Krug around, sometimes hovering just above the ground, other times carrying him and his entourage high above the heads of the cheering people below.

Krug, as usual, is taking it all in, absorbing the moment and lapping up the accolades. His slick black hair contrasts sharply with his silver suit and blood-red tie. His rotten teeth make for an odd disparity with everything else about him, which is all glitz, wealth, and style. All it takes is a glimpse of Krug, and the memories come flooding back, and, in retrospect, they're all embarrassing. We thought this man was our noble hero leading the fight against the dreaded Eastern Order who had so mercilessly bombed our town nearly to the ground. This was our president. Our representative. The one who knew the truth and who was committed to keeping us safe.

Growing up, we had each other, and we had the constant reports from Krug about the war against the Eastern Order. When we were recruited and after the smoke cleared, we still had each other, but we also had the aftermath of all the deception we're still struggling to sort out in our heads. This man, this so-called leader, used us and made all of our lives a lie.

Now, standing triumphantly atop his heli-barge, Krug waves to the adoring throng lining the San Francisco streets and cheering from row after row of balconies and rooftops. Krug looks almost misty-eyed as he nods his appreciation to the men, women, and children who are all holding up their left hands, first two fingers spread out, ring and pinky fingers tucked down, and with their thumbs extended to form the "K" symbol in honor of their beloved leader. They pump their hands in the air, shouting, "Krug!" over and over again.

"This is what everyone is seeing on their viz-screens right now," Wisp explains. "Not just us here, but everywhere. The residents of the New Towns. The Wealthies in the Arcologies. Even the poor Scroungers and Survivalists in the radioactive deserts all around the country. Those people don't have schools, roads, hospitals, or anything. But Krug made sure they had viz-screens, drugs, and guns. Everything they'd need to brainwash and kill themselves so Krug wouldn't have to. So everyone gets to see their beloved President Krug swooping into town on his big shiny chariot." Wisp nods to Olivia, whose tendrils snake out into her console as a second image appears next to the first.

The new image tells a much different story. It's the same city. The same streets. The same time of day. Krug is still standing on his heli-barge, only this time, he's in a protective turret, surrounded by a security detail of a dozen enormous and heavily-armed men in their American flag camouflage uniforms. On the streets below, there are no cheering crowds. No saluting civilians. No adoring fans. In fact, the streets are strangely deserted. As Krug's heli-barge gets closer to the Armory, small groups of Patriot soldiers stand guard in front of red and white striped barricades along certain parts of the street. A few people here and there salute Krug with the raised "K" sign and cry out feeble cheers that sound strangely hollow on the nearly-deserted and blocked-off roads. Behind them, probably a half mile or so away, thousands of people fill the streets and chant in protest even as a line of Patriot soldiers, their weapons primed and raised, advances on them.

Wisp points from the first image to the second one. "This first display, the wonderful glorious parade, is what everyone is seeing on their viz-screens. But *this*, this second image…this is what's actually happening as we speak. You can thank Olivia and Manthy for circumventing the security protocols and allowing us to see the truth."

"Wait," Cardyn says, "the parade's not real?"

"You sound surprised," Rain says quietly.

Brohn clenches his jaw at the stark contrast between the two displays. "We knew he was a liar…"

"He's worse than a liar," Wisp interrupts. "He's a *lie*. A hoax. The ultimate self-made man. He's projected the fantasy of himself so many times onto so many people that he's come to believe in himself as his own god."

"How has no one figured this out?" Cardyn asks. "I mean,

either there's a parade or there isn't one. Krug is either loved or he's hated, right?"

"Not exactly," Rain says slowly. "Look, we spent our lives knowing only what we saw on the viz-screens. We never thought to ask if it was real. Who would we ask, anyway? How could anyone ever really know for sure? Our entire country is based on faith in the government. Not just in the people running it but in the belief that there is a government at all. Democracy isn't a tangible thing. It's an idea, and it can be manipulated like any idea, especially when so many people out there, people like us, don't have the resources, or sometimes even the desire, to challenge it one way or the other."

Unlike the rest of us, Wisp has been standing this whole time, bathed in the multi-color glow of the side-by-side images of Krug's arrival. Now, she plops down in one of the mag-chairs and leans back with her hands behind her head and her heels up on the table. "Very true, Rain. Besides, Card, it's not like no one's figured it out. We have. Others have. It's just that most people who wind up figuring it out are either shouted down, labeled as crazy paranoiacs, jailed, killed, or, like the vast majority, are shuttled into the New Towns where Krug can more easily control his message while keeping the believers and the doubters in a state of constant fear and conflict."

Cardyn bites his lip and looks frustrated. "It's not fair. And it's not right. We need to stop him once and for all."

Brohn stands up, his face contorted with rage, and starts heading for the door. "That's the plan."

---

## 22

During this week, I've been working with Wisp, Rain, Manthy, and Olivia on surveillance and strategy. After viewing the fake parade and feeling sick to our stomachs about it, we leave Olivia down in the Intel Room and head upstairs to the fifth floor to join the Insubordinates and Granden in their final round of training.

As Wisp accompanies us down the hall toward the stairs, Manthy complains of headaches again and asks me if she can go downstairs to spend some more time with Caldwell and the Modifieds instead of heading upstairs with the rest of us.

I look around in the hallway for a second before realizing she's talking to me.

"It's fine with me," I tell her, and I'm wondering why she thinks she needs to ask my permission to do anything.

She says, "Thanks. Do you want me to take Render?"

I say, "Sure" and hand him off to Manthy who coos over him and tucks him against her body.

Then, we all walk along to the stairway where Manthy heads down, and the rest of us jog up the two flights to the fifth floor where Granden and some of the older Insubordinates are supervising our small but fiercely determined army.

Since we already know the layout of the fifth floor and all of its rooms, it's easy to pop into one room or the other and join in the various drills, pep-talks, and battle sims.

It feels good to be reunited with Brohn. Although we've had a few hours each night together, we've spent most of our days apart this week, not including the other day when we were captured and held captive by Ekker, which doesn't count because we were prisoners, and Ekker's a psycho.

Once upstairs, I marvel at how the three combat trainers have continued to sculpt this rag-tag band of underground rebels into a squadron of deadly efficiency.

"They've really vaulted this thing to a whole new level," I say, looking around at what has practically become a professional operation.

In the open rooms and even in the hallways, groups of Insubordinates are practicing martial arts moves, guiding each other in the proper use of some of the surveillance equipment, and talking with barely-restrained excitement about the training and tonight's attack.

Even if we fail, even if this thing today goes horribly slanted, I'm proud of what Brohn and Cardyn have done here. Before my eyes, they have become master mentors and trusted guides in this strange time of uncertainty.

"Card and I are going to catch up with Granden," Brohn tells the rest of us. "Why don't you all have a look around? See all the hard work we've been putting in up here while you all goofed around downstairs."

We have a nice laugh together before splitting up and meandering through the busy crowd of excited warriors-in-training.

Down at the end of the hall, Rain and I join six of the Insubordinates in their target shooting. Although Rain isn't quite as good as Karmine or Kella, she still manages to show off a bit for the Insubordinates, who cheer her on before begging me to try, too. I take the Inferno stock twenty-two rifle and point it down the length of the shooting range. The Insubordinates and even Rain seem especially impressed with my abilities. To tell the truth, looking over at the accuracy-display on the wall over to my left to see my score, I'm impressed, myself. Based on the read-out, I just took twenty shots and earned a perfect mark.

I shrug at the results, but the Insubordinates look like they want to pick me up and carry me around the room on their shoulders.

I have to tell them, "I don't know—just a lot of practice, I guess" when they insist on knowing my secret.

Out in the hall, Rain pulls me aside before I have a chance to go find Brohn again. The wide hallway is alive with activity. Insubordinates bounce from room to room. Granden is on the far side of the hall demonstrating a sophisticated flanking and infiltration technique on a rotating holo-display for a group of stern, serious-looking girls. Cardyn is just coming out of the room across from us. He gives me and Rain a happy wave before moving on to the next room where he and Brohn have been conducting martial arts training.

"Seriously," Rain asks me. "How did you do that? And don't tell me it was just a lot of practice. I can't remember the last time you shot a gun."

"It's not like I was bad at it in the Processor."

"You were terrible at it in the Processor," Rain nearly squeals.

"Okay. Listen. I've been feeling more and more connected to Render lately on a mental level even when we're not officially connected. I don't know if I'm borrowing his abilities, sharing them, or inheriting them. Either way, those projected holo-targets were a hundred meters away, but they might as well have been three feet away. Rain, I could honestly make out every pixel of the projection."

Rain looks excited and asks me to go on.

"Okay. I'm remembering something Ekker said to me about our so-called 'powers' as Emergents becoming enhanced by our proximity to each other."

"Proximity?"

"Yeah. You know, how we were all sort of squished together in the Valta after…the attacks. At first, I dismissed it as Ekker being a ranting, power-hungry lunatic. But the fact is, I feel different when I'm around you guys. It's not just normal confidence, either."

"Maybe it's security from being in a group."

"Maybe. But I think there's even more to it than that. I think Ekker was telling the truth. More and more, when I'm around you, I actually feel better. More alert. More alive. Not just happy to be with you. It's like I'm becoming a better version of myself."

Rain beams at me and gives me an unexpected hug. "Kress, 2.0."

Brohn pokes his head out of the room across the hall and invites me and Rain in. "If you two aren't too busy chit-chatting, maybe you would like to join us in here for our last round of hand-to-hand combat training?" He's wearing black tactical cargo pants with an army-green, short-sleeve compression shirt. His hair is tousled, and his face is shiny with sweat. As usual, he looks like he's been working twice as hard as the kids he's training.

"We'll be right there," Rain calls over.

Brohn beams and pumps his fist before turning and striding back into the room.

"You go ahead," Rains says to me. "I'm going to try the shooting range again. I may not be at your level anymore, but maybe I can still teach these kids a thing or two."

I tell Rain, "Okay" and start to follow Brohn into his training room.

Rain calls out to me before I get to the door. "No matter what happens tonight, Kress, I want you to know that you make me feel like a better version of me, too."

I answer her with a grateful smile, and she goes skittering back into the shooting gallery, her black ponytail bouncing rhythmically behind her.

Turning and wading through the torrent of burbling Insubordinates, I cross the hall and enter the room where Brohn is going over some pretty sophisticated details about the application of the centerline philosophy while engaging in a Hand Immobilization Attack. I lean against the wall and watch with what I know must be an oddly wide smile on my face as Brohn leads nine Insubordinates through these techniques of the Wing Chun fighting style. They're just about to break for sparring when Brohn notices me and calls me over.

"Feel like giving them a last-minute demonstration?" he calls out.

I look around, acting like I don't know who he's talking to. "Me?"

"Come on," Brohn says, waving me over. "Let's show them how it's done."

I plod over with pretend reluctance to the center of the room as the Insubordinates form a ring around me and Brohn.

With our guards up, we circle each other, sizing each other up, scoping out weakness and any flaw in the other person's guard we might exploit. I attack first, stepping into Brohn with a quick hop forward and a snap of my fist, which he deflects while simultaneously delivering an elbow strike, which I dodge, and then we are nearly nose-to-nose, our wrists and forearms sliding against and rotating around each other as we demonstrate the "sticky hands" technique. We push and probe for openings, our muscles firing at high speed until our hands and arms are a blur.

As we engage, our bodies forming a kind of improvised dance, Brohn narrates our techniques and strategies.

"Watch the quick footwork...Keep your hands loose to

disguise your attack. A clenched fist, a tense shoulder, shifting hips...these are all telegraphs, giveaways about when and where you plan to strike...Notice that it's not punch, parry, block, return punch. In close-quarters, hand-to-hand combat, the offense and the defense happen at the same time...we're aware of touch sensitivity, the micro-adjustments our opponent is making...Our kicks are low and practical, not high and flashy... Oh, and no one ever does a back-flip in the middle of a fight."

The laughs and cheers from the Insubordinates are interrupted by Wisp who appears in the doorway causing everyone to snap to attention.

"It's time," she says.

WITH THE INSUBORDINATES, WISP, AND ALL THE OTHERS GEARED up, Brohn, Cardyn, and Granden draw me aside to a table full of weapons and clothes, and they outfit me with the equipment I'll need.

"Sig Sauer 2040s," Granden says. "Like the ones we trained you on in the Processor."

"I remember."

I lean forward so Granden can strap a gas-powered 12-gauge over my head and onto my back.

"And this is a Dissimulator," Brohn explains. "It will mask your heat signature and take on the color spectrum and contour of whatever's around you. It's a one-shot deal, though, and we don't have very many of them, so use it wisely."

"Dissimulator. Use it wisely. Got it."

I clip the small device to the shoulder of my black and gray tactical recon vest.

"And your comm-link. To stay connected with Wisp."

I press the charcoal-colored button onto my neck just behind my ear.

"Will this thing even work?"

"Olivia and Manthy added a booster program to the communications code. Let's just hope it's enough."

Wisp sidles over and tells us she has to go over some last-minute planning with Granden. "I'll be five minutes," she says with a sweet smile. "Just down the hall. Then we'll get this little army of ours ready, riled up, and on the move."

I have a nice moment of being pretty close to overwhelmed with pride in who we are, what we're fighting for, and frankly, with how bad-ass we all look.

The Insubordinates are all dressed in black military style cargo pants and black compression shirts with impact pads on the elbows and shoulders. On top of that, everyone's wearing black and gray tactical vests with an array of pockets, pouches, and holsters of assorted sizes on the pants and on their service belts. There's even a crisp gold outline of some kind of symbol embossed on the breast pocket of each of the Insubordinates' invasion-force combat vests. At first, I can't make out what it is. Then I look closer at the insignia.

It's a raven.

"We got one for you, too," Cardyn beams, holding a vest up in front of me and making it dance in the air.

"How did you arrange all this?"

"Wasn't us," Triella says. "We owe it all to the Major."

Saying he'll see us in a minute and bouncing from group to group in the expanse of the fifth-floor corridor, Cardyn is a machine of efficiency. As I meander through the crowd and take in all the rowdy excitement, he organizes a group of a few dozen Insubordinates into their smaller squads. Meanwhile, Brohn's voice fills the large, crowded hallway as he calls out orders and directs everyone where to go and what to do.

"The three of you, you sort out these weapons," he says, broad-shouldered and standing a head taller than most of the people in the room. "Count them up, match them with their ammo, make sure all the magazines are loaded up and ready to go. You four are responsible for coordinating communication. You answer to Rain."

A few newcomers—kids not more than about thirteen or fourteen years old—admit to being nervous. "I don't remember how to eject the clip from the guns," one of them moans.

Cardyn comes to their rescue and gives them a quick, last-minute lesson. "First of all, it's a magazine, not a clip," he laughs. "Here, I'll show you."

The younger Insubordinates are wide-eyed and yippy, naïve to the bone but excited about being a part of something so much bigger than themselves. The older ones look edgy but more nervous, maybe even reluctant about what we're setting out to do. They don their military gear at the supply table in near silence while the younger Insubordinates leap and bounce around them.

Stopping to chat with Rain, I spot Jerald, Ethan, Sabine, and Orion, the four Insubordinates Brohn and I had coffee with the day Ekker captured us. This is the first time I've seen them since that day, and Jerald comes bounding up to me and Rain, gushing about how excited he is "to be involved in this great cause with such great warriors."

"We're hardly warriors," Rain corrects him. "And it's the cause that's great, not the handful of us who were lucky enough to survive the apocalypse out there."

"We heard about you and Brohn," Jerald says to me.

I blush at first, thinking he means about me and Brohn up here in the shooting range the other night, but he looks distressed as he puts his hand on my shoulder. "I'm just glad you were able to get out of there alive," he says.

"Well, we wouldn't have gotten out without a lot of help," I say, nodding toward Rain and breathing a sigh of relief.

Ethan and Orion join us at one of the equipment and weapons tables where I'm still loading my gun and strategically placing a 2040 Colt M45R4 in my hip holster with an eleven-inch tactical knife, a ballistic propulsion blade, and extra ammo into the various pockets of my belt and recon vest.

"Remember what you've been taught," Brohn tells a large group of Insubordinates who have pressed forward around him. He slips one of his handguns from his hip holster and raises it up at an imaginary enemy. "For most of the guns, you'll line up the two sights with your target. Keep one hand on the handle with your other hand underneath for support. When you shoot, don't *pull* the trigger. *Squeeze* it. Keep your eye focused downrange. Remember, there'll be some kickback, some smoke, and some hot shells but nothing to worry about."

Over in the far corner down at the other end of the hall, Cardyn and Manthy are chatting with some kids who look to be about our age. Manthy touches Card's arm as they talk, and I can feel Card blush from here.

After all the milling around has settled into a quiet, anticipatory hum, Wisp jumps up onto a wooden stage-like platform four of the Insubordinates have dragged from one of the nearby rooms and into the middle of the wide hall.

Brohn, Rain, Granden, and I stand on the floor next to the makeshift stage, positioning ourselves to one side with Cardyn and Manthy on the other. Standing on the floor next to me with his legs wide and his arms crossed, Granden's eyes scan our milling and excited troops like he's on the lookout for anyone who's distracted or too afraid or conflicted to contribute. He's got nothing to worry about, though. Everyone in this wide and well-lit hallway is on the same page. It's a blank page, one with nothing but potential and pure possibility.

From her perch on the platform, Wisp calls everyone to attention. She's practically royalty around here. The last remaining buzz in the hall stops the second she raises her hand.

"We've all come a long way from a lot of different places," she calls out. "We've fought. Some of us have been hurt. Some have died. I won't give you a bunch of clichés about how the ones we lost are in a better place now. It's our job to make our own world into a better place. Our friends died to help us take a step in that direction. We owe it to them to keep moving forward, to keep taking those next steps. But I've taken you as far as I can. I've helped bring us together. I'll still be here as your Major, but the next steps require abilities I just don't have. Lucky for us, we have a few people with us who do. Here are the ones, your Conspiracy, who'll lead the way."

She calls out to me, Brohn, Cardyn, Rain, and Manthy, and I'm glad she didn't refer to us as "Emergents" in her little intro. That would've been embarrassing. Plus, the pressure associated with being some kind of evolutionary freak of nature tasked with saving the world is more than I need right now.

Wisp hops down from the platform to stand next to Granden. I'm still amazed at what an interesting couple they make. He's twice her size and looms over her like a sequoia over a button mushroom, and yet she's the one radiating all the energy and power.

Brohn steps up onto the platform to where Wisp was just standing. He reaches his hand out to help me up as well. It's not necessary, of course, but it's a nice gesture, and I'll never object to having my hand in his. Manthy seems content to stay where she is, standing on the floor off to the side. Although she doesn't follow the rest of us up onto the platform, she does take a half-step forward to receive reverential salutes from the crowd of Insubordinates standing shoulder to shoulder under the hall-way's vivid purplish-white lights.

With the Insubordinates amassed before us, I nod to Brohn to take the lead. "Go ahead," I say through the side of my mouth.

Brohn leans down and kisses me on the cheek, and a bunch of oohs and aahs rise up from the crowd. Brohn puts his hands up and takes a small step back. "Thanks, but they're all yours, *Kakari Isutse*."

"Great," I mutter.

I've never spoken out loud in front of more than maybe seven or eight people at a time. Now I'm standing here in front of nearly fifty kids and a few adults of every age, shape, color, and size, everyone dressed in black, gray, and gold, heavily armed, hastily trained, and all thinking with the naïveté of youthful optimism and unbridled belief in our cause that we'll all be coming back here alive.

A few of them pump their fists in the air and chant my Costanoan nickname: "*Kakari Isutse!*"

I clear my throat. "Over this past week, Wisp has brought us all together. Brohn, Cardyn, and Granden have trained you. Rain has developed the battle plan and given you your assignments. With Render's help, Olivia and I have gathered the necessary intel. Now it's just a matter of following the plan Wisp and Rain have laid out. You've got to trust the intel. If you deviate, if you get nervous or decide to go off on your own, this plan will fall apart. If you fail, we all fail."

Most everyone nods or says "Yeah," and a few murmurs go up from the crowd.

"For as long as most of us in here have been alive, Krug has kept us divided and afraid. He rolled out his Eastern Order boogey man and played on our worst prejudices and our most embedded insecurities."

The murmurs turn into a louder buzz with some of the Insubordinates nodding. A few start to clap.

"Then he sat back," I continue, "and accumulated wealth and power and laughed at us while we fell into cycles of poverty and despair..."

A few more claps burst forth from the crowd.

"...while we amassed enough alcohol, drugs, and guns to kill each other in the privacy of our own broken-down neighborhoods..."

Now some of the Insubordinates shout out their agreement.

Cries of "Down with Krug!" and "No more lies!" ring out and start to catch on and spread through the assembly like a virus.

"...while we got tricked into blaming ourselves for our misery... while we got brainwashed into believing there wasn't enough for everyone. Not enough resources. Not enough wealth. Not enough safety, good schools, jobs, or opportunities to live a decent, healthy life. Krug and his businesses raped the planet to manufacture and sell goods to us we didn't need and then had the nerve to blame us for buying those very same products that polluted and destroyed the environment. And the worst part is, we bought it. We bought the products. And we bought the lies. I was one of the ones he tricked. I grew up in fear and surrounded by death and deceit. Well, that stops now. We're stronger together than we are apart. That's the strength Krug fears: the strength of family. The strength of unity. The strength of loving our neighbor more than we love ourselves. The strength to see through his tricks, to admit we've been duped, and to do something about it. The strength of not being afraid anymore."

Now the shouts from the crowd are rising to a crescendo.

"This isn't about peaceful protests," I cry out, my voice rising as I go. "It's not about informing the masses, election turn-out, or pushing for reform. We're past all that. We're not a political movement. We're not out to change anyone's mind. We are prepared to do what it takes—one block, street, and city at a time —to expose the lies and to bring down the dictatorship our democracy has become."

"But we can't do it alone," Cardyn shouts out to the crowd from where he's standing by the edge of the platform next to Rain. "And neither can you!"

"And we can't do it all at once!" Brohn adds over the growing tumult of the excited crowd.

At the back of the hall, out past the last of the Insubordinates, I spot Caldwell coming through the far door with a familiar companion perched on his shoulder.

Glistening in his new golden armor and feeling not perfect but at least on the mend, Render flutters over the heads of the Insubordinates in an explosion of dust and feathers and alights on my upper arm. Ducking down, the crowd gasps and then bursts into peals of laughter and cheers. I reach into my side pocket and toss Render a small protein cube, which he gulps down with a sharp snap of his black beak. I raise my hand to quiet the rowdy throng.

"What we *can* do starts here," I continue. "It starts with this plan in this neighborhood in this city. And it starts right now."

Render tilts his head back and punctures the open air in the crowded hallway with a series of sharp clicks and *kraas*!

"This isn't a coup because this isn't our government. Not anymore. By its very nature every Conspiracy is an act of rebellion. It's time to fulfill our purpose and live up to our name!"

Everyone offers up vigorous nods. Dozens of them shout, "Yes!" and pump their fists in the air.

With the hallway now filled to overflowing with adrenalin and with all of us whipped into an energetic frenzy, Wisp signals to Granden, and the two of them lead us thundering down the stairs, out the back door, and down into the network of tunnels that will lead us directly to the Armory and straight into the biggest fight of our lives.

## 24

THE NEXT HALF HOUR IS A BURBLE OF EXCITED ENERGY AS WE HIKE
our way toward the enemy and past the point of no return.

Along a short but silent and solemn march through the dimly-
lit subway tunnels and dried-up sewer access passageways, we
begin to fan out with groups of Insubordinates peeling off one at
a time from our ranks. Following Wisp's and Rain's plans to the
letter, several teams duck down different branches of the subter-
ranean network. One team climbs up a metal fourteen-step
safety ladder that ends in a hatch opening into the cellar of an old
beer distillery less than two blocks from the Armory. Another
team, their black gas-piston assault rifles clutched to their chests,
runs ahead of us and into a service elevator that will take them all
the way up to the roof of the military surplus store across the
street from the Armory. A third team gets the go-ahead from
Wisp and scampers up a set of damp concrete steps leading to a
trapdoor beneath one of the tool and supply sheds of a local
elementary school just around the corner from the Armory.

Wisp leads me and my Conspiracy to another set of stairs,
through an unlocked emergency door, and up an access ramp
that opens out into a mag-car parking garage below an office

building. According to Wisp, the Patriots—acting on bad intel and thinking it was a base of operations for the Insubordinates —took over the once-busy building about two weeks before we got into town. Although they claimed it was "a legal and peaceful exchange of title to the property," more than fifty people who worked in this building mysteriously "disappeared." Now, the garage is ghostly and almost empty with a few vehicles hovering on grav-pads in front of a bank of charging stations and a few older-style military jeeps resting on their rubber wheels in designated parking spots over by the service elevators.

Thanks to the on-the-ground surveillance Wisp has been conducting over the past couple of months, the specs Olivia has been able to pilfer from the city's urban and zoning systems databases, and the intel Render and I have provided from our endless, crisscrossing flights around the city these past few days, I know every inch of this area, inside and out. Combined with the holo-sims and the detailed information Granden, Brohn, and Cardyn have spent the week drilling into the heads of the Insubordinates, most of us could probably navigate these conduits and corridors and conduct this raid with our eyes closed.

Of course, given the enemy we're up against and the severity of the stakes, eyes wide open is probably our safest bet.

From the parking garage, Granden heads toward a stairway behind an emergency door while Wisp leads my Conspiracy up a maintenance tunnel and through a delivery entrance that opens onto the patio of a café nestled behind a small hotel. A haze of white light comes from behind the curtains of a window on the second floor, but the rest of the hotel is dark. With the café closed for the night, the patio is empty except for a stack of chairs and a few round tables tethered together against the back wall. The manager left an hour ago, and the custodial staff doesn't report until tomorrow. Again, thanks to Render and to my own oddly acute memory, I know the names, faces, and schedules of at least two dozen people who have been in and out of here over the past few days.

Slipping out the back door of the parking garage, Wisp leads us through a small laneway and out to the sidewalk, where we crouch down behind a long concrete barrier set out by the Patriot Army to cordon off this part of the street around the Armory. Two soldiers—overloaded with a variety of bulky rifles and handguns—are on guard duty, but they have turned their attention to a pair of teenagers who are engaged in what looks like a squabbling lovers' quarrel under the light cast by a green-tinted halo-post on the corner. As the argument gets louder and as the soldiers trot off to investigate, we scamper across the street in a crouch and plunge over a low stone wall lining the perimeter of the park where the Patriot Army conducts some of their military training exercises.

Wisp taps her comm-link and whispers, "Settled and primed." Out under the halo-post, the two teenagers suddenly stop their bickering and sprint off, leaving the two soldiers on the empty corner to share a head-scratching moment before returning to their guard duty.

In the quiet of the city and in the pitch-dark shadow of the Armory, our teams have now assumed their positions. Wisp taps her comm-link again, but nothing happens. She scowls and taps it again. When she still doesn't get a signal, Manthy crawls over and puts her hand behind Wisp's neck, her palm covering the comm-link. Her eyes widen, and she nods. "Got a signal," she whispers, her hand on Manthy's forearm in a gesture of thanks.

Wisp nods her head at a few quick and quiet reports and gives us a closed-fist signal, confirming that the nine teams of Insubordinates are all in place.

A couple of days ago, up on the fifth floor and on Rain's advice, each team gave itself a nickname. I suggested just calling them "Team 1, Team 2, etcetera," which caused Rain to roll her eyes and call me boring.

"Fine," I said. "What do you suggest?"

One of the Insubordinates—a tall, strong, but strangely mousy girl named Clover—put up her hand, and, when Rain called on her, Clover suggested they name themselves after various neighborhoods, streets, and landmarks of San Francisco.

They all thought it was a great idea, so, after Rain gave them her endorsement, that's what they became.

Tonight, lurking in shadows and peering down from rooftops, we have nine teams of five Insubordinates each plus my Conspiracy with all of us connected by comm-link and coordinated by Olivia back in the Style and by Wisp and Granden out here with us in the field.

The team of Insubordinates calling themselves Team Marina is up on the roof of the two-story military surplus building just across the street from the Armory. Team Bayview is camped out in a small courtyard of an apartment building a block away. A diversion team, Team Presidio, is stationed on Mission Street with another squad calling themselves Team Van Ness set up to run interference over on 15th Street, where we know a three-person night-patrol of Patriot Army soldiers will be on very sleepy guard duty after a long day of escorting Krug and his personal attaché around San Francisco.

Team Golden Gate and Team Alcatraz are set up to seal the barracks where the enemy soldiers are bivouacked, with Team Trolley stationed out back to commandeer the military vehicles on site. Team Ashbury is responsible for breaking into the small control shed out back and disabling the power-coupler controlling the Armory's external vehicle and pedestrian doors. They're also in charge of coordinating with Olivia to disable the building's three-stage communications generator.

"We can't have the Patriots calling for backup," Wisp explained during one of the recent training sessions. Team North Beach, the most heavily-armed and, frankly, gung-ho of all of us, will be the first ones through the front doors while my team sneaks into the Armory from the north side, worms our way inside, and seizes control of Command Headquarters.

Thanks to Render's amazing senses and my increasingly eidetic memory, we know exactly when every change of guard happens, who's going on duty, and who's coming off. We know exactly how many Patriot soldiers are currently out on patrol and how many are in the Armory.

For Ekker and the Patriot Army, that's the disadvantage of following protocol and adhering to strict military precision. It's predictable.

We're not.

We don't have the Patriots' numbers—there are over two-hundred of them on active duty in the Armory at the moment—and we can't match their weapons, their ruthlessness, or even their training.

Other than our actual combat knives, handguns, sniper rifles, stun-sticks, and concussion grenades, our best weapons are a touch of desperation, a bit of fear, and a whole lot of crazy. Plus, it doesn't hurt that our leader is a military genius and that her big brother is bullet-proof.

With everyone in position and with the Armory now quietly surrounded, we wait for Wisp's signal.

Tucked invisibly behind a landscaped cluster of boxwood and purple hopseed bushes, I can tell, even through the sparse moonlight speckling its way between the canopy of trees overhead, that everyone's on edge, which shouldn't be surprising considering what we're about to do. Cardyn has peeled off one of his gloves and is nibbling at the dry skin around the edge of his thumb. Rain keeps peering through small gaps in the vegetation and over the stone wall around us, her eyes riveted on the contingent of Patriot guards patrolling the darkened sidewalk across the street. Manthy looks droopy-eyed and seems small and weighted down by the cache of weapons packed into her tactical vest. Even Brohn looks fidgety, although he gives me a confident smile when our eyes meet through the midnight gloom.

Personally, I'm beyond terrified. I've had to fight for my life before, but it was always in the heat of the moment, a foray into spontaneous combat in defense of myself or my friends. Being part of a planned attack like this carries with it a whole new host of headaches. What if our plan is flawed in ways we haven't anticipated? What if Ekker knows what we're up to? After all, he did find the Style, even if he didn't technically find us. If it weren't for Wisp and Olivia's transformational magic trick that hid us all from that raid, we would have easily been captured or killed.

Given all that, we're going into this with a lot of confidence that may not be warranted.

On the other hand, I remind myself, we have brilliant tacticians and expert trainers on our side. We have the moral high ground in a rebellion against tyranny. And, for what it's worth, we have the Emergents.

*Who knows?* I ask myself by way of consolation in a time of crisis. *Maybe we can actually pull this off, defeat Krug and Ekker, liberate the city, expose the government's lies, and be back to the Style in time for breakfast.*

I must've smiled a little at this thought because Wisp gives me a playful elbow to the arm and asks me what's so funny.

"Nothing," I tell her. "Just fantasizing about best-case scenarios."

"Those are the best kind of scenarios to fantasize about," she whispers back to me through the dark.

Brohn crawls toward us and turns to sit next to me with his back against the low stone wall that curves around our little hiding place. His updated m4A4 carbine rifle with the attached M420 grenade launcher module rests on his lap. "Remember what we used to say back in the Valta whenever everything was going good?"

"Sure. 'For now, at least.'"

"After today, we're going to have to change that to 'for now and *forever*, at least.'"

"I can live with that."

"I think we all can," Cardyn pipes in softly from the other side of Brohn, where he's down on one knee redoing the laces on one of his boots, his HK416 assault rifle resting next to him on a patch of soft, wet grass.

"This is going to work," I insist.

"Not that I disagree," Brohn says, "but what makes you so sure?"

"Because if it doesn't, we won't get to use your awesome new 'now and forever' line. And that would be a terrible, terrible shame."

Brohn stifles a low laugh with the back of his hand before reaching out to clip the strap shut on my leg holster. "Can't have your gun slipping out mid-fight now, can we?"

I say, "Thanks," and I'm just getting ready to remind everyone that we only have two minutes before we initiate our attack when I hear Wisp next to me mutter, "Uh oh," and I curse myself for having upset the gods of war with my confidence and bravado.

"What's wrong?"

Wisp points over to where a male figure is approaching us in a stealthy crouch through dark swirls of midnight fog. Ghost-like, he glides between two rows of trees lining a narrow foot-path in the small, pitch-black park.

I get ready to raise my gun, but Wisp puts her hand on my forearm and shakes her head. "It's okay. I know him."

The man, dressed in a San Francisco police uniform, inches over and slides to a quiet, kneeling stop in front of Wisp.

"Kress. Brohn. Cardyn. Rain. Manthy," Wisp whispers, pointing to us one at a time. "This is Captain Huang. He came over from the city's Special Weapons and Tactics team."

"It's an honor to meet you," he says under his breath, stuttering like a hyperventilating, over-enthusiastic groupie and shaking each of our hands in turn. "I've heard a lot about you."

While he stares at us for what feels like an hour and a half, I finally ask him under my breath if he's here to stop us.

He shakes his head hard, his chins jiggling, and I worry for a second his head might fall clean off his neck. "No. The Major and Granden and I have been in touch over the past couple of months. All hush-hush and very unofficial, of course. And no. We're not going to stop you. In fact, we're here to help you."

Captain Huang is a pear-shaped, stocky man, bald and flush with friendliness. He's also rosy-cheeked, probably from scurrying all the way over here in the middle of the night under the noses of the Patriot Army. Squatting in front of us in the dark, panting and sweating, he seems practically giddy.

"Thank you," Wisp says, her voice quiet but clear. "When we talked a couple of weeks ago, you said you didn't know if you had support on the force."

"We didn't," Huang says tipping his head toward me and my Conspiracy. "But then *they* got here. Anyway, word got around, and…well, consider Mission, Richmond, Park, and the Northern District Stations at your disposal. Ingleside and South are going to sit it out, but they won't stand in your way."

"You're sure?"

"Don't worry. Granden is out making the rounds as we speak. He's got connections even above my pay-grade. He won't let anyone sabotage your operation."

Leaning in and whispering, Rain asks Captain Huang, "If you don't mind my asking…why? I mean, why are you helping us? The Patriot Army is part of the government. And so are you."

Captain Huang holds up a hand to cut her off. "Just because they call themselves 'Patriots' doesn't make them Americans."

Wisp holds up a finger for us to wait a second, taps her comm-link, and nods. "It's time," she says. "I'll coordinate from here with Captain Huang. Granden is working with the local authorities, as Huang says. I'm giving the go-ahead to the other nine teams right now. The rest of you know what to do." Wisp's thin black wristband gives a quick blink. "Now get going—this is it!"

On Wisp's cue, my Conspiracy slips around to the side of the Armory where the two guards on duty have left their post to aid their fellow Patriots, who have just entered into in a furious gun battle with Team Bayview about fifty yards down the block.

On a rooftop on the far side of the street, Team Marina lays out a blitz of cover fire with their retrofitted McMillan Tac-50 2040 sniper rifles. A blizzard of bullets rains down, sending soldiers scattering for cover as the deadly slugs plunk huge divots into the surface of the street and along the Armory's façade.

The deafening howl of emergency-alert klaxons from the Armory joins in with the rest of the escalating pandemonium. As we hoped, the diversions attract the Patriots' attention everywhere except where we are. Despite the flashes from muzzle fire in the gun battle out front, the explosions from Team North Beach's blaze-grenades, and the searing brightness of the Armory's external security beacons, my team is amazingly and thankfully pretty much invisible.

In the confusion and under the cloud of dust and debris being kicked up, we slip easily up to the now-unguarded middle door on the east side of the building. Thanks to our feathered, flying spy, we know the combination they use on the input panel, and we know they never change it. Rain punches in the code, and, sure enough, the door unlocks and slides open.

Once inside, we skitter past an unmanned office, through a set of glass double-doors, and into a small supply room.

We all get Wisp's voice in our heads telling us that Teams Golden Gate and Alcatraz are at the Munitions Depot and Team Ashbury is about to take control of the Communications Center. Those are tough but manageable jobs. Both of those divisions are staffed mostly with lower-ranking, barely-trained soldiers. Still, it's a good first victory, and Brohn and Cardyn exchange a congratulatory handshake.

Our assignment is Command Headquarters. We know from our recon missions that it'll be where Krug is set up and it'll be the first thing the Patriots lock down once they realize they're under attack, which, unless they're blind, deaf, and dumb as a box of hair, they're aware of by now. Besides being the brains of the Patriot's local organization, Command Headquarters is also the hub of operations and the most important room in the facility. It's also the most protected. It's from there that the Patriots will initiate their complete takeover of the city starting in just a few hours when Krug's reinforcements arrive.

That gives us a practically non-existent window of time to get in, take it over, and secure the room while coordinating with the simultaneous attacks currently underway against the Munitions Depot and the Communications Center over on the west side of the huge facility.

I take the lead and guide us out of the supply room and up the service staircase tucked away in the interior of the Armory. It's just one flight up the unguarded narrow stairway that ends on the mezzanine level at a landing lined with green lockers, storage totes, and custodial supplies. I immediately recognize it in minute detail from Render's stealthy exploration of the space.

Brohn starts to make his way toward the door that will lead us out to the open, second-floor walkway overlooking the vast floor of the Armory, but I grab him by his arm and hold him back.

"Not that door," I whisper, pointing to the door of the storage closet set in between two of the banks of lockers. "That one."

"You're sure?"

"I'm sure."

The door is locked, but Brohn solves that problem by snapping off the handle and reaching in with his finger to disengage the interior locking mechanism.

We enter what appears to be a closet, but which I know is an old pass-through leading straight to an unused conference room, which leads to an access corridor, which is, conveniently, just on the other side of a synth-steel wall from Command Headquarters.

Once we're inside and have made our way across the empty conference room, Manthy does her trick on the electronic lock on the next door. It surrenders to her and opens with a light sigh. We step into the access corridor and scurry along its dark length to the small control room annex where we know that a single soldier, Lance Corporal Ferregetti, will be tucked away at his little monitoring station.

Rain steps forward and lunges into the room, but the chair where Ferregetti is supposed to be sitting is empty. One by one, we follow Rain into the empty room. "What the hell?" Wisp exclaims. Then, turning to me, she asks if I'm sure this is the right station, and, if so, where is the guard.

Before I can answer, a voice rings out from behind us. "Drop your weapons," the man stammers. "And don't…don't move!"

I twist around to see that it's Ferregetti, looking dangerously nervous behind the huge four-barreled rotary machine he's got trained on us.

"How can we drop our weapons if we can't move?" Cardyn asks, stepping between us and the quivering soldier. His voice is even and oddly calm, and I'm pretty sure he's lost his mind. He must sense that we're about to take our chances as we reach for our weapons because he waves us back. "There's a way out of this, you know," he tells Ferregetti. "Krug is using you for his own good, not for yours. Break the hold he has on you. Be honest with yourself. About why you're here and what kind of person you really want to be. Honesty is the mark of true strength. It's what will get you out of here alive."

The puzzled young man, short but thick and with a scraggle of a black goatee adorning his chin and upper lip, lowers his gun, raises it, and lowers it again. He gives a painful squint with each motion, alternating between wanting to drop the big weapon and needing to fire it. "I can't," he says, through clenched teeth. "I have a duty." It takes visible effort, but he raises the big gun one more time. With his sleeves cuffed above his elbows, I can see his forearm muscles flex and fill with blood.

In a flash, Rain shoots him once in the leg to immobilize him and once in the hand, causing the clunky gun to clang to the ground.

Before I even know what's happened, Brohn is on the man, his hand clamped over the wounded soldier's mouth. In one swift motion, he whips a pair of immobilizer zip-cuffs from his belt and slaps them onto the groaning soldier while Manthy draws one of her stun-sticks from her belt and presses it to the man's neck, causing him to twitch like a freshly-caught fish until he slumps down to the floor and moans himself into unconsciousness.

"How...?" I start to ask Cardyn, my eyes wide. I'm not sure whether to cheer or dismiss what just happened as a bizarre dream I'm sure to wake up from at any second.

Brohn claps Cardyn on the shoulder. "See?" he says to me. "I told you he was good at getting people to do his bidding."

Cardyn looks disappointed. "But I didn't get him to do anything. He still would've killed us."

"But you got him to pause, to think. You have abilities," Brohn says. "A gift. Raw, maybe. But it's something to work on."

I'm still looking back and forth from Cardyn to the downed soldier. "How...?" I ask again, but the rest of my Conspiracy is already ahead of me and on their way to the last door between us and the Command Headquarters, our ultimate objective.

Her head cocked, Manthy drags her palm along the area around the door that we know opens into the rear of the big room. She raises her head and lowers it again, her ear to the wall, concentrating until she taps into the system she's looking for. At first, I think it's a trick of the light, but Rain nudges me. She sees it, too. Manthy's eyes have gone black, like mine apparently do when I connect with Render.

Neither of us has time to contemplate this, though. We have a job to do.

With the muffled sound of gunfire and explosions coming from all around the Armory and with agitated shouts coming from the other side of this door, we draw our weapons, exchange what we hope isn't our last look goodbye, and prepare to burst into the room.

25
---

THE DOOR WHOOSHES OPEN, AND WE LEAP INTO A SCENE OF CHAOS and panic. Patriot soldiers are scrambling around, rushing from one monitor to the other, trying to respond to orders barked at them from Ekker on the far side of the room, and practically crashing into each other in the confusion as they try to sort out what's happening outside.

Our infiltration is quick, intense, and we've caught everyone in this room completely by surprise. Their arrogance makes them dangerous but also vulnerable. Thinking the local police were on their side—or at least under their thumb—and that the little pockets of rebels scattered throughout the city were too uncoordinated and insignificant to warrant real attention, this place isn't half as well-defended as it should be.

In a fraction of an eye-blink, I absorb every detail of the expansive space:

An enormous, two-leveled room. A huge bank of holo-displays on one wall. Four command consoles in the middle. Three rows of monitoring ports. A dozen bundles of conduits and a system of silver bulkheads running the length of the ceiling. A central tactical display station. A curved wall of red projected surveillance holo-screens showing the action outside and down on the main floor below.

There are nineteen Patriot soldier, Ekker, and the mystery woman in red, her face concealed by the hood of her jacket.

And, there in the flesh in front of us for the first time, dressed in his signature shiny silver suit and crimson tie, is President Krug.

In all the times I've seen him, whether it was on the viz-screens in the Valta or on the holo-projection of this morning's presidential parade, I always imagined him as a giant. Something mythological, a mountain of a man who could and did crush underfoot anyone or anything that dared to get in his way. Standing way over on the far side of the room, cowering behind Ekker and the Patriot guard, he's small, vulnerable, and nothing like the monster of my imagination. As I look at him, I'm taken back to something my dad once said to me: "It takes a small man to be a monster."

In the second it takes for us to break in and survey the scene, the soldiers spring into action with the ones from Krug's private detail leaping into a protective circle around him on the far side of the room. Dressed in the blue combat pants and the red and white camo jackets like the other Patriots, but sporting full tactical body armor and black armbands with one white star on each, designating them as elite presidential guards, the six men of Ekker's personal entourage fire at us before he has even finished shouting out the order.

Manthy and I dive behind a control console and fire our weapons at the soldiers from around each corner.

Cardyn and Rain dive for cover, too, only they dive behind Brohn. The hurricane of gunfire thunders in the room, and our advantage of surprise is long-gone. Despite what I already know, I'm shocked to see bullets bouncing off Brohn's body. He turns a shoulder in the direction of the blasts and crouches over Cardyn and Rain as they return fire, hitting several of the soldiers who reel backward and crash into the cluster of monitoring ports in the middle of the room. Absorbing a horizontal storm of gunfire, Brohn struggles to stay on his feet, his face contorted in agony. Clearly, bullet-proof isn't the same as pain-proof.

From our places of cover, we pick off the startled and scrambling Patriot guards with lethal precision. With expert marksmanship, Rain takes down three of the men, one after the other. The men pitch violently forward, crashing against another one of the Patriot soldiers, who loses his balance and sends a spray of bullets pinging into the ceiling.

I call out for Manthy to cover me as I sprint out from behind the control console. She drops her Sig Sauer, pulls her two FNX five-seven pistols from her shoulder holsters, and lays down a spray of cover fire that sends most of the enemy soldiers diving for cover. The ones who try to stand their ground and return fire are met with well-placed shots that drop them one by one.

Before we can get to Ekker and Krug on the far side of the room, Ekker, his arms over his face, leaps from behind his cover and presses a black button on the console on the far side of the room, and a floor-to-ceiling energy barrier shimmers to life between us and them.

We direct our fire at Ekker and Krug, but the energy field absorbs the brunt of our blasts, and our bullets plunk harmlessly to the floor.

Ekker grabs Krug by the arm and disappears through the far door with the woman in red and Krug's remaining guards and Patriot soldiers.

Brohn taps his comm-link and connects with Wisp. "We have the Command Headquarters. But Ekker and Krug got away. We're going after them!"

Rain calls out, "Manthy!"

Eyes clamped shut, Manthy slaps both hands down on the central console on our side of the energy barrier.

Her eyes go black—this time I see it clear as day—and the

screen fizzles away. The five of us rush out of the Command Headquarters through the door Krug and the others just escaped through. Breathing hard, we sprint down a narrow corridor, around a sharp corner, and up to a door that's still closing slowly on old-style hinges. We burst through the door and out onto the mezzanine walkway that runs in a circle around the lengthy perimeter of the Armory's wide-open interior.

With Krug and his crew galloping down the long walkway, we prepare to go after them, but we have to stop and duck as bullets blast into the wall behind us.

Down below, the Insubordinates and the San Francisco police are engaged in a major firefight with the Patriot soldiers who have regrouped and are firing at the Insubordinate infiltration teams from behind parked vehicles and up on the mezzanine across from us. We're in somebody's sights, but in the chaos of the battle, I can't tell right away where the shots are coming from. Fortunately, neither can Krug and his men, which means they have to come to a sliding stop in their tracks and duck down just like us, or else risk getting mowed down.

"Team Portola was supposed to secure this level!" Cardyn shouts.

In a defensive crouch, Brohn points down the long track to where Krug is inching toward an open staircase on the far side of the Armory. His soldiers alternate between firing at us and firing down at our people on the Armory floor.

With the barrage of gunfire all around us, there's no way we can get to Krug, but we also can't let him escape up the open, five-level steel staircase that zigzags up the entire height of the Armory.

"They're trying to get to the stairs," Rain calls out. "They going to try to get to the roof! We have to stop them!" But she knows as well as the rest of us that chasing after Ekker and Krug right now would constitute a group suicide pact of epic proportions.

A swarm of bullets whizzes around our heads, and we all roll behind a low stack of iron-gray storage bins piled up against the wall.

Our inability to move is infuriating, but we're pinned down, and any attempt to charge at Krug would put us directly into a lot of lines of fire. Our only saving grace is that he's pinned down, too. But he won't be for long, at the rate his men are regrouping and staging a major counter-offensive that has us on our heels.

With the Patriot soldiers lunging for fresh firepower from their weapons lockers, I'm considering suggesting we drop the whole plan and go into full panic mode when the massive double doors down below us and on either side of the giant Armory slide smoothly open.

The Armory doors let in a lot of things: fresh San Francisco midnight air. The sound of shouting and gunfire from the skirmishes underway outside. And two armies storming in from opposite directions to save the day.

Through the south side doors, armed Insubordinates accompany an entire battalion of local police officers. Side by side, they run in as one before splintering off, leaping behind parked jeeps, desks, and other barriers firing their weapons at the startled and suddenly outnumbered Patriot Army.

From the north side, a completely different, unarmed, but equally lethal army sweeps in. When I see them, it's all I can do to suppress a jubilant cry.

It's an army of a hundred *kraa*-ing birds, bursting into the Armory in a furious, swirling swarm, led by a large black raven with glistening, golden armor.

26

RENDER AND THE HUNDRED RAVENS ACCOMPANYING HIM BLAST into the Armory from the north with most of the Insubordinates and what appears to be a good percentage of the San Francisco police force—led by Captain Huang himself—charging in from the south. The shouting people storm in like a human wave of white-water rapids, churning in an advancing mass, their array of guns and rifles blazing.

Bursting forth in a ferocious black storm cloud from the opposite direction, the ravens consume the open space, flocking and darting as they disorient, attack, and terrify the flailing enemy soldiers. In the chaos, many of the Patriot soldiers begin shooting randomly, their bullets zinging wildly through the Armory.

From up here, we see swarms of marked police mag-cars glide to a stop in an intimidating cluster at the north and south entrances of the Armory. In an instant, the dark of night outside explodes in a firework of red and white emergency lights, their flashing beams creating a strobe effect inside the facility.

Adding to the roar of the shoot-out, platoons of shouting

police officers take positions behind their vehicles and fire at the Patriots. The soldiers whip around to face the unexpected assault from behind. Weapons are drawn and firing wildly on both sides. It's a cacophony of chaos, with the Patriots now outnumbered and outgunned. What had just been a hopeless and deadly situation for us has just been turned on its head.

Realizing what's happening, many of the Patriots drop their guns. Some of the men try to run, only to be corralled at the exits by our containment teams. Although many of the scrambling and disoriented soldiers try to force their way out and fight back, the Insubordinates have been trained too well for them, and they dispatch the Patriots with the moves they've been taught by Brohn, Cardyn, and Granden. The Insubordinates practically dance through the befuddled Patriot soldiers, treating them to what looks from up here like an excruciating buffet of straight punches, leg-sweeps, palm heel-attacks, elbow strikes, round-house kicks, forearm thrusts, stinging jabs, and a wide variety of painful takedowns. With what amounts to an almost eerie efficiency, as soon as any Patriot soldier hits the ground, an Insubordinate or a San Francisco law enforcer is on him, applying restraining cuffs, or, when necessary, finishing the soldier off with a well-placed stun-stick to the base of the neck.

It's not all clean and bloodless, though. Some of the Patriots steel their jaws and re-load their weapons, determined not to go down without a fight. From positions behind parked vehicles, metal supply trunks, equipment lockers, and maintenance stations, the remaining Patriots continue to fire. Ducking down and snaking through the cluster of office cubicles, our teams continue their assault.

Still pinned down, we watch helplessly as the battle rages below and as Krug begins to make his escape down the long walkway and toward the metal staircase at the far end of the facility. His group's progress is impeded by Team Van Ness, the team Ethan is on. Ethan and his fellow Insubordinates aim their weapons and order Krug's soldiers to stand down. As confident as they are, they're no match for Ekker, who has his gun out and begins firing before anyone even knows he's moved.

He drops three members of Ethan's team with precision shots to the head and single-handedly takes down the other two team members as if they were standing still.

Rain screams out, "No!" and we're about to dash over to help when another hail of gunfire, this time coming from behind us, pins us down again.

Cardyn and Rain spin toward the group of Patriot soldiers who are shooting at us from behind a stack of heavy-duty steel crates on the mezzanine level about thirty or forty yards in the opposite direction. Dropping to the floor and laying down return fire, Cardyn and Rain yell at me and Brohn to go after Ekker and Krug. "We'll cover you!"

Evading a flurry of gunfire, Manthy rolls over to the wall and reaches her hand up to the input panel by the nearest door. With her palm slapped down on the panel on the wall, she cries out to me and Brohn. "I'll keep the landing gates and the rooftop doorway open for you! Go get him!"

With Cardyn and Rain blasting cover fire at the soldiers behind us, Brohn and I bolt down the walkway. Running full-tilt with the sound of gunfire all around us, we follow Krug and his entourage up the staircase, our boots ringing out like church bells against the metal steps. The electronic safety barriers designed to close off each of the four landings spark and fizzle and, thanks to Manthy, stay in their open, inactive position. As we near the top, just as Brohn and I are closing in, two of the soldiers turn and fire at us.

Brohn tugs me behind him and takes a bullet to the shoulder that staggers him, but he keeps his balance and continues pressing on to the next landing.

As the soldiers stop and take aim again, a swarm of ferociously *kraa*-ing ravens engulfs the two men like ravenous jackals on an antelope carcass. One of the men flails backward, hits the guardrail on the landing, and plummets to his death amidst the fighting armies below. The other man drops to his knees and disappears, screaming, under the razor-sharp talons and piercing beaks of the swarming birds.

Brohn and I dodge around the scrum and continue to clamber up the stairs after Krug.

One of the Patriot soldiers turns and looks down at us, his gun pointed right at my head. Render, his black feathers and golden armor flashing in the air, swoops in and knocks the soldier off the staircase before he has a chance to fire.

The man falls past me and Brohn in a blur, and we watch as his body slams with a bone-shattering crunch, joining his dead partner on the floor below.

Render is already banking and heading back into the fray before I even have a chance to thank him.

I do manage to send him one question: *Aren't you supposed to be in recovery mode?*

His voice in my head says, *Strength in numbers*, before he banks off to rejoin his raven army.

As Brohn and I resume our pursuit of Krug, Ekker, and their entourage, I realize the potentially fatal flaw in this course of action:

There are only two of us.

Brohn doesn't have to worry about getting shot, but Ekker could turn around at any time and fire at me. Or, if he manages to get close enough, probably kill me with his bare hands.

Still surrounded by his remaining guards, Ekker, and the woman in red, Krug is ushered through the giant synth-steel rooftop door, which swings shut and tries but fails, thanks to Manthy, to lock shut behind them.

Brohn leans in with his shoulder, and we burst through the door to find ourselves out on the flat part of the Armory's roof.

Krug's glistening chrome heli-barge, its humming mag

boosters creating distortion waves in the magnetic field around it, is tethered to a landing post, its silver ramp extended out to the edge of the roof like a raft at a dock.

Gunfire sprays at us from the heli-barge and forces us to dive for cover behind a raised ventilation shaft. With our backs to the cold metal, bullets whiz above and around us.

"We can't let them get away!" Brohn shouts. "Follow me!"

Taking a deep breath, he leaps up and charges toward the barge with me tucked in a crouch right behind him. One of the Patriot's bullets skims past Brohn and pings off the armor inserts in my sleeve by my upper arm. It hurts, but not enough to slow me down.

Up ahead of us, surrounded by his guards and with the help of the woman in red, Krug scurries up the ramp and onto the heli-barge.

Led by Ekker, four of the soldiers accompanying Krug turn around at the edge of the rooftop to advance on me and Brohn.

The first soldier charges ahead of Ekker and throws a punch at Brohn. Brohn sidesteps the blow and slugs the soldier hard enough in the side of the head to dent the man's helmet. The soldier staggers but recovers quickly and lashes out with a spinning back-kick, which Brohn easily evades. The second soldier— a gun in one hand, a ten-inch, serrated combat knife in the other —circles around behind Brohn while the other two charge at me in an effort to separate us. With me and Brohn split up and surrounded, the men close in on us.

One soldier takes a huge swipe at me, his knife blade flashing in the moonlight. I dodge the attack and crack his elbow with the heel of my hand while using his momentum to guide him into his partner. The two crash together, but one of them gets a shot off as he falls. The bullet glances off the chest-protection armor under my vest and spins me part way around.

Distracted, I catch my heel on a length of pipe running along the rooftop and stumble backward. One of the soldiers turns away from Brohn and steps toward me. I regain my balance fast enough to duck the man's fist thundering toward my head, but not fast enough to elude another soldier who's slipped around behind me.

With Ekker entering the fight and lumbering toward him, Brohns screams out, "No!" as the soldier who has snuck up on me strikes me with a hard kick behind my knee, causing me to stagger down. He follows that with a thundering forearm strike to the back of my head that makes me see stars and sends me toppling forward as he snags me by the collar and starts dragging me by the back of my vest toward Krug's heli-barge.

I'm kicking wildly at the air and clawing at the man's hands, but he's got to be twice my weight and ten times my strength. I can't shake myself loose.

Another soldier sprints down the barge's ramp and grabs me by the ankles, and, together, the two men haul me onto the heli-barge as Krug barks out orders from where he's standing with the woman in red behind a wall of huge men.

"Secure her! And go help Ekker with the other one!"

Five soldiers leap from the heli-barge onto the Armory's roof and charge over to where Brohn and Ekker are face to face, circling each other, fists clamped into wrecking balls. Swirls of wind whip through the night sky and stir up a vortex of debris along the rooftop. In the distance and over the soldiers' shouts and the throbbing hum of the barge's engines, I hear Ekker tell Brohn to give up.

"I've done a lot of things in my life," Brohn snarls. "Giving up isn't one of them."

"Mine is a better way," Ekker shouts. "I can give you the chance to be the first and best of your kind. With your power, you are primed to be the future of humanity."

"The future I want for humanity isn't power," Brohn says. "It's peace."

"That's a boy's dream," Ekker cries as he lunges forward. "This is the world of reality. This is the world of men!"

Ekker and Brohn are both strong and fast. Brohn sidesteps Ekker's attack, and the two launch into an epic struggle, throwing and blocking jarring punches and savage kicks. Ekker locks Brohn's arm in a hammer-grip, but Brohn disables the move with a pinpoint strike to a pressure point on Ekker's wrist. Ekker loses his grip, and Brohn attacks with a blinding flurry of fist and elbow-strikes that sends the other man stumbling back and slamming up against a large iron exhaust pipe protruding from one of the venting ports on roof.

Ekker is quick to regain his balance, and he catches Brohn with a couple of quick jabs and a haymaker that lands solidly on Brohn's cheek. Brohn's head turns with the impact, but he stays in full combat mode and even manages to offer up a little smile. With Ekker stunned and nursing what appears to be a bloody and badly broken hand, Brohn dodges one more feeble kick before engaging in a furious counter-strike. An elephant kick to Ekker's midsection doubles him over, and Brohn presses his attack with a thunderous uppercut that snaps Ekker's head back and causes him to pitch forward onto his hands and knees, blood streaming from his nose.

I shout out to warn Brohn as one of the Patriots fires two shots into his back, which causes him to lunge forward and drop down to one knee. Seeing a window of opportunity, the soldier stalks forward, both hands locked on his gun with the barrel aimed right at the back of Brohn's head.

But before he can squeeze off another shot, Brohn has already spun around and slung his combat knife at the man. The knife spins in a glimmering silver blur through the air and burrows itself handle-deep in the soldier's neck just above his chest-protector.

Brohn stands and gets ready to resume his attack on Ekker, who is struggling to get to his feet when two more Patriot soldiers, guns and knives drawn, charge at Brohn from either side.

I have no choice but to watch helplessly from Krug's barge as I struggle and thrash against the two men holding me back. One of Krug's soldiers is about ready to clamp immobilizer cuffs around my wrists when he pitches forward, bounces off my shoulder, and plummets over the edge of the heli-barge. I watch as he drops five stories down and winds up a broken slog of human-shaped lasagna on the ground below.

His partner is spinning around to find out what's happened when a projectile rips through his jaw just below the bottom edge of his helmet. A stream of blood explodes from the other side of his head, and he collapses to the floor of the barge.

I look out to see Rain on the roof of the Armory—probably a hundred yards away, at least—squinting down the barrel of a sinister-looking sniper-rifle.

I'm just giving her a grateful thumbs up when a solid thump to the side of my head staggers me back.

Reaching out through a blurry haze, I claw at the clothes of my attacker as I crumple to the floor.

Standing over me, a rifle still gripped in her hands and her jacket askew, the woman in red's hood slides back to reveal a face I've known since I was six. It's a face I've missed so much. One I've cried over and wished so badly to see again.

But not now. Not like this.

Kella, her blond hair, long and matted, her eyes bloodshot and hollow, tosses her rifle to the floor of the barge and yanks out a pistol, which she aims at my head.

Stunned, I shout her name, and her eyes glaze over like a splinter of recognition has lodged itself in her brain. But she quickly shakes off any confusion and begins to squeeze the trigger.

Instinctively, as if I've been doing it all my life, I put my hand up and reach out to Kella with my mind. In a fraction of a second, my consciousness merges with hers. It's not the same smooth connection I have with Render. This one is shaky. Glitchy. Unsteady. Like a baby taking its first steps. The pain is intense, but I push on.

Disconnected from herself and stunned nearly catatonic, Kella lowers her gun, and, in a flash, fractured images from the last weeks of her life whisk by in a near-instantaneous tableau of lived moments through my mind:

Kella, captured by Ekker in the mountains while she protected Adric and Celia, giving them time to escape along with the kids they've been looking after for so long.

Another Emergent—a girl like Cardyn, who can nudge people into doing her bidding—captured and coerced by Ekker and turned against Kella.

Ekker's experiments on Kella in the basement of this very facility, in the very same prison-orb where he held me and Brohn just a few days ago.

Kella's raw-throated screams as the physical and emotional torture combined with the rewiring going on inside her head. They became too much to bear, and she surrendered her mind to Ekker.

Kella, my dear friend and companion in peaceful times and in the depths of battle, sobbing, contorted in agony, reduced to a slave inside her own head, struggling to escape but unable to break free.

*Come with me.*

I say this to her without speaking, my mind to hers.

But she resists me. She shakes me off.

So, instead of asking, I push her mind with mine. Hard.

Her eyes roll back, and she collapses onto the floor next to me.

Only a few feet away but oblivious to what's happening between me and Kella, Krug barks orders to his remaining soldiers. "Pull up the ramp! Get us out of here!"

All his presidential power is gone. He's desperate now. And scared. Nothing but a panicky child.

The hands of the pilot of the heli-barge tremble violently as he fumbles with the projected navigational controls. On its mag boosters and with its ramp fully receded, the heli-barge begins its smooth glide away from the Armory's rooftop.

Standing and lifting Kella up by the collar of her red jacket, I hook my arm around her waist, squeeze her to me, and rush to the edge of the barge, fully prepared to jump, even if it means she and I both plummet to our deaths. Anything is better than staying aboard this thing with Krug. But one of the soldiers, leaving Krug's side, snags me by my upper arm and drags me back, locking his arm around my neck as I reach out across the growing distance between the barge and the edge of the roof.

Right next to me, one of Krug's soldiers fires out at Brohn, who is sprinting across the rooftop right toward us. The burst of fire from the weapon so close to my ears sends me lurching to the side.

Brohn, his head down and with one arm covering his face, runs right toward us into the gunfire.

He slides to a stop at the edge of the roof, reaching a helpless hand out to me over the growing distance as the heli-barge, carrying me and Kella along with it, prepares to cruise away for good.

I'm wishing I could fly over to Brohn when a voice in my head tells me to do exactly that.

Remembering my impossible leap in the halo back at the Processor, and the time in the mountains when I managed to do the impossible, I wrench away from the soldier who's dragging me and Kella back toward the middle of the barge. A snap of my fist to his carotid artery just below the edge of his helmet followed immediately by a heel-of-the-hand strike to the bridge of his nose puts him down for the count. Lifting Kella up and hugging her limp body tightly to mine, I bolt back toward Brohn.

At the edge of the heli-barge and with Kella clamped to my hip, I leap. The two of us go soaring out as one across the distance, my arms curled over both our faces as bullets zing back and forth through the air around us.

We land in Brohn's arms with a heavy thud, and the three of us collapse onto the Armory's rooftop. The shock of landing nearly knocks the wind out of me but, considering Kella and I should both be splattered five floors down on the ground right now—and seeing as how I'm off the heli-barge and safe in Brohn's arms—I'm not going to complain.

A few feet away, Cardyn and Manthy stand guard over Ekker, who is battered and is now restrained with zip-cuffs, his head wilting into his chest in defeat. Four of the Patriots are on their knees or curled up on their sides, their hands cuffed behind their backs. The remaining soldiers lie still on the ground.

Rain, sniper rifle slung across her back, comes running toward us across the rooftop.

The second they realize the person lying barely conscious between me and Brohn is Kella, the rest of our team comes swarming over.

Cardyn, Rain, and Manthy slide to their knees around us, and we're all struggling to catch our breath in the middle of a convulsive fit of relieved laughter, confused speechlessness, and grateful tears.

I look back to see Krug's heli-barge growing smaller as it cruises away from us, heading out into the dark sky over the city.

From where he's kneeling with the rest of us at Kella's side, Cardyn bolts up like he's going to go chasing after Krug's barge, now a fading spot in the distance.

"So what does this mean?" he asks, his eyes jumping from Krug's barge to Kella to Ekker and back to us. "Is it over? Did we win?"

"It's over," Manthy assures him, reaching up to take his hand.

Kneeling with Kella's head resting on my lap, I brush a tangle

259

of blond hair away from her face. She's conscious, but her eyes are still unfocused. It's going to take a lot to undo whatever Ekker did to her. But she's here. She's alive. We're together.

"We won," I assure Cardyn. "We definitely won. For now, at least."

## 27

"So," Rain pants through a smile, her sniper rifle slung around on her back. "Am I the only one who saw Kress literally *fly* over here with Kella in her arms?"

"I don't know what you're talking about," I grin, pointing back to the edge of the building where Krug's barge was just docked. "If you time it just right, anyone can run on top of those magnetic distortion waves."

"Yeah," Rain grins as the others laugh. "Magnetic distortion waves. That's what it was."

"What happened to her?" Cardyn asks, kneeling with his arm around Kella's shoulders. "How'd she wind up with Ekker?"

"That's a story Kella will tell us when she's a little more herself," I explain to him and the others with a sad shake of my head. "I don't think it's going to be a pleasant one."

Cardyn, his eyes brimming with compassion, gives Kella's shoulder a gentle squeeze. "Maybe not," he says. "But at least she's alive, so we know it has a happy ending."

When he says this, I'm reminded of another part of Render's prophecy. He said we'd be "reunited with death." I wonder if this is what he meant, our unexpected reunion with Kella, who has been miraculously returned to us.

Kella looks around at us through unseeing eyes and tries to stand but can't. As we all get up and step back to give her space, Brohn scoops her up in his arms, her blond hair splayed out over his shoulder, and leads us back across the roof toward the door.

"Think they'll be okay here?" Cardyn asks, pointing to Ekker and to the bloodied, bound, and downed soldiers still squirming but immobilized in their zip-cuffs.

"Let's not leave it to chance," Rain says. She taps her comm-link to connect with Wisp. "We've got Ekker and a bunch of Patriots up here on the roof." There's a pause, and then she says, "No. Krug got away." Another silence is followed by, "Copy that," and she taps her comm-link to disconnect before turning back to us.

"Wisp is sending up a clean-up crew."

"I take it that means they've got things under control downstairs?" I ask.

Rain gives us a shrug followed by a sparkly-eyed smile. "Sounds like it. Let's go see for ourselves."

Following Brohn, who has Kella's head resting against his chest as he carries her across the roof, we step back through the big metal access door. Once inside, we look down from the top of the metal staircase to see the floor of the Armory, the size of two football fields and littered with discarded weapons and bodies, sprawling beneath us. The air is hazy and hot. A grayish-blue cloud floats lazily in the vast open space.

As we walk down the stairs and descend through the swirls of battlefield smoke, the aftermath of our rebellion hits us full-force. Mingled in with the red, white, and blue uniforms of the dead, unconscious, or zip-cuffed and captured Patriot soldiers are the black-clad bodies of a dozen Insubordinates and at least four or five uniformed San Francisco law enforcement officers. One of the Insubordinates leans against a wall near the bottom of the stairs. He's clearly exhausted and has his hand clamped over a wound on his upper arm. I don't know his name, but he manages to offer us a weak smile as we pass. Another Insubordinate, a girl I recognize as Triella, the one who asked us about our time in the Processor, is kneeling over an unmoving fellow Insubordinate. Triella looks up at us over her shoulder as we pass and shakes her head.

Seeing them makes me think about how we all knew the risks going in. That doesn't make it any easier to deal with the inevitability of injury and death. But I take some small comfort in knowing that the Patriots were fighting to preserve lies, disparity, and control, while we fought for equality, honesty, and the right to be free from fear.

There are plenty of gray areas in life. But here, there's no question in my mind who were the bad guys and who were the good guys in this scenario.

Battered and limping, we head across the ground floor of the Armory, weaving our way through the people, weapons, thousands of shell casings, and the rest of the debris from the intense fight. Out toward the middle of the huge space, we meet up with Wisp, who comes running over, the relief to see us alive clearly visible on her face.

Looking around, we can finally see the results of a week's worth of planning but a lifetime of struggle and pain. The Patriots of San Francisco have been defeated. Entire squads of local police are cuffing them and loading them in groups into prisoner transport trucks.

All around us, the Insubordinates are cheering, shaking hands, nursing wounds, and already exchanging exaggerated stories of their prowess in battle.

Above us, the railing running around the interior perimeter of the mezzanine level is lined with ravens, their shadowy feathered forms standing out like a queue of ominous gargoyles staring down at us with glossy black eyes.

Render flies down and lands on my outstretched arm. He's exhausted, barely hanging on after expending so much physical, emotional, and psychic energy.

"So," I ask him, gazing up at his raven army. "Who are your friends?"

He lets out four short, sharp *kraas*! and we all do a double-take. Maybe it's our exhaustion after such a pitched battle. Or maybe it's just wishful thinking or a belief in magic, but for a second, it almost sounded like his four barked syllables formed a single word: *Con-spir-a-cy*.

As we're contemplating this, Captain Huang limps up to us, his face a patchwork of scratches and blotches of dirt, sweat, and blood. "A few of the Patriots managed to slip past our clean-up crew," he informs Wisp. "But don't worry. We've got drone trackers on them. They'll be in custody before they know what hit them." Huang notices Kella in Brohn's arms and takes a step back, his hand on his sidearm. "I know her," he stammers. "I recognize the red jacket. She was with Ekker. She's one of them!" He pulls his gun from its holster, but Brohn stops him from raising it with a firm grip on Huang's wrist.

"She was with us first," Brohn says, his voice deep and resonant with the authoritative air of finality. "And she's with us now."

With Brohn's hand still clamped defiantly on his wrist, Huang looks back and forth between Brohn and Wisp, who both stare back like they're daring him to challenge them over Kella. Huang seems to get the picture, re-holsters his weapon, and holds his hands up. "You're the Major," he says to Wisp. And then, with equal deference to the rest of us, "And you're the Emergents. Whatever you think is best. You take care of your people," he adds with a sweep of his hand at the eerie quiet of the smoke-filled Armory, "and my people and I will take care of this."

"What's best," I suggest, my hand on Kella's feverish forehead, "is for us to get our friend out of here and back to herself as soon as possible."

At that, Wisp taps her comm-link and sends out instructions for all of the Insubordinates to rendezvous at the Style for debriefing, and then to assemble the next morning at Grace Cathedral to celebrate our win and to reflect on all the losses along the way.

"Now, let's get her back to the Style," Wisp says, marching toward the Armory's huge front doors. "The battle may be over, but we still have a lot left to fight for."

Since we don't need to sneak around underneath the city anymore, she leads us between the police mag-cars and their flashing lights, through the dimly-lit streets, past the growing number of wary onlookers slowly emerging from the nearby buildings, and on to the Style. Along the way, Kella, still in Brohn's arms, drifts in and out of consciousness.

Back at the Style, we bring her with us upstairs to our fourth-floor dorm room. Wisp arranges to have a sixth bed brought in, and we insert it into our spoked-wheel configuration before collapsing, all of us drained to the core from battle and worried about Kella, who soon starts to mumble in a half-sleep about Ekker and the righteousness of his cause.

It's a horrifying thing to hear coming from her mouth. I know this isn't her, though. This is the slave Ekker wanted to turn all of us into. Kella fought him as best she could, but she was alone then.

She's not alone now.

I reach a hand across to her, the same way Brohn has done so many times with me. After a time Kella goes quiet, her breathing evens out, and I fall asleep, hand-in-hand, with my dear friend.

## 28

*Saturday*

THE NEXT MORNING, AFTER THE DEEPEST AND MOST THANKFULLY dreamless sleep I've ever had, I wake up with the others, and we get ourselves cleaned and changed into fresh clothes. Kella is quiet, but she seems rested and much closer to being herself than she was a few hours ago. Cardyn is gigglishly chirpy and says how much he wants to leave the Style and go out to see the city we've just liberated. "I bet they'll throw us a parade," he says. Manthy teases him for his restlessness and calls him hyperactive, but he doesn't seem to care. Like Kella, Brohn is quiet. He gives me a smile to reassure me that he's fine. "Just having a contemplative moment," he says, dropping down to his bed and lacing up his boots. I nod my understanding before walking over to the armoire where Render's been perched for the night. With the first streaks of light leaking in around the edges of the windows, he *kraas*! out his desire to escape the confines of this room.

*Are you sure?*

*I'm sure I'll die if I don't.*

I don't know if he's serious or joking, but I'm not about to take any chances. I trot across the room and throw open the window. Render flutters over to the windowsill and hesitates for a second before launching himself out over the city. His wings are still weak, but the freedom to fly is giving him strength. He doesn't go far—only to the next building over. He alights on the roof, his golden armor glinting in the morning light, and he's happy.

Just then, Wisp pokes her head into our room and tells us it's time to leave the Style. "The others are already at the cathedral," she informs us. "Let's get moving."

We follow her down the stairs, and, unlike the other times we've left this building, we leave through the front door. It's an oddly refreshing thing. No sneaking out the back. No dropping down into old sewer and subway lines to avoid being detected and shot. Just us. Walking out the front door like normal people about to enter into a normal day in a safe city.

Once outside, we inhale the fresh air of victory and march on a zigzag through the city streets all the way to Grace Cathedral. Along the way, people going about their daily routines stop to applaud and shout out their thanks. Some of the braver ones run right up and shake our hands or hold us by the shoulders and tell us how grateful they are and how free they finally feel.

Cardyn turns to me. "Not exactly a parade," he pretend-complains. "But I'll take it!"

"Come on," Wisp urges, still all business. "We have more work to do."

We jog the last blocks past more cheering residents until we arrive at the church. Nestled between an apartment complex, three large office buildings, and some smaller businesses clustered into an office park, the cathedral practically screams, "Sanctuary." I'm a little nervous about seeing the place. After all, it was here that Ekker first caught me and Brohn, and we just walked past the exact spot where I was convinced Brohn had been shot dead at my feet.

Shaking off the painful flashback, I climb along with the others up the wide concrete steps and through the massive front doors.

Still a little dazed, Kella accompanies us, mostly hanging close to Cardyn, who has taken to mother-henning over her as she continues to try to orient herself to where she is and what's happened to her.

Inside, the cathedral is already packed to the rafters with happy and mostly well-rested revelers. The Insubordinates are milling around with everyone recounting their stories from last night.

We're all clean and polished and relatively stress-free for the first time in…well…ever. The enormity of what we did, of what we accomplished against all odds and what it means for the future of our nation, is starting to sink in. The clenched fist that's been residing in my gut these past few days loosens its grip, and the pulse in my ears slows to a steady thrum.

Team Presidio of the Insubordinates is traveling around the room offering changes of bandages and tending to those of us with minor injuries left untreated from the night before, while Team Bayview has recently arrived from St. Francis Memorial where they've spent the night overseeing and assisting the hospital's medical staff with the more seriously injured.

As we walk deeper into the church, Cardyn is literally dragged away from us by a group of Insubordinates. Giving us a smug "what can I do?" shrug, he goes melting into the crowd where he seems to have achieved celebrity status. Three clearly infatuated, star-struck girls from Team Ashbury go bouncing around him, yipping at him with all kinds of questions I can't hear, but I can see clear as day how much he's enjoying the attention.

Taking over for Cardyn, Wisp draws Kella aside and offers to watch over her. The two of them meander toward the front of the room, Wisp talking quietly to Kella as they go.

Brohn tugs on my sleeve. "Not sure how," he says to me over the din of the victorious celebrations, "but word's gotten around about him."

"About Cardyn?"

Brohn smiles in Cardyn's direction like a proud brother. "It's like a magic trick. Some kind of hypnosis."

"I don't know if you're giving him enough credit. He's cute. And funny. And sweet."

"And an Emergent."

"Maybe it's not a trick," I suggest. "Maybe it doesn't have anything to do with what he is. Maybe they just like him for *who* he is. I know I always have."

Brohn gives me a sideways glance. "Sure. And maybe you can communicate with Render because you're secretly a raven, your-self, disguised as a human girl."

Brohn stares for another second at Cardyn and at the adoring entourage around him before turning back to me and putting his hands on my waist. He winces when I sling my arms around his neck.

"I'm sorry," I say. "That must hurt."

Brohn slides his hands up to my forearms, preventing me from pulling away. "It doesn't hurt as much as you *not* holding me," he laughs.

I laugh, too, and I grip him in a tight hug that I know can't feel good on his bullet-ridden body, but right now, I'm too caught up in him—in *us*—to care.

The old church is massive, but the darkness in the air and the weathered wood beams hanging high overhead make it feel smaller and somehow sadder. It's been an exhausting week. I'm tired all over. I'm rubbing the sore muscles in my arms when Wisp climbs the steps at the front of the room and approaches the dais.

She raises both hands above her head and calls for everyone's attention. We all stop talking and turn as one to look up in admiration at our diminutive leader, the already legendary Major, who, before our eyes, has led us to safety from the brink of slavery.

Like the rest of us, Wisp has changed out of her tactical vest and black infiltration fatigues. She is now back in her baggy khakis and her oversized lime-green hoodie with the sleeves pushed up above her elbows.

"The city is secure," she begins. "The Patriot Army reinforcements were cut off just a few hours ago and were turned back outside of Oakland by three full precincts of local law enforcement and by a team of our own Insubordinates." Wisp makes it a point to look at me. "They say ravens were involved." Everyone cheers, and Wisp gives me a conspiratorial smile and a raised eyebrow, which I return with a grin and a knowing nod, even though I don't have any idea what this new information really means. It does seem that ravens are somehow becoming central to the Insubordinates and what has the potential to be a nationwide resistance movement. Who knows how many battalions might be in Render's army?

"But," Wisp continues, hanging her head as the cheers subside, "our victory here came at a cost." With her head still down and her hands gripping the edges of the lectern in front of her, her voice quivers. "We've sustained confirmed losses: Ethan. Kyle. Emeka. Naveen. Lennox. Nilaja. Tam. Aliera. Alexis. Varion. Naomi. And peace officers: Jackson. Anderson. Ventner. Carlssen. Duerte. There are more in the hospital up the road as we speak. Fellow warriors struggling to hang on. We lost good people. People who were afraid, like all of us, afraid of risking their lives to take on an army but who were more afraid of what would happen if they didn't. They channeled all that fear into power, power they used to help us to victory. Remember their names, their faces. Remember their spirits. Carry them with you.

Let their power become yours until all the good in the world is ours again."

The images of the people we lost—the Insubordinates and the peace officers—appear in a succession of holo-images floating in the air above Wisp.

All around us, eyes fill with tears, and the names of the dead are whispered over and over throughout the cathedral. In the still of the moment, Cardyn, with Kella back by his side, makes his way over to us, his head down as he rejoins our Conspiracy. We form a tight circle, our arms over each other's shoulders in a melancholy moment of remembrance, gratitude, and tears.

Brohn raises his head and gazes out over the somber crowd and at the holo-images hovering like ghosts above the pulpit. "They were good soldiers," he sighs, his voice breaking.

"And even better human beings," Cardyn adds, his head pressed against Kella's in an offer of support amidst the quiet fog of sadness roiling through the cathedral.

Brohn turns to me, Rain, and Manthy. "We'll tell you all about them someday," he promises.

I tell him I'd like that. I forget sometimes how much time he and Cardyn spent with the Insubordinates. Training someone isn't like writing code or programming a computer. At its best, it's about forging relationships, understanding the needs and desires, fears and motivations, and the strengths and weaknesses of the person you're working with. It's as much psychological as it is physical, and it's at least as much about emotion and empathy as it is about anything else. I spent the last week getting to know everything about Ekker, his army, and the ins and outs of the Armory and all about dozens of other strategic places throughout the city. Working with Rain, Manthy, Olivia, and Wisp, I became immersed in the nuts and bolts of our rebellion. Beyond the occasional passing encounters and conversations, though, I never really got to know the Insubordinates. Hearing the names of the dead called out fills me with regret: I wound up knowing so much about their city and their cause and so little about them.

Wisp raises her head and scans the throng of people before her. She pushes up the sleeves of her hoodie, which have fallen down again, and gives us all a smile. It's a complicated expression, one filled with pride about what we've accomplished, sorrow about all we've lost, and fear about what's yet to come.

"The big question," she calls out to all of us, "is 'what's next?' For some of you, it will be going back to your families, starting families of your own, getting on with your lives. For others, it will mean keeping the fight going, inspiring others, and spreading the word about what happened here. Krug has his army, but we have the power. No matter where you go or how you choose to contribute going forward, remember the foundation for this rebellion was the belief that lies will keep us under control for only as long as we let them. We were successful last night because we were prepared. But we won because we were right!"

With cheers going up and with the mood returning to celebratory, Cardyn leads Kella by the hand over to another group of Insubordinates while Rain excuses herself and weaves through the crowd in Wisp's direction.

Manthy turns to me and gives me a grin, something I don't think I'll ever get used to. The girl who used to slump around in the shadows with her head down, now seems taller, more alive. She has her thick tangle of brown hair pulled back into a casual ponytail and is sporting what has to be the prettiest smile I've ever seen in my life. I'm happy for her. I'm happy for how far she's come and for the amazing person she's turned into. No. That's not it, exactly. She's always been amazing. I guess if I'm being honest, I'm happy with myself for finally recognizing her amazingness.

Manthy looks from me to Brohn. She winces at the commotion going on all around us, the cheers, the hearty pats on the back, the hugs of sympathy and consolation. "Not a fan of crowds," she says as she walks around behind us. She trails her hand along my shoulders as she goes. When I crane my head around to catch her eye, she gives me a second mini-grin out of the corner of her mouth before disappearing into the exuberant horde.

"Where's she going?" Brohn asks, looking back over his shoulder to where Manthy has already slipped away.

"Probably just walking off the post-battle jitters," I say, although I know full well what she's up to. She's leaving me alone with Brohn, letting us finally have a moment together after so much time apart. It's her gift to me. I look out into the crowd and offer her a mental "Thanks" before turning back to Brohn.

"This isn't the end, you know."

"Of the war?" he says. "I know. It's just the beginning."

"I mean us. This isn't where we end. We have a future. For the first time, I really believe we have a future."

Brohn leans down and kisses me, and, for a second, it's like there's been no battle, no rebellion, no losses, and no gains—just the two of us, alone together in the middle of so many people and connected on a level beyond the simplicity of a lifetime of shared experiences. Brohn leans back, his hands on my hips, my arms draped around his neck, and he looks at me like we're the last two people on Earth. Which, to be honest, I'm glad we're not. As much as I've dreamed of spending the rest of my life in Brohn's arms, there's something even more satisfying about knowing we also have our Conspiracy and our expanding universe of friends. But above all, there's a brightening light of hope that this future I've come to believe in might be possible after all.

Brohn and I stand there, talking, reminiscing, and holding each other for not nearly long enough as the Insubordinates continue to chatter and shuffle around us until the spell is finally broken by Wisp who bounds over and apologizes for interrupting. Brohn and I both laugh and swallow her up in a massive hug.

"We always have time for the Major," Brohn insists, one arm over his sister's shoulder, the other over mine.

"So…what next?" I ask her.

"As much as we'd like to stay here and live happily ever after…," Brohn starts to say.

"There are a lot of people out there in a lot of places that could use our help," I finish. "What do we do about them?"

I give Wisp a sideways look when she says, "I don't know. And I don't know all the answers to the questions about who we all are. But you're not going to find any more answers here."

"Where, then?" I ask.

Wisp calls Cardyn over from where he's been chatting with some of his admirers, and he pads up to us with Kella, now looking much less pale and dazed than she did last night, walking along behind him. Then Wisp stands on her tip-toes to spot Rain and Manthy on the far side of the room. She whistles to them through her fingers, and they worm their way through the crowd to join up with us again.

With all of us together, Wisp tells us to follow her, which we do. Ignoring Brohn's questions about what she's up to, Wisp leads us through the crush of the celebrating army, into the lobby of the cathedral, and, finally, out the big double doors and down the steps to the street where she points to an enormous Patriot troop transport rig sitting in the middle of the road.

"Feel like taking a road trip?"

## 29

OUT IN FRONT OF THE CHURCH, DENNIS KAMMET, THE PATRIOT Army vehicle specialist who helped get us into the city, slides out from underneath the massive rig and promises to help us on the next leg of our journey as well. Wiping his hands on a rag that he then crams into his back pocket, he pats the side of the truck.

"It's all yours. This is what Krug and his inner circle rode in on before he boarded his heli-barge for his little cruise around town. Krug is all about luxury anyway, and he hates to fly, thus... this. Technically, it's a P2040 Military Tender on an eight-by-eight wheeled chassis. Some people know it as the Aparcarlypse. It's also been called the Carmageddon and the Survivor Driver. Only two of them were ever built. This one and one back East in D.C."

"We're going to take a road trip in this?" I ask.

Rain turns and gives me a little sideways wink and a chirpy giggle. "Sorry about that, *Kakari Isutse*. Not all of us can fly."

As I blush, Cardyn asks where, exactly, Wisp expects us to go.

"Granden and I spent last night working that out," Wisp answers. "There are various places you'll need to visit. Chicago. Philadelphia. Maybe a few others. And some off-the-grid cities.

Think of it as a vacation, only instead of fun and relaxing, it'll mostly be super dangerous, endlessly terrifying, and you'll be lucky to live through it."

"You know," Cardyn says, "for such an inspirational leader, you can be a real downer sometimes, you know?"

"What can I tell you? I dropped out of cheerleading school."

Our laughter is interrupted by Brohn, who holds up a hand. "Wait. Did you say, 'cities *you'll* need to visit'?"

"Yes."

"You're coming with us, right?"

Wisp shakes her head. "I want to. I really do. But what I want to do and what I *need* to do are, unfortunately, in two very different places."

"Your place is with us," Brohn insists, looking suddenly crestfallen. I can't blame him. He was taken away from his sister. Then he returned to the Valta and thought she'd been killed. Then he found her again here in San Francisco. And now, a week after that wonderful discovery, she's saying they have to part ways again.

Rain steps forward to agree with Brohn. "If we're going anywhere, you've got to come with us."

"Right," Cardyn adds, pointing up to one of the cathedral's pinnacles where Render is quietly perched and spying on us. "You're officially part of our Conspiracy now."

"I'm sorry," Wisp says. "If you stay here, Krug and the Patriots will track you down, and everything we just fought for will be for nothing. No. You can't afford to wait around here for that to happen, and I can't leave here without finishing what I started. I have my mission. You have yours. Just because we'll be apart doesn't mean we won't be together."

Brohn looks down at the ground then up at the sky like he's looking for an answer, any answer that's different from the one he reluctantly knows is right.

"We'll see each other again, Big Brother," Wisp promises, and

Brohn nods before swallowing her up in his arms.

"What about you, Granden?" I ask. "Will you be joining us?"

Granden shakes his head. "Like Wisp, I need to stay here. We need to make sure everything we worked for and everything we accomplished doesn't backslide."

"And that someone needs to be you?" I ask. I've grown fond of Granden over this past week. I've not only forgiven him for his part in our lives in the Processor, I've come to appreciate what he did and how much he risked for us. We had no way of knowing it at the time, but all the training he put us through—the struggles, challenges, and the often painful lessons—he wasn't doing it so we could fight the Eastern Order, and he wasn't doing it so we could be lab rats and eventually super-soldiers in Krug's Patriot Army. He wasn't even doing it to oppose his father. No. Granden trained and supervised us out of duty, but he freed us out of friendship. Because he wanted to. Not for some great cause, but for us. Because he saw how much we needed each other, how much of a family we were. Unlike Ekker, he wasn't interested in us as Emergents or obsessed with what we could become. He was willing to sacrifice his own career, his own life even, so we could go on being what we were.

"I'd love to come with you, Kress," Granden says, his hand on my shoulder. "I really would. No one wants to take down Krug more than I do. But we need to help Captain Huang and the other city officials to keep the Patriot Army from coming back. Our victory here is the foundation the rest of the rebellion will be based on. Once it's the strongest foundation possible, Wisp and I can move on. Maybe we'll even meet up again someday."

"I'd like that," I say. "You're the one who got us here. You risked your life to help us. It only seems fair we return the favor."

Wisp reaches up and puts her hand on Granden's shoulder. "Granden is going to help keep the city secure. He can't do that alone, even with the help of the local authorities. A lot of what needs to be done has to be done under the radar. Off the books.

You need to get the revolution going out there. We need to keep building things here."

"Me, too," a voice says from somewhere behind Cardyn.

We all turn to look. It's Kella.

"I'm going to stay, too."

"You can't," I cry. "We just found you."

Kella looks like she might start sobbing, but she steels herself and steps over to stand next to Granden and Wisp. "They need me here."

"It's true," Wisp says after a long, pain-filled moment. "What you did for the Insubordinates in less than a week was more than amazing. But we need to keep training new recruits. And no one's better than Kella at marksmanship and in-the-field combat operations."

Granden nods his agreement at this claim. "You've trained with her," he reminds us. "You know how good she is."

"But that was before..." I start to say and then think better of it. No sense in re-opening the Ekker wound quite so soon.

"I can do this," Kella assures us. "I want to." And then she smiles for the first time in a long time. "Don't worry. Like Granden says, I have a feeling we'll meet again."

I smile and take her hand. "I've got the same feeling."

"We all do," Brohn adds, stepping forward to shake her hand. She pushes his hand away and throws her arms around his waist as we all laugh—even Manthy—and step in for one of our great group-huddle hugs.

As civilians from the city start to gather around, many of them clapping and nodding their appreciation, we stand next to the truck, shaking hands with the Insubordinates, giving and receiving hearty slaps on the back, and exchanging a litany of praise and congratulations.

As the Insubordinates pass on and as our goodbyes begin to ebb, Wisp tells us it's getting late and that we need to get moving.

We swarm Granden with an onslaught of handshakes and

hugs before moving on to Kella.

"You were with us the whole time," I promise, tapping my temple with my finger and putting my hand on my heart. "You always will be."

Kella offers up a feeble smile. I can tell she's in pain from her experiences with Ekker, and I know her recovery won't be anywhere near just around the corner. But maybe staying here with Wisp and Granden—being part of something new, helping to build on our rebellion from the safety of this newly liberated city—maybe that's exactly what she needs.

Standing out there by the truck in front of Grace Cathedral, I keep saying goodbye to everyone. I can't seem to stop. None of us can. Even Caldwell has taken a break from his supervision of the Modifieds and has come by to see us off. He steps forward to give us each a quick, tentative, but kind-hearted handshake. He lingers the longest with Manthy, holding her hands in his, saying how proud he is of her and how much he knows she's going to mean to the world.

The hugs and well-wishes seem to go on forever, and no one is complaining. For her part, Kella accepts our outpouring of emotion with a kind of smiling but stunned stoicism. I'm still getting traces of her consciousness from when I connected with her on the Armory rooftop last night, but the images are faded and scrambled now. I feel her gratitude and her relief, but that's mingled with a haze of bleak trauma and even with regret about losing Ekker. The major parts of the hooks he had in her may be gone, but some barbs remain.

Finally, with more effort than we expended yesterday in the throes of battle, we force ourselves to let go.

One at a time, our faces wet with tears, we leave Kella, Granden, and the Insubordinates behind, and Wisp starts to climb the ladder into the truck.

"Now let's have a look at your new digs," she says. "I'll show you around before you go."

Still sad but laughing at the whirlwind of emotions I know we're all experiencing, we line up behind Wisp and begin to follow her into the behemoth of a truck. Before it's my turn, Render flutters down on wobbly wings and lands at my feet. I bend down to pick him up and tuck him under my arm. Usually, he'd be perched on my shoulder or flying around looking for food or a game to play, but he seems to need to be carried at the moment.

Despite his obvious fatigue, even he seems impressed by the massive vehicle. I don't blame him. It's an imposing and impressive sight that makes our other truck, the one we drove all by ourselves from Reno to Oakland, look like a hover-bike. It's got body armor, wheels as tall as Wisp, and inside, according to Kammet, it's got a water-storage tank, a fully-stocked pantry, and a dozen sleeping bunks that slide out of recessed compartments in the walls. Plus, as Kammet continues to boast from behind us, it's got an integrated communication network system and medi-repository complete with an array of clinical supplies and diagnostic instruments.

Once on board, we marvel at the interior of our new mobile home.

"Okay, I take it back," Cardyn gushes as he climbs the short set of extending steps and ducks through the steel-framed doorway on the side of the truck. "This thing is awesome!"

"And huge," Rain points out, scanning the living quarters and offering up a series of impressed nods.

"It's room you're going to need," Wisp promises. "This army of ours is just getting started."

"As long as I don't have to bunk with Manthy," Cardyn moans.

"There's plenty of room for you *under* the truck," Manthy says, and there's no doubt it's a threat.

Ignoring my two constantly bickering friends, but grateful for the shift in mood, I walk around the truck's spacious interior with Brohn at my side. The belly of the truck is practically a palace. It's got a fully-stocked kitchen with a glistening marble countertop, two collapsible Cherrywood tables, four comfort-loungers, a bank of viz screens on one side, and a four-seat game console complete with a cache of VR-sims and holo-ball challenges on the other. In terms of comfort and distracting things to do, it's literally the best place I've ever been in my life. When Brohn and I get to the back, we encounter a narrow metal ladder.

"Where does this go?" Brohn asks, peering up to where an open portal rains light down on us.

"That's the Communications Pod," Wisp tells us. "There's a surprise for you up there. Go on up."

I shield my eyes with my hand and look up into the pod before I clamber up with Brohn right behind me. We step into what looks like a small but fully furnished conference room where I see a familiar but very unexpected face.

"Olivia?"

Climbing up behind Brohn, Wisp giggles at our surprise and delight.

"You can't do this next part without her. And she refused to stay behind anyway."

"And you were able to disconnect her from the console in the Intel Room?"

"And secure me up here," Olivia finishes. "Yes."

She spins around in her swivel mag-chair in the middle of a buffet of consoles, monitors, and controls. Even her three hovering orb-monitors have come with her.

"What's up there?" Rain calls from down below.

"Our saving grace," Brohn calls back.

Rain and Cardyn, with Manthy dragging herself along behind, climb up into the tidy compartment and squeal their delight at seeing Olivia.

Rain and Manthy hug her on either side, and her tendrils wriggle and caress their shoulders until Wisp reminds us all that this is only the beginning, and that our next mission awaits.

# EPILOGUE

"I NEED TO GET BACK," WISP SAYS, GESTURING BACK DOWN THE Pod's access ladder. "And you need to get going. But before we go our separate ways, though, we need to send a message."

"Message?" I ask.

Wisp nods. "Time to spread the truth." She turns to Olivia. "Are you ready to broadcast?"

Olivia says, "Nearly" and leans over her work station, her back to us, her tendrils woven into her monitors with lines of red code scrolling through the air in front of her.

Wisp turns to us and looks suddenly serious. "Most of the cities and their infrastructures have been wiped out with the populations consolidated in a few major cities: San Francisco, as you know. But also Chicago. Philadelphia. New York. New Orleans. Atlanta. Washington, D.C. The smaller cities are mostly gone. The medium-sized ones are on their way out and are being left to fail, turn into pits of violence, or become ghost towns. A lot of the land in between has been scorched by years of bomb-ings, battles, and radiation fall-out. We've seen some of it. Granden's seen it all. Millions have been exiled, imprisoned, or killed in the name of Krug's war against the Eastern Order. It's not going to be a pretty picture out there."

Olivia swings around in her swiveling mag-chair to face us. "I forget sometimes how isolated you were. Wisp is right. The country isn't what you think it is. A lot has changed during your time in the Valta."

"We've seen some of it," Brohn reminds her.

"Right," Rain says. "Someone even shot at us in Reno."

"Just to watch us die," Cardyn sings out.

When Olivia looks confused, Manthy, along with an eye-roll for the ages, explains that it's a line from an old song and apologizes for Cardyn being, and these are Manthy's exact words: "a maniacal, human-shaped maggot sandwich."

Olivia laughs her tinny laugh and then, with a series of indicator lights blinking to life behind her, swings back around to her monitors to announce the successful completion of her communication patch.

"It'll have to be a pretty basic message," she instructs us. "Quick. Simple. To the point. I can set it so it runs on a continuous loop on as many bandwidths, communication hubs, and network feeds as I can access. The Patriots will shut it down as soon as they get wind of it, and it won't get to everyone, but word about you has already started to spread. People will pay attention."

Wisp asks me if I'd like to do the honors.

At first, I hesitate. After all, I reminder her, she's the Major. But she shakes her head, and a round of, "Yes, Kress. You should be the one" from Brohn, Cardyn, and Rain, and a gentle nudge from Manthy prompt me to step forward.

Finally, nodding my consent, I tip my head toward the transmitter on Olivia's console. I take a breath and clear my throat, ready to talk to the world.

"We have defeated the Patriot Army in San Francisco," I begin. "The city is free. The Eastern Order is fake. Krug is a liar."

And then, after Olivia checks the scrolling read-out and asks if we're ready for her to initiate the broadcast, Brohn puts a hand on my shoulder and tilts his head back toward the transmitter.

I nod again and lean down toward the communications monitor with one more message:

"Krug. We are the Emergents. And we're coming for you."

END OF BOOK 3

# WANT TO READ MORE ABOUT KRESS AND HER CONSPIRACY?

*The Emergents Trilogy*

Book One, *Survival:*

In the year 2043, with the nation destroyed by war, seventeen-year-old Kress and her Conspiracy of friends embark on a dangerous cross-country mission to locate and recruit Emergents, fellow teenagers who have begun to exhibit strange evolutionary abilities.

Not all Emergents are ready to accept who and what they are, however. Some have even started using their abilities for selfish or evil ends.

Now Kress has to figure out who is friend and who is foe as she risks everything to expose the government's lies and take down the tyrannical President Krug once and for all. Picking up where the *Resistance Trilogy* leaves off, the stand-alone *Emergents Trilogy* follows Kress and her Conspiracy on a daring quest to restore democracy and truth to the country.

Available now!

# NEW SERIES: SEEKER'S WORLD

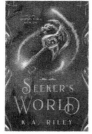  

On her seventeenth birthday, Vega Sloane receives a series of strange and puzzling gifts. Among them is a key shaped like a dragon. The question is: What exactly is it meant to open?

All of a sudden, the peaceful town where Vega grew up is crawling with shadows, strange beings and unlikely allies.

Vega soon discovers that many of the ancient stories she once considered myths and legends are true, and that a magical world exists beyond her own…one that only the chosen few can see. It's a world where cruel beings stalk the lands and magic lives on the air, where the Blood-born prove their worth in an ancient academy that trains those born with special powers.

# ALSO BY K. A. RILEY

## Resistance Trilogy

*Recruitment*

*Render*

*Rebellion*

## Emergents Trilogy

*Survival*

*Sacrifice (Coming in November 2019)*

*Synthesis (Coming in 2020)*

## Transcendent Trilogy (Coming Soon!)

*Travelers*

*Transfigured*

*Terminus*

## Seeker's World Series

*Seeker's World*

*Seeker's Quest*

*Seeker's Fate*

## Athena's Law Series

Book One: *Rise of the Inciters*

Book Two: *Into an Unholy Land*

Book Three: *No Man's Land*

For updates on upcoming release dates, Blog entries, and exclusive excerpts from upcoming books and more:

https://karileywrites.org

Made in the USA
Monee, IL
25 January 2021